W9-BHR-815

ALSO BY MARK SALZMAN

Iron & Silk
The Laughing Sutra

THE SOLOIST

THE SOLOIST

Mark Salzman

RANDOM HOUSE
NEW YORK

Published in the United States by Random House, Inc., New York.

Library of Congress Cataloging-in-Publication Data
Salzman, Mark.
The Soloist / Mark Salzman. — 1st ed. p. cm.
ISBN 0-394-57010-3
I. Title.
PS3569.A4627E28 1994
813′.54 — dc20 93-3956

Manufactured in the United States of America
2 4 6 8 9 7 5 3
First Edition 1994

Book design by Victoria Wong

For Martha L. Salzman

ACKNOWLEDGMENTS

It is my privilege to thank several delightful people for their help with this book. For questions about music and the professional musical life I turned primarily to Martha Salzman, harpsichordist, music teacher and cherished mother. This book's dedication reflects my gratitude to her for having taught me to enjoy music, to work hard but not too hard at all things, and to value kindness above all else.

I also benefited from the advice and hilarious anecdotes of the cellist Yo-Yo Ma, who is as warmhearted, gracious and articulate as he is talented. Dr. L. Jolyon West of the Neuropsychiatric Institute of UCLA treated me to invaluable insights from his experiences as one of our premier forensic psychiatrists, gave me a crash course in the history of the insanity defense, and offered terrific solutions to problems I was having with the story—all in one unforgettable afternoon. Karen Gee, deputy public defender, Ryan H. Rainey, deputy district attorney, and Luis Li, lawyer and mountaineer, tutored me from scratch about how trials work in California. Karen was good enough to read the nearly finished manuscript during one of her rare vacations, and then return it with such detailed comments that I considered submitting her notes to the *Yale Law Review.*

Others who kindly shared their expertise on subjects ranging from life in organized Zen communities to the optics of lunar eclipses are Tek Young Lin, James and Van Loc Tran Doran, Shiho Ito, Drs. Christine and Armand Guigui, John Ahouse and Joseph Salzman. I owe special thanks to Victoria Steele, head of the Special Collections Department at USC Library, who worked tirelessly to help me locate the best possible materials and informants whenever I had questions or problems. She is a real treasure, as anyone who has had the pleasure of meeting or working with her will attest.

More than a dozen good friends and an almost equal number of family members agreed to read early drafts of the manuscript in spite of my preposterous requirement that they be honest with me only if they loved it. All of them managed to compliment the book so skillfully that I hardly realized I was being corrected, and for this I am deeply grateful. I would like to give special mention to two friends—both artists in the very best sense of the word—who gave the manuscript more attention than I can adequately thank them for, and whose thoughtful compliments resulted in the most corrections: Timothy Steele, poet, and Terry Sanders, filmmaker. My editor at Random House gave me excellent advice that strengthened and clarified the story and made this, at last, a real book. I also want to acknowledge my incalculable debt to Eric Ashworth, Rebecca Saletan, Neil Olson, Michael Siegel and Andrew Reich, without whose guidance and persistent efforts on my behalf I would probably have gone back to working in Chinese restaurants by now. I would also like to thank Professor Hugh M. Stimson for his friendship, his good-natured prodding, and for his singularly heartening concern for this and other projects of mine over the last sixteen years.

Finally, I must say that it would not be possible to thank Jessica Yu—filmmaker, writer and wife—enough for her assistance during the two years it took to write this book. As always, she gave unfailingly constructive advice and criticism from beginning to end, and if she ever got tired of hearing about or discussing the book, she never let it show. She is an inexhaustible source of brilliant ideas and has a priceless sense of humor; fortune smiled on me when we crossed paths.

THE SOLOIST

1

This morning I read an article suggesting that Saint Theresa of Avila, a sixteenth-century Spanish mystic noted for her ecstatic visions, suffered from a neurological disorder known to cause hallucinations. I found the article while browsing through my colleague Martin's bookshelves the other day. He subscribes to more journals and magazines than our department library, and enjoys having visitors to his office, so I wander down the hall at least twice a week to read and chat with him. I expressed surprise over the content of the article, but Martin said he'd suspected as much for years. "I'll bet it's just a matter of time before they prove that most of those saints had their wires crossed. Along with a lot of artists. They're pretty sure now that Van Gogh had a kind of brain disease that made him see everything as if it were saturated with yellow light. I wouldn't be surprised if it turned out that William Blake was epileptic."

Maybe scientists will discover that musical genius is an allergic reaction to sound or a symptom of a vitamin deficiency in the brain. If so, I'll have a lot to think about; as a child I was accustomed to receiving standing ovations in thousand-seat halls but now I play for an audience of one—

and she can't tell me what she thinks. Was I stricken or healed when my gift faded?

I'll be thirty-six years old this spring, which is young for a retired concert soloist but old for a virgin. I started out as a musical prodigy. When I was three years old my mother took me next door to meet our new neighbor, a young schoolteacher who had just moved to Poughkeepsie. I remember that she had a wandering right eye, which frightened me. While she and my mother talked I slipped away and discovered a small upright piano in an adjacent room. Although I'd never seen a piano before, within minutes I was able to pick out the melody of a song I'd heard on the radio. By the time my mother noticed my absence and came looking for me, I had worked out the harmony as well.

That event—the discovery that I had a musical gift—had as profound an effect on my parents as it did on me. Originally they had planned to have more children, but in view of my gift my mother decided it would be best for her and my father to focus all of their attention and resources on me. They practically starved themselves to rent a piano and pay for lessons with the best teacher in the area. By the age of five I played well enough to give a recital, for which I was paid twenty-five dollars—my professional debut. It looked as if I was going to be a pianist, but then, at age six, my mother took me down to Manhattan to hear Janos Starker play the Haydn D-major concerto, and on the ride home I begged her to let me switch to the cello. The piano was a lovely instrument, but the cello sounded like a living, breathing animal with vocal cords made of amber. Five minutes into that concert I knew I had to sing through that animal's voice.

I progressed with the cello so quickly and with such feverish intensity that by the time I was nine there were no cellists left in our area qualified to teach me. My mother and I ended up moving to Germany so I could study with Johannes von Kempen, a brilliant cellist best known for his interpretation of German music, particularly Bach. My father stayed behind in Poughkeepsie—partly because he didn't want to lose his pension and medical benefits by quitting his shipping clerk's job, but also because he said he couldn't live in Germany again—so for that period I saw him only when I traveled to the United States to give concerts and every winter when he would come to Europe and meet us in Switzerland for the holidays.

The hardest part about that move was being torn away from my friends in school. Up until that time I had led a fairly normal social life; few of the other children knew anything about classical music or were aware of the attention I was getting from adults for my playing, so although I was occasionally teased for not playing kickball or dodge ball (my mother had forbidden me to play any sports for fear that I might damage my fingers), I remember having a good time in school. Once we moved to Germany, however, I studied with a private tutor whose salary and living expenses were enthusiastically provided by a wealthy lover of music, and my playmates were all adult musicians. I spent most of my time with Maestro von Kempen, and he was almost ninety when I first met him. Once we moved to Germany my mother discouraged me from having any contact with children my own age, because she thought their immature games and interests might distract me from my studies.

Whenever I complained of loneliness my mother would tell me that God had given me a special gift, and as painful as it was for her to be so strict it would be unforgivable if she allowed me to throw it away. She claimed that all of the sacrifices I was making as a child would be rewarded many times over when I was an adult, when, she assured me, everyone would want to play with me and be my friend. When I became a teenager and began to show an interest in girls, she told me to keep my mind on music, and guaranteed that if I followed her advice the day would come when the most beautiful and cultivated women in the world would line up at the chance to date me. I remember her once saying, when I was sixteen, "You're young still—just a child! And your stock's gonna keep going up, Renne, it will. Why cash it in too soon? You wait and see, you'll thank me someday."

My mother saw to it that I followed this advice whether I wanted to or not. When I was seventeen we traveled north to Sweden, where I had been invited to play the Lalo concerto with the Stockholm orchestra. During one of the rehearsal breaks the conductor's daughter, a year older than I and herself a musician of some talent, invited me to have some coffee with her at a pastry shop just across the street. My mother had gone shopping during the rehearsal, so I figured it would be safe. Those thirty minutes were remarkable; even though we could barely communicate with each other I felt as if we had eloped, and my senses were as heightened as during a concert. I felt the snow collapse under each of my footsteps, I enjoyed my pastry as if it were the first time man had tasted fruit or custard, and every strand of her blond hair spread out against her camel-hair coat looked like spun gold. Deliriously happy, I asked if we could repeat our date the next day. She agreed, but I made the mistake that night of urging my mother a bit too strongly to go shopping again the next afternoon. She became suspicious and returned to the hall early, then panicked when she learned I was not there. Thinking it would come as a relief to her, the conductor said that there was nothing to worry about, that I was with his daughter, but she did not welcome this news. As soon as I walked in the door she pulled me out of rehearsal, embarrassing me terribly, led me back to our hotel and made a frightful scene. She scolded me with uncharacteristic bitterness and told me never to try to deceive her again. In spite of my acute shame I managed to ask what was wrong with having coffee with the conductor's daughter—what could happen, after all, during a thirty-minute rehearsal break in downtown Stockholm, a city we would be leaving in just two more days? My mother looked at me the way Caesar must have looked at Brutus, then her face went utterly blank. In a frozen voice she asked if this was how I was repaying her for all her years of sacrifice.

"Fine, then," she said before I could answer. "You don't need my advice anymore. You're a famous musician now, a big shot, and I'm in the way. What do I know about anything? Who cares that I gave up having my own life, or other children, just to let you have this chance? Fine. You do what you want." She actually started packing a suitcase. Her reaction terrified me; even at that age I didn't have any experience with independence and my will to defy her collapsed immediately. Only after I had tearfully apologized and promised at least two dozen times never to see the girl again did she finally soften and agree to stay with me for the rest of the tour.

By this time I had traveled all over the world, had played with some of the finest orchestras in Europe and America, had made several recordings and was treated like royalty wherever I went. Musically speaking, that early part of my life did appear to be charmed; onstage or off, I honestly felt that I couldn't hit a wrong note even if I tried. I remember once thinking during my accompanist's solo that if I were to lift my cello by the neck and break it over his head, the thud would have been in the key of our piece. I played without any fear or self-consciousness at all; I had received such unreserved praise and attention, and from such an early age, that it never occurred to me to question my abilities. And I loved performing.

Yet I was not satisfied. After every concert, throngs of older people would crowd backstage to shake my hand or kiss my cheek, and with tears in their eyes they would say I was a miracle, a gift from God, and that they hoped to live long enough to hear me play as an adult. Music critics, music lovers, conductors, my teacher and, most of all, my mother joined this chorus, telling me over and over again that playing the way I did as a teenager meant that as long as I kept working hard adulthood would soon bestow upon me emotional qualities that would make me the premier cellist of my generation, if not the century. For this reason, and because I wanted so badly to choose my own friends and have a romantic life, I could hardly wait to get older.

My life changed course abruptly when I was eighteen. My mother and I had returned to Poughkeepsie by then; Professor von Kempen had had his final stroke and passed away the year before. At his memorial service I had not let myself cry; I believed that he would have wanted me to show restraint. Also, I hoped that if I acted like a grown man I would hasten the process of maturity that was going to make me a finished product, a master cellist rather than a child prodigy, the maestro's true successor rather than his potential heir. I knew that he believed my success would restore validity to his life's work. Less than a year later, however, while preparing for a concert tour through South America, I started to notice what appeared to be a hearing problem that affected my sense of pitch. I made it through that tour but with great difficulty, and for the first time in my life I received mixed reviews. Within a few months the problem became so acute that I could barely play at all.

My natural gift for intonation turned against me. My ear began to examine each note so intensely that even a variation of a single cycle in pitch bothered me. Not even I could play with that kind of acoustic precision, which made it nearly impossible for me to concentrate on the melodic line, and as a result my playing became fragmented and weak. Concerts became interminable humiliations instead of being euphoric experiences for me.

Eventually I had to cancel all of my engagements, many of which had been organized years in advance. It was an enormous inconvenience for the halls and orchestras, and it put me in a terrible position. At an age when most young men and women feel their lives are just beginning, I felt mine had ended. I wanted to disappear completely, and for all practical purposes I did. I lived at home with my parents until I was twenty-four, practicing obsessively and thinking of nothing else but overcoming my musical problem. Having once been able to sing through that magnificent animal the cello, with all the power and freedom it gave me, I couldn't imagine living without that ability.

I was terribly lonely, but I felt unwilling or unable to establish new relationships with anyone until my gift came back. To use my mother's analogy, my stock had plummeted to such depths that I couldn't possibly cash it in at such a loss; I was stuck. I didn't feel like a real person during this period; I didn't resemble the person I saw myself to be. I felt like a ghost, or an image in a distorted mirror, and I didn't know how to present myself to others. I yearned for an intimate relationship with someone, but felt especially self-conscious and disappointed with myself around women. The women I was attracted to, I assumed, would not want to associate with a failed musician.

Meanwhile, I had come to resent my mother for isolating me from other young people and for giving me such an exaggerated sense of entitlement. I also resented my father for letting my mother do it; once she had convinced herself that cultivating my talent was a religious duty, he had largely withdrawn from the issue of my upbringing. Living at home with them allowed me to practice with relatively few distractions, but eventually I became convinced that the only way I could find my voice again was by building a whole new life for myself, this time without anyone else telling me what to do. So I moved to Los Angeles, where the music department of a large university offered me an immediate appointment and the promise of a manageable teaching load.

For ten years very little happened to me. I hardly remember anything about this period, except how impatient I felt with many of the students, who seemed more interested in their social lives than in music. Even Bach, who was remembered by contemporaries as a man of nearly infinite patience and mild disposition, could lose his temper when confronted with musicians who didn't practice enough. Once, while rehearsing a cantata, Bach listened in horror as the church organist lost his place during a simple passage. Enraged at this needless crime against music, Bach tore off his wig, threw it at the organist and shouted, "You ought to have been a cobbler!" Ours being a litigious society, I managed to refrain from throwing things at students, but if dreams came true and university teachers had more control over students' professional decisions, Southern California would have found itself overrun with cobblers by now.

I plodded forward with my job and my grueling daily practice routine until early last year, when my life changed direction once again. It started the weekend that Yo-Yo Ma visited our campus to give a master class, and after watching him do more in one afternoon to inspire my students than I had been able to do in the entire year, I came home to find a summons for jury duty in my mailbox.

2

Mr. Ma taught for over two hours that day, then surprised everyone by giving an impromptu performance for the students and faculty. His energy appeared to come from an inexhaustible source; his playing showed no signs of wear from all the teaching, and he didn't seem worried about exhausting himself before the concert he was giving downtown the next evening. He answered questions afterward and proved to be an endearing and irrepressibly humorous speaker, which explained why I had heard laughter all afternoon coming from the practice room he used for his master class. I had been in my office down the hall in case they needed someone to quickly locate or photocopy any music during the lesson.

After this, the chairman suggested that we all move over to the Faculty Lounge for drinks, where we had to split up into several tables. I felt sorry for Yo-Yo, having to entertain the faculty after spending three long hours with our students—I don't know if anyone even asked if he would have preferred to go back to his hotel—so I sat with a group of students at the farthest table. I remember that the only part of being a concert musician that I disliked was the socializing afterward. I loved making music onstage, but I hated having to sit through postconcert dinners with groups of people who wanted to know all about me, or who wanted to tell me all about themselves, and who inevitably seemed disappointed to find that I was not as fluent in conversation as I was in the language of music. I pleaded with my mother to decline those invitations, but she insisted that it was important for me to "mingle." The truth, I realize now, is that the dinners and luncheons and teas were important for her, not for me. Since she couldn't actually sit onstage with me during concerts, those social occasions were her only chance to get the attention she felt she deserved as my mother, since anyone wishing to speak to me had to meet with her approval first.

Yo-Yo must have been telling funny stories the whole time because his table never stopped laughing. I looked over a few times and caught glimpses of him gesturing with his hands as he talked. At one point I think he was imitating Arthur Rubinstein. Whatever he was doing was obviously funny, and he was laughing just as loudly as everyone else at his antics. His sense of humor was so contagious that, I heard later, it even inspired Larry Axelrod, a notoriously serious bassoonist, to tell a joke.

After the drinks we said our good-byes and I joined the others to thank Yo-Yo and see him off. When it came my turn to shake his hand he surprised me by calling me Renne, the familiar version of my name. He remembered it from the only other time we'd met, sixteen years before, after one of my recitals in New York. That night he had come backstage to compliment me and we had a brief conversation before my mother pulled me away to meet a conductor. I remember liking him instantly, especially since we were the same age, and I hoped we could build a friendship, but my mother purposely kept me away from him. This was just after he had chosen to attend Harvard rather than one of the famous music schools in order to get an all-around education. It turned out to be a very wise decision, but at the time some people grumbled that he wasn't being serious enough, and that his music would suffer for it. I think my mother was afraid that if I spent too much time with him some of his rebelliousness might rub off on me and I would do something rash, like ask to live on my own or choose my own friends.

After seeing Yo-Yo off I went back to my apartment to get in some practice before dinner. On my way inside I checked the mailbox and found the usual pile of junk mail and a letter from the Superior Court of Los Angeles County. Even though I had no reason to worry, my heart started pounding as I opened it. It turned out to be a trial jury summons, requiring me to appear for a period of at least ten days starting the second week in May, just around graduation time. My relief that it was only jury duty quickly turned to annoyance. I'd assumed that teachers were exempt from the process.

The thought of having to sit in a stuffy courtroom for days, listening to evidence and legal mumbo jumbo, watching people get upset or perjure themselves, then debating a verdict with a bunch of strangers filled me with anxiety. Just watching coverage of trials on the news made me tense.

I poured myself a drink and put the summons aside. I had to practice. I got tuned up, ran through a few bowing exercises to get my shoulders loose, then jumped right into some music. I had hoped that Yo-Yo's surprise performance would have some residual effect on my playing, but this was not the case. The pattern was the same. The first few minutes I played were my best; I felt relaxed and largely unaware of my fingers on the strings, the way we are unaware of our feet when we walk. But then, a few bars into the piece, I heard myself come in flat on a note. All of a sudden I became aware of my fingers as they struggled to find the exact center of the note. This little distraction was enough to cause me to come in sharp on the next note, which made me even more conscious of my fingers. They started to feel cold and numb on the strings, and I had to stop. When I tried to do a simple scale to get my intonation back, I could hear the flaws in pitch so acutely that it became hopeless; only a machine could produce notes pure enough to satisfy my ear. Trying to find the right pitch with my fingertips, which now felt like giant frozen sausages, became like trying to guide a badly frayed shoelace through the eye of a needle. Only force of habit kept me at it until dinner.

For probably the thousandth time, I wondered what advice Professor von Kempen would have given me if he were still alive. I remembered that once, when I became frustrated that my fingers were not long enough to reach a certain extension, my frail teacher edged forward on his hard pine chair until I was afraid he would slide right off. "Every musician," he said as if reciting a prayer, "discovers that God has given him faulty equipment. That's where the difference between an ordinary musician and a great artist lies—how they face their shortcomings." As always, he spoke to me in his archaic Bavarian dialect, with his eyes fixed on mine, and tapped my knee with his cello bow for emphasis. "The common man is shackled by them, Herr Sundheimer, but not the great artist! He finds creative ways to make use of his flaws, and thus he transcends them." He closed his eyes then, nodding slowly and pursing his lips in thought.

I was barely ten when he gave me this lesson, so unfortunately the greater part of his advice went over my head. When he offered these obscure lectures, which was fairly often, I would make an effort to seem interested, but I was really only waiting for him to give me concrete suggestions. I wanted solutions to the musical problems, not observations about spiritual poise. Eventually he showed me that I could make the extension if I released my thumb from behind the neck of the cello at just the right moment—a simple adjustment.

I have been trying to find creative ways to make use of my hearing problem ever since it began, but without any signs of transcending it. Maybe von Kempen was only talking about certain kinds of shortcomings. Perhaps if he had lived a little longer he would have recommended I stop playing the cello and find another outlet for my creative energies.

I spoke to Martin, our senior violin instructor, to see if he knew how I could get out of jury duty. We have a money pool going in the department that will be won by the first person who can, without purposely trying to do so, bring up a subject in conversation that Martin isn't shockingly informed about. I've heard him give advice about living wills, tax-free investments, computer software and new types of surgery for carpal tunnel syndrome, which is the bane of so many pianists and string musicians; once, when I told him I was thinking about buying a new car, he remembered how *Consumer Reports* rated the model I was interested in. Sure enough, when I mentioned jury duty his eyes lit up.

The only drawback to asking for Martin's advice is that he

doesn't quite stop at the answer to your question. If you ask what *Consumer Reports* thought of the Ford Probe he'll tell you, but not without also telling you how it rated every other car in that price range, mentioning along the way that *Car and Driver* came to entirely different conclusions. True to form, he managed to launch himself from my problem with jury duty into a vigorous critique of the jury system itself. The gist of his commentary was that while the original concept of being judged by one's peers had been a nice idea, it clearly wasn't designed with today's society in mind. "In the eighteenth century," he explained, "this country had a small population of highly educated people. Now we have a huge population, and most of them are poorly educated and don't know how to think for themselves."

I asked if he didn't think that having ordinary citizens sit on juries helps keep the law in touch with common sense and with the community's sense of justice, but he asked me right back who I thought ordinary citizens were. "Look at how many people vote Republican," he lamented, "or how many picket abortion clinics, or how many read *USA Today*! There's ordinary citizens for you, Reinhart. You want their brand of common sense? I'd rather have a judge settle my case, I can tell you that."

As a rule, I try to avoid talking with anyone about the collapse of society. My own view is that apathy is an acceptable, if not admirable, stance because it actively reduces frustration and despair and to that extent makes the world a better place. As soon as I could get a word in I told Martin that in spite of my feeble defense of the jury system I wanted to avoid participating in it and wondered if he knew how I could avoid serving. He said that it would be easy for me to get out of it; all I had to do was say that a graduate student of mine was giving a thesis recital and that he would be severely inconvenienced if I was pulled away for any length of time. I merely had to go to the courthouse the first day of my summons, Martin assured me, state my excuse to the clerk and they would let me go.

3

A few weeks after Yo-Yo Ma's visit to the university, and just before my appointment for jury duty began, I received a letter from an elementary-school music teacher down in Long Beach. Mr. Ralph Douglas wrote to inform me that ". . . because of your stature, I feel you are the right person to contact with regard to a musical genius I have discovered."

I got a perverse kick out of the reference to my stature, since I'm five-six.

"Kyung-hee Kim is only nine years old, but he is nothing less than a giant," Mr. Douglas gushed, pursuing the size theme. "He is musical, he can sight-read any piece of music you give him regardless of the difficulty, and he has a huge sound! I discovered him two years ago by accident. I needed members for the school orchestra, so I passed out a few instruments in my regular music class to see if anybody would get interested. Kyung-hee was last in line, and all I had left were a triangle and a cello. How lucky for us that he did not choose the triangle! I have been giving him lessons for only two years, but already he sounds like a professional! Even though I'm not a cellist myself, I confidently predict that Kyung-hee will be the next Rostopovitch [*sic*]."

Well.

Right away I suspected that this was a mildly talented boy judged through the ears of a wildly enthusiastic school-band instructor. If the boy had a real gift, it would almost certainly have been recognized by someone other than Ralph by now. Why hadn't the boy's parents—or Mr. Douglas, for that matter—found a real cello teacher for him by this time? And finally, though it was a small point, I wondered how seriously we could take Mr. Douglas's prediction with regard to Rostropovitch if he couldn't even spell the cellist's name properly.

I wrote Mr. Douglas back and thanked him for his letter, but explained that I taught only through the university, except for master classes every other summer at Tanglewood. A few days later, however, I received a telephone call from a woman who identified herself as Kyung-hee's mother. Her English was extremely limited, but she managed to say—loudly—that I was the only teacher she wanted for her son, and that once I heard him play I would change my mind.

I politely explained to her that my schedule would not permit it, but either she was not to be discouraged or she didn't understand what I said. "What time Kyung-hee come your house?" When I said that I simply wasn't interested in teaching children, she didn't say anything.

"Hello?" I asked, wondering if we had been disconnected.

"Yes?" she asked. "What time?"

Annoyed as I was, I remembered hearing my mother plead over the phone with a conductor to grant me an audition in his hotel room. It had embarrassed me terribly, but it had worked; he eventually gave in. I played while he ate his room-service breakfast and I went on to solo with his orchestra. That concert turned out to be the one that really got my career started. Thinking about this weakened my resistance, so I told Mrs. Kim I would hear her son, but with the understanding that it would be just for a few minutes. I really don't know why I gave in, for I felt that even if he was talented, I wouldn't be the right person for him anyway. I just hoped he wouldn't be an absolute disaster. My nightmare was that not only would he be a perfectly ordinary nine-year-old cellist, but when I had to say I couldn't teach him the mother wouldn't take no for an answer. If the boy did have something, I planned to send him on to Laura Kantor. She'd been working with several young cellists and I'd heard they were coming along well. I couldn't imagine how she did it, though; I felt uncomfortable around children even under the best of conditions. I could never figure out how to talk to them without either seeming condescending or hurting their feelings by talking over their heads. When I was a kid I used to despise it when adults would patronize me, but as soon as I grew up I found myself doing the same thing and feeling guilty about it.

4

The weekend before graduation I celebrated my thirty-fourth birthday alone, as I had nearly every year since moving away from home. I didn't want to just stay in the apartment, so I drove up to Santa Barbara and stayed at a bed-and-breakfast place my mother had particularly enjoyed the last time she and my father visited. It's right on the water, with red fuchsia growing all over its white stucco walls. In full sun it almost hurts your eyes to look at it. I made sure to get a room facing the ocean.

I spent the day shopping for a suit. I like new clothes, but I dislike having to shop for them. I hate spending money on things like clothes or furniture—practical things. I get that, I'm sure, from watching my parents despair over the monthly bills when I was very young. There was a time when we lived well, but that was when I was being paraded around Europe, and it was all other people's money anyway. As soon as my career slowed down, my patrons withdrew from sight.

In the end I didn't find a suit that I liked enough to buy, but I did find, in a used bookstore guarded by a sleepy miniature dachshund, a beautiful volume of photographs taken in space accompanied by quotes from astronauts describing their experiences. One quote in particular, from a Russian cosmonaut, caught my attention. He said that what struck him most about being outside the atmosphere was the silence. "It was a great silence," he wrote, "unlike any I have encountered on Earth, so vast and deep that I began to hear my own body: my heart beating, my blood vessels pulsing, even the rustle of my muscles moving over each other seemed audible. . . ."

This immediately made me think of the kind of silence I used to love, the instant before I would start a piece and the audience would quiet down to absolute stillness. I always held the bow over the strings for a few seconds too long, just to relish that incredible vacuum, when a hall filled with hundreds of people could become so quiet. No one ever, ever sneezed, coughed or budged until I offered release with the first note.

The astronauts careen through infinity at five miles a second, moving, working and even floating outside the capsule, but always surrounded by absolute silence. What does that do to someone? I wonder. To stare into all that velvety blackness and see the earth hanging in the middle of it, a sparkling, round ball floating in near-perfect emptiness, where sound has no meaning at all.

The book reminded me of the period in my childhood when the race to put men on the moon was at its highest pitch, and like most young boys, I dreamed of being an astronaut. Unlike most young boys, though, I actually trained for it. I asked my father to bring home a wooden crate from the warehouse just large enough for me to fit into, but not too large—I wanted to get used to being cramped. I appointed the crate with cushions, a blanket, a clock, snacks, a water bottle, a thermometer and a homemade periscope, and "trained" by setting the crate in front of the television set and watching my favorite programs through the periscope, which extended upward through a small hole in the top of my "capsule." I began by sitting in the crate through an entire half-hour program, and decided to increase my sitting time by five minutes each day.

As with my cello practice, I approached this astronaut training with purposeful intensity. At the end of a month I was up to three hours a day and still going strong. Understandably, my mother was deeply concerned. She tried to talk me out of doing it, but with no success; the idea of piloting a sleek bullet through the dark vastness of space fascinated me to the point of obsession. I was determined to increase dramatically my tolerance for sitting in cramped spaces, so that word of my training would reach the directors at NASA and inspire them to grant me early acceptance into the space program.

My training came to an abrupt end when my father happened to say at the breakfast table, "Reinhart, vat you are doing in that box all day? You don't got to practice sitting still, you sit still plenty once you get up there in space, you don't got to practice that. If you want to be astronaut, what you got to do is learn how to fly airplane. You do that when you grow up, not eight-years-old boy."

My mother chimed in, "That's right, Renne, you don't have to torture yourself sitting in that little box for hours! You could hurt your eyes looking through that tube! Please, Renne! Besides," she added, leaning toward me and speaking quietly, "they may not ever let Jews be astronauts, you know. It's sad, but with music at least you know you'll have a future."

"Oh, they'll send Jews into space, all right," my father muttered. "They just won't let them back down."

I'm sure that my father, who could find a way to be pessimistic or cynical about nearly anything, did not intend to frighten me when he said that, but when I climbed into my box and closed the lid later on that day, I began to imagine what it would be like if the rocket went off course, or if NASA decided that in fact they didn't need me to return, and I had to gradually suffocate in complete darkness. This thought disturbed me so much that I not only discontinued my training, but could not sleep at night for months afterward unless all the lights in my bedroom were on and the door was wide open.

After dinner in Santa Barbara I watched a movie, then took a short walk along the beach on my way back to the hotel. It was chilly but calm by the water. The gibbous moon, low in the western sky, cast a perfect column of reflected light on the ocean from the horizon to my feet. I was lost in thought until a rogue wave, with a heroic dying effort, made it farther up the beach than any of its predecessors and soaked my shoes.

Back in the room I found a bottle of champagne in an ice bucket waiting for me. An attached card said, "Happy Birthday to our dearest Reinhart, love Mother and Dad." The first time I played at Carnegie Hall, when I was fifteen, the conductor let me have a sip of champagne that night at dinner. It was Moët et Chandon, and my mother never forgot that I liked it. Every year she makes sure I get a bottle for my birthday. I had told them I would be at the bed-and-breakfast place over the weekend, but I didn't think she'd go to the trouble of having a bottle sent to my room. I should have known better, I suppose.

I wasn't really in the mood for champagne, but I couldn't very well leave it sitting there overnight. It would have been depressing to wake up the next morning and pack, all the time having to stare at the unopened bottle floating in its bucket of water. I drank as much of it as I could, opened one of the windows and tried to listen to the ocean. But I couldn't keep my attention on the sound for long. I kept thinking how much I wished I could quit my teaching job without having to worry about money. In a way it was odd that I was so determined to give concerts again, because a lot of active performers would have envied my life now; I didn't have to travel, struggle to maintain a grueling repertoire, deal with booking agents or publicists, or sweat out reviews. I taught three days a week and could have played the cello all day long on the other four for my own enjoyment if I liked. Unfortunately, playing onstage for an audience was the only kind of enjoyment I wanted.

I longed to concertize again—I'd longed for it every single day of the sixteen years since I'd had to stop—and occasionally I thought I was ready to try, but at the same time I was terrified of repeating what had happened at my last concert. It was at a tiny recital hall in Chicago, where I was scheduled to play three of the Bach unaccompanied suites. I hit the first chord of the fifth suite, in C minor, but it sounded so out of tune that, furious with myself, I stopped and started again. The second time was even worse, so I checked the tuning of the instrument and started again, only to stop a third time. The audience became restless and started murmuring, and then I realized what I had done. Who in the history of professional music had started a piece three times? No one that I'd heard of; it was an almost unthinkable failure. I managed to stay composed long enough to put my cello down on the stage. My hands and knees shook terribly as I bent down to place the bow across the cello. I walked across the stage, got through the stage door and then felt myself slowly shatter into a million pieces.

5

After I returned to Los Angeles I called home to thank my parents for the champagne. My father answered, catching me by surprise because my mother almost always answered the phone. My father didn't like speaking when he couldn't see whom he was talking to; it made him fidgety, he said, and it was true. Whenever I saw him having to talk on the phone he would pace, play with the cord or doodle on the backs of envelopes. The phone was in the kitchen, and my mother, who was fanatically conscientious, always stacked the bills on the kitchen table so that she would be forced to take care of them immediately. This led to another reason why my father didn't like talking on the phone: my mother would get unreasonably angry and scold him because marking up the envelopes made her nervous—she felt you must never scribble on official papers. Maybe it had something to do with getting out of Germany as a young woman, when documents were all-important. Some of this must have rubbed off on me, because to this day I have to photocopy all my music and pencil in my notes on the copies. I have never been able to bring myself to write on a published sheet of music or in a book.

"Hello, Dad. It's Reinhart."

"Ah . . . happy birthday."

"Thank you. How are you, Dad?"

"Ach, same tings. You?"

"Fine. The semester's over. It was quiet this year."

"Good, good . . . Momma's upstairs. Hold on."

My mother got on and immediately apologized for not being closer to the phone when I called. "But your father, he's stripping the wax in the kitchen, and the smell! I don't even know why he's doing it; the floor was fine before. You got your champagne? Those people—they acted like they were doing me such a big favor, but that's what they're in business for. You don't know what they wanted to charge me for—"

"It worked out fine, Mother. It was in my room when I came back from taking a walk by the ocean. It was perfect; thank you so much."

"You think I'm gonna forget my only boy's birthday? Imagine, thirty-four years already! It seems just a few days ago we were traveling around so much, yes?"

"Yes, it—"

"Remember London that time it snowed? And that cab-driver who says we never make it to the hall on time? You were so cute, Renne, with that little black hat and the coat on! You were just like a little old man. Here I was, I was going to kill that driver, and you were so quiet! And you were the one giving the concert, yeah?"

"Yes, I remember that."

"And how were the students at the end of the year? Good ones this time?"

"No, not this year."

"Ah, Renne . . . you remember Mrs. Sprenkle, yes? She

sent us an invitation this year. All her students had a recital, but you know your father, he wouldn't go. Last week I had them over for dinner and your father wouldn't say a word the whole night. He can't stand them. . . . Ach! Did you hear what he just said?"

"No."

"He says he can't stand anybody! You see? He never wants to have any fun."

"He's always been quiet, Mother."

"Reinhart! He's not a quiet man, he's just acting old, that's what. What's he gonna do when he's *really* old, huh?"

She told me what she had cooked that night, what Mrs. Sprenkle said about the Finkelsteins' daughter, who is supposed to be showing a lot of talent with the piano, and how Rabbi Siegel asked all about me when she bumped into him in town. He still remembered how, when I was only four years old, I was able to hear the chants only once and then sing them from memory.

As always, as soon as she mentioned my childhood her voice became almost reverential. "So, Reinhart," she asked, and I could have finished the sentence for her, "how is your music? You practicing hard still? Practicing too hard, I think, yes?"

"There isn't much to tell you, Mother. It's about the same."

There was a pause at the other end, then a sigh. "Ach, Renne . . . you work so hard. I just know God must be testing you. You working so hard like that, believe me, it will change for you. I know it will! God tests us to make us stronger, Renne. Maybe you should take a vacation, hm? Maybe someplace warm, or back to Europe somewhere?"

"We'll see. Mother, did you find out about Dad's pension plan yet?"

"Ah, you know your father, every day I'm asking him, every day he's putting it off. He's afraid to ask. Don't worry about that, Renne. What we care about is, are you happy? That's what matters most, Renne. When you have kids, you'll know. Believe me."

I was afraid that she might start asking if I was dating anyone, so I told her I had to hurry out for a dinner engagement, thanked her again for the champagne and tried to sign off.

"Wait a minute, Renne, I want to check . . . did you get your plane tickets yet?"

"Mother! It's only May! There's still half a year left, I have plenty of time."

"You don't know with these airlines, Renne! Things get crazy before you know it, and remember what happened to us in San Francisco. You don't want something like that to happen for Yom Kippur, do you? You haven't been here in three years, Reinhart. Is it asking too much that you get your tickets early so I can—"

"All right, Mother, all right. I'll make the reservation this week."

"Don't forget, Renne. That's all your father and I look forward to these days. We haven't seen you in so long. . . ."

"I promise—this week."

"We miss you, Renne. Happy birthday! Don't work too hard. You were always so serious, you should try to enjoy yourself more, yeah?"

"Thank you, Mother, I—"

"So did you enjoy yourself up in Santa Barbara? At that nice place? I wish I could go there again."

"Why don't you, Mother? You and Dad could come out to visit for a week. And get out of the humidity."

"Are you kidding? Your father's going to retire soon—we have to start saving now. We've already waited too long. But you're so young, you should be doing that every weekend! Renne—"

"Mother, I have to get to dinner. Thanks again for the champagne. It was very sweet of you."

"We think about you all the time, Renne. Happy birthday—I know this year it's going to happen for you. I just know it."

6

That Sunday afternoon the Kims showed up twenty minutes before their appointment, and sat out in their car, a filthy station wagon camouflaged with rust and primer, until exactly five o'clock. Since I wasn't busy I thought about going out and inviting them in early, but decided not to; if they were the sort of people who took pride in such matters, I didn't want to spoil their gesture of arriving precisely on time. My university students sometimes show up for lessons ten minutes late without any apology at all, or arrive early and ask to use my phone.

At last the family got out of the car and hurried up the sidewalk to the apartment. They rang the doorbell, and, after a pause of two or three seconds, rang again. Clearly they were anxious for me to hear their little boy. When I opened the door, Mr. and Mrs. Kim stood with their tiny son in front of them. An older sister, who looked twelve or thirteen, stood a few feet behind them all and stared at her shoes. Mrs. Kim poked her son sharply, and he said, without a trace of emotion in his face or voice, "Hello."

He had his thin arms wrapped around the neck of his cello case. Even the quarter-size cello was as tall as he was. He wore a brand-new suit and tie, but his shoes were badly scuffed. He appeared sorely in need of good food, fresh air and some exercise; he looked terribly small, even for a nine-year-old. He had a pitifully uneven haircut, and wore a pair of unattractive glasses that did not quite sit level on his face. One didn't have to strain to imagine the sort of teasing a child like this must receive from his classmates. He didn't look at me, but instead focused his eyes on a point a few yards behind me, at about the level of my knees.

Mr. Kim looked apologetic for intruding on my schedule. He wrung his hands in front of him and bowed his head several times. I extended my hand to shake his, and he seemed momentarily surprised, or perhaps embarrassed. When he did shake my hand, his palm felt as if it were made of wood. Both his hands were heavily callused. While he cut a trim, athletic figure and had handsome, masculine features, Mrs. Kim's appearance made a less positive impression. She had a thick body and a round, bland face. Her eyes were tiny slits above her cheeks, and she trained them on me as if I, not her son, were the one being auditioned. She clutched her purse in front of her with hands that were also badly weathered. Meanwhile, Kyung-hee's sister hung back and made no attempt to draw attention to herself.

I invited them all in and led them to the studio, where I had set up the smallest chair I could find next to the piano. Even that was too high for the boy, however. When he sat in it his feet dangled helplessly toward the floor. When I said I would try to find something more suitable, his sister said in an unpleasant monotone, "He doesn't care what kind of chair."

Kyung-hee took out the quarter-size cello and the little

bow, tightened the hairs, then shyly held the cello out toward me.

"His hands aren't strong enough to tune it," his sister declared—with some satisfaction, I noticed—but Kyung-hee showed no signs of embarrassment.

The tuning pegs were so poorly fitted that the cello was in fact almost impossible to tune. When I handed it back, he managed to avoid making any eye contact with me. I sat down and waited, but he just stared at the floor with his mouth slightly open. His appearance was so pathetic that I actually felt irritated looking at him. I was angry at his parents for giving him such an execrable haircut, and I was angry at him for not making the slightest effort to treat the occasion with some dignity. I couldn't wait to get him out of my house.

At last his mother said something to him in Korean, and without any sort of mental or physical preparation that I could detect he raised his bow and started sawing awkwardly at the first notes of a transcribed Mozart sonata.

The first few notes only confirmed my suspicions. He played the cheerful little piece without any signs of cheer at all—just what you might expect from a child with quick fingers but a deaf musical ear. Why the cello? Why me? That was what I was thinking when an extraordinary thing happened. Suddenly the music seemed to hit him from behind, from *outside* him rather than from his own body. By the tenth or fifteenth bar of music, even on that dreadful cello he played with such authority that I had to close my eyes; I couldn't bear to desecrate the music with the sight of that expressionless little boy.

Most of the child prodigies you read about in the paper or

see onstage are gifted mimics rather than artists, and the ability to imitate wears thin pretty quickly. A true prodigy—someone in whom the emotions of music actually resonate and find expression at a very young age—is rare. Many people think it is an impossibility. They assume that with so little life experience, no child could possibly comprehend the complex emotions of a piece of real music. When they hear about a Yehudi Menuhin or a Mozart they assume it must be a trick, a subtle deception of some kind. Nevertheless I know from my own experience that the emotions in music are musical emotions, and develop according to their own rules of chemistry and experience. They resemble and can strongly evoke the emotions we associate with profound life experiences, like sexual love or the death of a parent, but you don't need to have those experiences to "feel" music properly.

I could tell immediately and beyond any doubt that this boy felt the music. His interpretation was simply too fresh, too original to be explained by imitation. It had to come from some inner source, even though I had the impression that the music came from all around him.

When he finished the piece, he immediately fell limp again. His shoulders drooped and his mouth hung open again. I glanced at his parents to see their reaction to all of this. Mr. Kim was looking at me with a worried expression; he seemed unsure about how to judge his son's talent. Mrs. Kim, not wanting to take any chances, said something to Kyung-hee in Korean and the boy started a new piece.

The same thing happened as before: he began dreadfully—it was another light piece, the sort favored by elementary-school instrument teachers—but within a few bars managed to connect with whatever source he had drawn upon before, and positively soared. Mr. Douglas was wrong, of course; the boy was no Rostropovitch yet. He needed to learn technique from a real cellist, and simply had to undo whatever it was that made him look and play like an imbecile at the beginning of his pieces. There was plenty of room for exploration and growth, but it was obvious that the boy possessed a talent of incredible proportions.

Unable to contain my curiosity, I asked him if he had ever played any Bach. When he shook his head, I played Pierre Fournier's recording of the Bach unaccompanied cello suite in D minor on the stereo for him. I wondered how he would react to profound music, as opposed to the pieces Mr. Douglas had been teaching him.

When it ended I looked closely at Kyung-hee to see his reaction. His eyes were as round as saucers. I found a clean edition of the piece, set it up on a stand for him and asked him to try to sight-read it. The result was awesome. Some of the passages were technically beyond him, but without missing a beat he improvised solutions that were remarkably successful. When confronted with triple stops that he could not reach, he followed the melody, choosing the key note rather than the harmony. It was a spectacle that any musician would have cherished; he was getting his first taste of Bach, and it was transforming him right in front of my eyes!

I had strangely mixed feelings. When he finished I said that hearing him play had been an unforgettable and delightful experience. I know that when I was his age I would have been overcome with joy if my teacher had talked to me like that, instead of his usual habit, which was to pat me on the head or bow stiffly in my direction, but Kyung-hee's face registered neither pleasure nor embarrassment.

I didn't know what to do. I had planned, if he was indeed talented, to give his parents Laura Kantor's number, but I couldn't do it. After an awkward silence I turned to the Kims and heard myself say, almost as if in a dream, that I would be happy to teach Kyung-hee, and that I would charge them fifteen dollars for each lesson. I did not say that my usual fee for private lessons started at one hundred dollars. Mr. Kim said something, and then he and his wife had a lively discussion in Korean; from their gestures and so forth I got the impression that Mr. Kim thought fifteen dollars was way too much to spend on music, while Mrs. Kim seemed to be telling him he was being unreasonable.

She apparently won the argument, because at a certain point he just shook his head and looked at the floor angrily, and Mrs. Kim turned to me and asked when I would be available. I felt it was crucial that we get Kyung-hee's basic technique cleaned up immediately, so I suggested that at the beginning we meet twice a week, Sunday mornings and a weekday afternoon. Later, when I was sure that the worst of his habits had been corrected, we could reduce it to once a week. Mrs. Kim shook her head and told me that Kyung-hee and his sister were needed at the family dry cleaners on Saturday and Sunday, and both parents worked all day on weekdays, so what about weekday evenings? I wanted to wring their necks for making a child with a gift like this provide cheap labor, but decided to keep my mouth shut, at least at this early stage. We agreed on Monday and Thursday evenings. I gave Kyung-hee the Bach suites and told him that for the next few days he could poke around in them as he liked, and that we would start serious work after the first lesson. Then Mr. Kim said something to his wife. She nodded, then said she and her husband had a question for me. Pointing to her son, she asked, "When he can make concert?"

Only with great effort did I manage to keep a pleasant smile on my face. "You and Kyung-hee will have to make that decision," I said. "My recommendation, though, is that you move slowly. Talent like his can be ruined if you push it too fast."

Mrs. Kim nodded, but I thought I saw a hint of disapproval cross her face, though it may just have been that she didn't understand me. They left, and from my living-room window I watched them go out to the car. Mr. and Mrs. Kim appeared to be arguing again about something, and their daughter pulled one of those hand-sized video games out of her pocket and started playing with it. I watched until their car disappeared down the block, but as far as I could tell, none of them had said anything or paid any attention to Kyung-hee. He appeared to be in his own little world.

7

I had to get up well before dawn the next morning to practice before leaving for the courthouse. This spring I was focusing my efforts on chromatic scales, hoping to get my intervals so true that even my hearing couldn't detect faults there. Chromatic scales are notoriously difficult, and even when you do them properly you feel you may go insane from listening to them. After an hour of torture I had breakfast, then followed the map on the back of my summons to the court parking lot, where jurors board a shuttle for the downtown courthouse.

I'd walked or driven past the Criminal Courts Building probably a hundred times since moving to Los Angeles, but I'd never paid any attention to it until that morning. It's a square building that looks like a giant beehive; one could imagine behind each of its tiny windows a larval bureaucrat, feeding on carbon paper and waiting to mature into a clerk, a paralegal or a judge.

I passed through the security check along with a Spanish-speaking family that looked as if they had all been crying, then joined over two hundred other prospective jurors in a huge, dimly lit room where we had to check in at the clerk's desk.

My earlier suspicions about the courthouse actually being an incubator for bureaucrats proved resoundingly true. I gave the clerk my name and she handed me a pamphlet about jury duty, then brushed me aside to take the name of the next person in line. After half an hour, when everyone had checked in, I returned to her desk and asked whom I should speak to about being excused from duty. She said that I was supposed to do this before I checked in; because I had now checked in, I had to serve for the rest of the day. I asked how I was supposed to have known to give her my excuse and she pointed to the jury-duty pamphlet, the one she'd handed me immediately before checking me in. Before I could gather my wits enough to protest the obvious problem with this system she informed me that if I got called to a trial I would have a chance to speak to the judge and he or she could excuse me. Other than that, I would just have to wait out the day.

So I waited. I counted floor tiles, I read two-year-old magazines about aquarium care, I discovered sections of the newspaper I never knew existed, but mostly I avoided making eye contact with anyone. I didn't want to get drawn into any of the conversations I was overhearing around me, such as whether or not an Armenian jewelry-store owner was justified in shooting a black child barely thirteen years old who tried to rob the store wielding a toy gun; how uninspiring the candidates for the upcoming local elections were; and why Proposition 126 would be the death of Los Angeles. I didn't even know what Proposition 126 was. We broke for lunch, then returned again in two hours. By four o'clock I thought I would lose my mind from the boredom, but then my name, along with seventy-four others, was called and we were told to report to Department 135.

As we entered and took seats in the gallery I was struck by

how unimpressive the courtroom was. The judge's bench looked as if it was made of cheap veneer paneling, the American flag in the corner was on a flimsy stand and some of the ceiling panels were slightly ajar. The whole atmosphere reminded me of a junior high school auditorium rather than a hall of justice. The custodian instructed sixteen of us to sit in the jury box.

We had to stand for the judge's entrance—a distasteful ritual, I thought, in light of what you read every day about lawyers. Judge Davis stood over six feet tall and must have weighed at least three hundred pounds. He had short white hair, several chins and a wide mouth with downturned edges. I was immediately reminded of a magazine article about people who look like their pets; in it was a photo of a large man holding his English bulldog. Judge Davis could easily have joined the two of them in the picture without spoiling the effect. He cleared his throat loudly and called the court to order, introducing the case as *The State of California* vs. *Philip Weber.* The charge was second-degree murder. "This charge," he warned us, "is not to be taken as evidence of guilt. It is an accusation, not a declaration; all of you are to presume that the defendant is innocent until proven otherwise."

I couldn't believe it: Martin the encyclopedic violin teacher had told me, along with many other things that I hadn't asked to know, that the chances of my being selected for a big trial were infinitesimal. I should have guessed right then and there that I would somehow end up on a murder trial.

Instinctively I looked for the place where I thought the accused murderer would have to sit once the trial started, and realized to my horror and fascination that he was already sitting there. He was a young man, in his early twenties or so, pale and thin, and he had an enigmatic smile on his face. He sat straight, with his head erect and shoulders relaxed, watching the judge but seeming oblivious to the rest of us.

He didn't look like a murderer at all; he looked like a missionary from Salt Lake City. I became curious to know what he had done. Was it a brutal, shocking murder—did he stab his parents in their bed?—or would it turn out that he was driving too fast and had been involved in a fatal traffic accident?

My wondering was interrupted when Judge Davis leaned forward onto his elbows and delivered a stern lecture on the importance of jury duty, how seriously we should view our responsibility, and how little patience he had for people who tried to evade that solemn responsibility with frivolous excuses. His voice coming down from that platform had a sobering effect. I think everyone in the courtroom sat up straighter when he spoke. After his speech he riffled through some papers on his desk—he had gigantic, fumbling hands—then looked us over the way I imagine Marine drill instructors examine fresh recruits.

"This case may take time," he said warily. "Is that going to cause undue hardship for anyone?"

At first no one moved, then I heard a few people shift in their seats, and finally one woman coughed politely.

"Let's start with you," Judge Davis said, settling back into his chair and looking at her closely. "Who are you, ma'am?"

"I'm Janice Parks."

"What's the problem?"

She said that her husband worked the night shift at a piping factory and would have a fit if she wasn't home to cook an early dinner for him before going to work. Judge Davis clearly did not think much of her excuse; he turned slightly purple and boomed, "Do you understand it's your duty to serve, Mrs. Parks?"

"Yes, but—"

"Have you ever been accused of something you didn't do, Mrs. Parks?"

"I . . . I guess so, maybe," she stammered.

"How would you feel if you were accused of something serious, and were arrested for it, but when it came time to pick a jury all the ordinary people, your neighbors, weren't willing to do it because they had to cook dinner on time. What would you feel then?"

She didn't respond. "Not being able to cook dinner doesn't sound like undue hardship to me," Judge Davis snapped, dismissing her excuse with a wave of his thick hand, then he asked, "Who else? Who else feels they cannot serve? Raise your hands."

An older man writhed painfully in his seat and raised his hand. "Who are you? What's the problem?" the judge asked again. The poor old gentleman winced and said he had just thrown his back out the day before, which made it impossible for him to sit for long periods of time. Judge Davis seemed unimpressed, but when the man produced a note from his doctor in support of his claim, he was allowed to go. Another man said he couldn't deal with the testimony if it was going to be about murder; he was dismissed. A woman had plane tickets out of the country that she had purchased months before; she was also permitted to leave. A self-employed man, a screenwriter, described the extreme financial hardships jury duty would put him through, but when Judge Davis asked him to prove that he was currently working on a project that absolutely could not be delayed, the man said angrily, "All right, all right. Forget I mentioned it."

The more this went on, the more I felt my resolve weaken. Not only was my excuse of having to oversee a graduate recital fraudulent, but I was beginning to think that jury duty might be a good idea. It would force me to keep away from the cello for at least ten days, which would be the longest I'd gone without practicing for many years, perhaps even since I had first started playing. I'd tried before to take vacations from music, but my resistance always broke down after two or, at most, three days. Since I'd already handed in the semester grades, I was finished with teaching until September. There was only the Korean boy, and his lessons were at night anyway. By five o'clock no one was offering excuses anymore, so Judge Davis adjourned the court for the day, reminding us to be punctual the next morning, and then, after banging his gavel impressively, squeezed himself through a narrow door behind his desk to his chambers.

That night I tried to work out a lesson plan for the Korean boy for our first few weeks. It was a bittersweet task; the thought of passing on to him the knowledge I'd received from my teacher both excited and depressed me. It would have been different if I had felt more warmly toward him, if only he were more expressive or more clearly enthusiastic about studying with me. But he didn't seem to need or want my knowledge or approval. If I was going to share everything with a student, and eventually be surpassed by him, at least it should be someone I liked. At the same time, I wanted to transcend that feeling and make the most of the opportunity to teach him. It was partially for his sake, because I knew my having been a child performer would make me especially qualified to guide him, but also for my own sake. Kyung-hee was a rare case, and I knew that it would be deeply satisfying as a teacher to have the sort of communication that becomes possible with an exceptionally talented young person.

I went through my old cedar chest and dug out my notebooks and sheet music from my years in Germany; I hadn't looked at them since I was a teenager. Going through those materials made me think of my old teacher, his dark house and the smell of his pipe tobacco. "Herr Professor," as I called him, always smoked a pipe during our lessons, and had Frau Schmidt, his housekeeper, bring him coffee in a tall iron pot that was hopelessly dented and blackened from use.

One day von Kempen and I were in his house on Ederstausee, a large reservoir near Kassel, when he suddenly broke off the lesson to take me for a walk in his garden. He wanted me to see a flower that had bloomed just that morning; he had been trying to create a new variety of rose, and this was the first hybrid of its type. Because of a youthful equestrian accident, von Kempen had a badly crippled knee and could not walk without a cane. He had quite a collection of walking sticks from around the world; one, my favorite, even had a fencing sword hidden in it. When he taught, though, and had to get up for anything, he preferred to use his cello for support. I used to shiver at the sight of him hobbling around the studio with that ancient cello under his arm, but now I find that image strangely attractive.

That afternoon, using the cello as a crutch, he took me out into the garden to see the new rose. When he pointed it out to me I tried to seem interested, but he sensed my impatience. He asked what I was thinking at that very moment and I answered honestly that I wanted to finish the piece we were working on. He coughed disapprovingly and ordered me to put my eye right up to the flower so that my whole field of view was consumed by the brilliant orange-red petals.

As I did so he said, "Herr Sundheimer, look at all that color! And the pollen dust, which attracts a certain kind of bee that carries it to the other flowers and fertilizes them. Imagine the complexity of it, the perfection of the design! Isn't it amazing that God produces such things? Herr Sundheimer, right now you are looking at something that has never existed before today, not in all the time since the beginning of the universe. When it fades, it will never exist again—it is absolutely unique in the world. Doesn't it now seem more precious than when you first noticed it?"

"Yes, Herr Professor."

"Yes," von Kempen said, "and that is the way to approach music. Every piece, every time you play it, is unique and irreplaceable. You should open your ears and heart to every phrase, every note, and squeeze every drop of beauty you can from it. Take nothing for granted!" The maestro loved cigarettes almost as much as his pipe, and particularly enjoyed them while sitting outdoors in his garden. He removed one from a handsome silver case, lit it and puffed happily for a while, then handed me a pair of nail clippers from his pocket and told me to cut the flower at the stem. When I had done so he threaded it through the buttonhole of my jacket. "There you are," he said. "With all that uniqueness concentrated in one suit of clothes, you ought to have the lesson of your life!" and he led me back inside.

I couldn't possibly have re-created such moments with my college students; had I tried to do so, I would only have made a fool of myself and embarrassed them. It was a matter partially of their age, and partially of musicianship. You have to be either very young or uncontrollably musical not to find such expressions of sentiment maudlin. When I was a student I was both very young and very musical, which allowed my otherwise reserved teacher to express himself with abandon.

Strangely enough, in spite of our close relationship and the unrestrained warmth he showed toward me at all times, I never came to feel entirely at ease around him. I was not afraid of him, and certainly didn't dislike him, but I think that his advanced age, his old-fashioned manners and obscure dialect, and perhaps the fact that we worked together in a foreign country kept me from ever feeling completely natural in his company, and from being able to adequately return the candor and affection he showed me. How I wish I could see him now, even if for only an hour! As an example of my awkwardness, one afternoon during our lesson I realized I had to go to the bathroom, but I felt embarrassed to interrupt the lesson for this reason. I watched the minute hand on his old grandfather clock creep toward the hour, debating wildly whether to blurt out my problem or try to wait until the end of the lesson. The worse my discomfort grew, the more embarrassing the situation became. The longer I waited, the more convinced I was that he would sense the urgency in my voice and think me an idiot. After an eternity of silent agony, with only three minutes to go before the hour, I could stand it no longer. I wet my pants but kept playing, hoping he wouldn't notice. When the clock rang four o'clock, von Kempen—who never kept me overtime out of kindness to my mother, who always waited for me downstairs—stood and bowed as was his habit at the end of lessons. I returned the bow, holding the cello in front of me, and kept it in front of me all the way out to our car, where at last I burst into tears of shame. Instead of being sympathetic, my mother was furious.

• • •

When I went to Germany to study with him, von Kempen was grateful for the opportunity, and it showed in his whole bearing toward me. At that point in his life he had not concertized for twenty years after having made a firm decision to commit himself entirely to teaching. I, on the other hand, was teaching only to fill in the gaps until I could get back on the stage. I had mixed feelings about taking on a student who would require so much attention, especially one with so little personal charm. I worried that teaching him might drain me and extinguish my last hopes for coming to life again as a performer.

Looking at my notebooks and seeing in my childish handwriting the excitement I felt during each of my lessons, I grew angry with myself for being so selfish and not rejoicing in Kyung-hee's talent as any music lover should. Once someone came into the dressing room backstage after one of my concerts and rudely asked von Kempen if it ever bothered him to see such a young student get so much attention. The old man stood up from his chair (it was always painful for him to stand, but he insisted on such formalities) and said, "Sir, I assure you it is an honor and a pleasure to teach this boy, but even if it was not, it would still be my responsibility to do so. How I feel about it is entirely irrelevant." I wanted to have that kind of dignity, but it did not come so easily to me.

8

The next day Judge Davis began the trial by introducing the two lawyers, starting with the accused man's counsel, a public defender named Anna Doppelt. She wore a meticulously pressed gray business suit, no jewelry except for a pair of small gold earrings, and her hair was fastened straight back with a dark barrette. She seemed to be wearing no makeup, but could have used a bit here and there; she had thin lips and dry-looking skin. She appeared to be about my age, in her mid-thirties, or maybe even younger. Her desk was covered with large but orderly piles of yellow legal pads with writing all over them. In spite of appearing overworked, she seemed eager to get on with the trial.

"And representing the state," the judge said, sounding a bit friendlier, "the prosecutor, Assistant District Attorney Jack Graham." Mr. Graham was an older man, probably in his late fifties. He was somewhat overweight, wore a pair of reading glasses, and his tie didn't quite match his shirt. He had a pleasant, friendly look to him. From the way the judge introduced him, I suspected that they had worked in the same courtroom before.

Next the judge read twelve names off a computerized list,

and twelve prospective jurors from our group rose to take seats in the jury box. The rest of us stayed in the gallery. The judge announced that he would now initiate a procedure known as the voir dire, or "telling the truth." He explained in a rapid monotone that the men and women in the jury box would answer a series of questions, displayed on a large sign in the front of the courtroom, to see whether they were fit to be the jurors of the case. The first three questions were fairly predictable: name, occupation and marital status. The last questions surprised me: each juror had to state the occupations of their spouses and grown children, and had to describe any prior jury-duty experience in painstaking detail.

When one man mentioned that he worked as a janitor at the L.A. Times building, Judge Davis interrupted him to ask what newspapers he read. Had he read anything about this case? No. The judge interrupted another juror, a frightened-looking older woman who mentioned that her husband had been a police officer, to ask if she had ever been the victim of a crime. When she answered that she had been mugged once, only blocks away from this very courthouse, several people laughed quietly and Ms. Doppelt glanced at Judge Davis, who appeared to stifle a grin. He thanked the woman without further comment and moved on to the next prospective juror.

When all twelve had answered the printed questions, the judge invited Ms. Doppelt, the defense attorney, to voir dire the jury. She centered one of her yellow legal pads in front of her, took a deep breath and went down the line, asking questions for nearly two hours. I noticed that she scrutinized those jurors who seemed overly conservative or religious. When she finished, Mr. Graham, the prosecutor, did the same thing. He seemed especially wary of people whose work had even the most tenuous association with psychiatry or psychology. When all of the questioning was finished, Judge Davis invited the prosecutor to begin the next procedure. Mr. Graham nodded and gestured toward the juror sitting closest to the bench, a former schoolteacher who had once been a social worker, and said, "Thank you, Your Honor. We would like to thank and excuse juror number one, Mrs. Berger." She was led away without any comment from the judge and replaced with someone from the gallery. That person, a Mr. Lenahan, answered the questions on the printed card, identifying himself as a retired police officer. He was interviewed by the two lawyers and was promptly dismissed by Ms. Doppelt. Another juror was called to the box, went through the questioning procedure and was allowed to stay.

This went on all morning, past lunch and into the afternoon. Among those dismissed was a woman who admitted she had read about the defendant in a tabloid magazine article titled "Zen Monster Kills Guru," and had already made up her mind that the defendant belonged behind bars for what he did. From this interview I deduced that it had been a cult murder. The woman who had been mugged near the courthouse was sent home, as was a man whose wife worked at a hospital, had been assaulted by a patient there and had had to see a psychologist as part of her therapy before returning to work.

After Mr. Graham dismissed a young woman who had recently finished law school, Judge Davis read my name from his list. By this time everyone involved was looking tired of the selection process. After I had answered the printed questions, Ms. Doppelt raised her head from behind a pile of documents she was studying and asked me if I knew about the case from reading the papers or hearing about it otherwise. I said no. "Mr. Sundheimer, if someone had, let's say, an epileptic fit, and during his seizure he killed someone with a blow of his hand, do you think he should be punished for that?"

"I wouldn't say so, no."

"Why not?" she asked, nodding slowly.

"Because . . . I should think he had no control over it—over his movements, I mean."

"In other words," Ms. Doppelt suggested, "he didn't intend to kill anyone, right? Is that what you mean?"

"Yes . . . I suppose that was what I meant. . . ." She made me nervous; I couldn't tell if she was pleased by my answer or only setting me up for an embarrassing dismissal.

"Good," she said at last, looking at the other jurors as well as at me. "Let me just point out here that the law states that a person who is too sick—mentally sick—to form the intent to kill cannot be convicted of murder. He or she should be found not guilty by reason of insanity, then committed to an institution for treatment and held there until deemed fit to return to society. Does anyone here disagree with that? Does anyone think that's being too lenient?"

No one raised a hand. She seemed satisfied with my answers and turned the questioning over to the prosecutor. Mr. Graham stood up to stretch his legs, looked at me and smiled. His glasses were the old-fashioned black-rimmed type, and I noticed when he stood that his shoes needed polishing. He was an extremely charming man. He spoke gently, with a Southern accent, and used expressions I'd never heard before; during one interview a woman seemed to be giving contradictory answers to his questions about her occupation, but instead of getting angry he smiled and asked,

"Ma'am, I just want to make sure we're reading out of the same hymn book here—when you've finished with jury duty, will you be going back to selling merchandise over the phone or to writing novels?" I've always liked Southern English; it has a more musical cadence than the other varieties. I believe that all of us in the jury box wanted him to like us.

When he came to me, Mr. Graham leaned back in his chair, adjusted his glasses and asked if I knew anything about or had any impressions of foreign religions, such as Buddhism? No, except that I presumed it involved meditation. Did I have any religious beliefs that would make me feel uncomfortable hearing about Buddhism or would make me unable to be objective about the concepts of a foreign religion? No.

He asked about my education, so I mentioned that I'd been tutored privately in Europe while studying music.

"Do you give concerts now, Mr. Sundheimer?"

"Recently I've been teaching more than concertizing."

When I told him where I taught, and that I offered a music-theory course along with my tutorials in cello performance, one of his eyebrows rose up suddenly. "Really? Is your theory course difficult?"

His question caught me off guard. "Well . . . no," I stammered, "not if the student has taken the prerequisites."

"Forgive me for asking," he drawled, "it's just that one of my daughters goes there and I'm trying to help her find a course to bring her grades up."

The sound of laughter erupted in the gallery. I was too nervous to realize it was a joke until it was too late for me to laugh or even smile. Then Mr. Graham asked about my parents and close relatives. Any history of mental illness that I was aware of? No. Did I think that mental illness excused a person from any responsibility to society? Before I could even begin to think about that one, the defense attorney objected that the question was designed to prejudice the jury, and the judge agreed, instructing me not to answer.

The prosecutor showed no signs of annoyance and looked as if he might have been finished with his questions, but then he cocked his head to one side and asked, "You made a record, didn't you? When you were just a boy."

I answered that I had. I'd actually made several records, but since most of them were out of print, I didn't mention them.

Mr. Graham nodded with recognition and, after a moment's pause, indicated that he had no further questions. I had passed my test.

9

The first thing I did when Kyung-hee and his mother arrived was to ask him to try sitting in the little fold-up chair I'd bought for him over the weekend. It was just the right size, although I seemed more excited about it than he or his mother did. I wanted him to learn to sit properly. You cannot control the cello with your feet dangling above the ground. He had to learn how to use his legs to move the instrument as he went from string to string.

I'd been wondering how he would respond to my suggestion that we start from scratch. For the first half hour, all we did was discuss how to hold the cello without using the left hand for support, how to rotate it from side to side easily, and how to use gravity rather than arm strength to give the bow stroke its power. The purpose behind all good technique is to find the optimal balance of musical force and muscular relaxation. Like most cellists with poor training, he was as stiff as a board when he played.

I was pleased to see that he didn't show any signs of impatience. On the other hand, he didn't necessarily show signs of comprehension, either. He did whatever I asked him to, but that frozen expression of his—the slightly open mouth, the eyes never seeming to look at anything in particular—gave me the disturbing feeling that he might be obeying me mechanically without really grasping the underlying principle. I pulled my French edition of Pablo Casals's autobiography down from the shelf and read aloud one of his better-known quotes: *"Dans la vie il faut montrer du caractère et de la gentillesse."* I translated it as "In life, one must show both strength and gentleness," and I explained that as cellists, we try to apply this theory to our playing.

I asked Kyung-hee if he understood why it was important to be gentle as well as strong. He didn't answer or even look at me. Thinking he might not have heard me, I asked the question again. This time, after a long pause, he managed to nod stiffly.

"Can you tell me why we try to play that way?" I asked. He obviously heard me, but this time was either too nervous or too confused to answer. "I mean," I tried again, speaking in as friendly a manner as I could, "can you think of a time where you had to be gentle rather than strong?"

"Yes," he said at last, without elaborating.

"Would you tell me about it?"

After another long silence, he finally said, "If you try to hold a cat hard, it goes away. But if you hold it soft, it stays there."

"Yes, exactly," I said, encouraged that something had come out of him. "That is why we—"

"Mr. Douglas has a black cat," he blurted out, interrupting me. I felt a twinge of annoyance. When I was a child, I never dared interrupt an adult, much less a teacher. I think if I had interrupted von Kempen, he would have died of shock. Still, I wanted the boy to loosen up and express himself more freely, so I stifled my reaction. "Does he, really?" I asked.

"Uh."

"Well . . . I suppose everyone should have a pet, shouldn't they? I read in a magazine that just touching a cat or dog lowers your blood pressure and makes you feel more relaxed. Which sort of returns us to what we were talking about before, doesn't it?"

"My mom won't let me have a cat," Kyung-hee said. Before he could explain further, his mother, who was sitting only a few yards away on the sofa, spoke to him firmly in Korean. Kyung-hee lowered his head and fell silent again. He didn't look contrite or bitter when she scolded him; he just seemed to withdraw. I decided to save the Socratic method for another day and explained that in order to play the most difficult works with apparent ease, one must work very hard at the beginning to develop a precise, smooth technique that wastes no movement or energy. I told him that both Yehudi Menuhin and Arthur Rubinstein ignored technique early in their careers because they felt that sheer talent would carry them, but had to undergo years of painful retraining later in their careers to undo their sloppy habits. After this cautionary advice, I told him that although he might think me cruel to give him all these exercises, he'd certainly be grateful later.

"Now, Kyung-hee, let's start with scales. You know your scales, don't you?"

Silence.

"Kyung-hee, do you know what scales are?"

Another long silence, then at last he nodded.

"Why don't you tell me what you know about scales, Kyung-hee."

He fidgeted in his chair, then at last said in a tiny voice, "They're all over fish."

Evidently he had not been taught scales. Incredible! No wonder his parents didn't think to find him another teacher; he'd obviously been teaching himself by sight-reading, and Mr. Douglas had probably just been sitting back amazed and taking credit for it. I set a book of scales on the stand, explained how they worked and had him run through a few. As I expected, he had an extremely hard time, not only because his technique was improper but because they weren't melodic; there wasn't anything for him to hang on to. It seemed to take all the power out of him. As painful as it was for him, though, it would have been crueler for me to indulge him and let him go on playing instinctively. Better to get the basics straight now. I showed Kyung-hee how to finger the scales, and told him that for the next week he should do nothing else but them and the bowing exercises I gave him.

"What about this?" he asked, pointing to the Bach I'd given him last time. I sympathized because I could well understand how he must feel right now after discovering Bach only a week before. But if he gave in to this temptation, as soon as he started playing he'd fall right into his old habits: his bowing would get inconsistent, his left hand would clench up and his whole body would go tense again. So I repeated that he wasn't to play any music until he had mastered these exercises.

I stood up as a signal that the lesson was over, but Mrs. Kim cleared her throat. I turned to her and she said, "Last time you give him that." She was pointing to the Bach. "He playing that every day, all week. You should hear."

I really didn't want to set a precedent of letting her decide the content of our lessons, but at the same time I didn't want to alienate her, especially so early on. "All right," I said, sitting back down and looking at Kyung-hee. "Would you like to play some of it for me?"

I can't say that Kyung-hee showed signs of wanting to play anything, but he picked up the Bach gingerly and opened it up to page one. I should have known! Children always start at the beginning. He looked at it for a moment, then started the prelude to the G major suite. I noticed that this time he was more engaged in the music from the beginning than he had been the first time I saw him. Maybe it was just that he was relieved to be done with scales for the day.

As I predicted, his bad habits all came back in an instant—but the music! Just like the first time I heard him I had to close my eyes to really hear him, and it was something. That prelude, divine in its simplicity, is really just a series of arpeggios, which may help explain why the Bach suites were mistaken for exercises, and went virtually unplayed for nearly two centuries. Fortunately Pablo Casals stumbled upon a copy of them in a tiny music shop in Barcelona when he was thirteen years old. It was the discovery of his life; they were to become his favorite music. For twelve years he studied and worked every day at them, and was nearly twenty-five before he first played one of them in public. Casals often said that he felt that Bach was the Shakespeare and Rembrandt of music rolled into one, and that Bach's music expressed every nuance of the human experience. Von Kempen went even further, believing that Bach's musical inspiration was divine in origin, and that to play Bach properly was an act of religious devotion.

Kyung-hee made the arpeggios sound like waves out in mid-ocean, gentle in appearance but with enormous power under the surface. He gave the piece just the right balance of agitation and calm. He wanted to go on and play the Allemande, but I asked him to stop for the day. I was anxious to have some privacy after a very long hour with him; I had never had to teach anyone such basic technique before. After he and his mother left I sat by myself in the studio for a long time, feeling exhausted.

10

The voir dire continued for a whole second day. This part of the selection process took me by surprise. I always thought a jury was supposed to be a randomly selected group of law-abiding taxpayers. Anyone can see how the courts would want to sift out the obvious misfits, but allowing lawyers to try to stack the jury in their favor seemed odd to me.

After lunch on this second day of jury selection I was feeling drowsy; by now we had ten confirmed jurors, including me. Six were women: a widow whose husband had worked for the Jet Propulsion Lab in Pasadena, a retired Jewish lady who used to work as a practical nurse at an old folks' home, a large black woman who did secretarial work in the file room of an office building, an older Hispanic woman who worked as a nurse's aide at a hospital, a housewife whose husband was a pharmacist and another housewife whose husband worked "in sales." For men we had a leathery-skinned fellow who worked outdoors reading gas meters, a retired janitor from a high school in Eagle Rock and another retired man who used to be a plant manager at GM, a huge complex where they build cars. I was struggling to keep my eyes open when the judge called for someone to replace the latest dismissal, a man sitting next to me who was a biologist and who insisted that psychiatry was "not a real science," and that he could not take psychiatric testimony seriously.

The new prospective juror, I noticed as she made her way across the courtroom, had an excellent figure. She had a dark complexion and shadows under her eyes—something I've always found attractive. She looked Hispanic, or perhaps Middle Eastern, and appeared to be around my age. She wore a bloodred sweater. The clerk led her to the empty seat next to mine, and I felt myself blush as she sat down.

How many times I've wished I could suppress that reaction! When I was sixteen I soloed with the Seattle Symphony and, as usual, everything went beautifully. I received a standing ovation and was called back onstage for an encore. After I took my final bow—one aspect of performance that I'd never had a gift for; in fact, I'd had to take lessons from a dance teacher to learn how to bow without looking like a broken electric toy—just as I straightened up, the concertmaster congratulated me by kissing me on the cheek. If she had been older or uglier it might have gone without a hitch, but this particular concertmaster was young and very attractive, especially in her black velvet evening dress. When she kissed me, my face, illuminated by a row of powerful stage lights, turned such an intense shade of crimson that the audience acted as if it was the most endearing thing they had ever seen and cheered me for it. It was the only time in my life I did not enjoy the sound of applause.

The judge asked the new juror to state her name for the court.

"Maria-Teresa Reiter."

I didn't want to be rude by turning and watching her

during her interview, especially since we were sitting only a foot apart, so I fixed my eyes on a point on the wall in the back of the courtroom and tried to look impassive.

Maria-Teresa explained that she was an ambulance dispatcher, was married with one child, and had never done jury duty before. From her exchange with the defense attorney we learned that she was a lapsed Catholic who knew nothing about Asian religions and had been the victim of a crime only once, when her car was broken into. She had not been in the car at the time, and lost only a tape player, a pair of sunglasses and her husband's basketball.

The prosecutor educed that no one in her immediate family suffered from mental illness, that she had worked for the ambulance company since finishing high school, and that she and her husband, who worked for the railroad as an engineer, were both politically moderate. She stayed poised throughout the questioning, and answered in a masculine, whiskey-flavored voice. During one of the breaks I discovered why: she was an unabashed chain-smoker.

Ms. Reiter made it through her voir dire, leaving only one more juror to be confirmed. After two dismissals—a woman whose cousin had died in the Guyana tragedy and did not want to hear testimony about cults, and a man who had been badly frightened recently by a "crazy" homeless person—the two lawyers focused their attention on a black man, Mr. Dwight Anderson, an ex-Marine who worked as an industrial investigator at a defense plant. Toward the end of his interview, at about four-thirty, a patch of sunlight that had been gradually making its way across the floor of the courtroom reached the jury box. As the sun fell the patch of light crept up our legs, then spilled onto our laps, and eventually reached chest level. The brilliant red fabric of Ms. Reiter's sweater drew my attention. The afternoon sunlight illuminated the soft wool and, from where I was sitting, made her sweater partially transparent, giving me a clear view of her breasts in three-quarter profile. They were at the very beginning of exquisite decline. It dismayed and embarrassed me that I could feel this sort of longing so suddenly and so strongly, and in such an inappropriate setting.

When I could stand it no longer I shifted my attention back toward the courtroom. To my amusement I noticed that almost all in my field of view, male and female, had their eyes on Ms. Reiter's chest. I looked around at the rest of the room and saw that only two people seemed oblivious to the spectacle: the court stenographer, who was facing directly away from us as she typed, and the defendant, who was looking right at me. He had a bland smile on his face, as if he knew exactly what was going through my mind. I shuddered and looked away; when I glanced back a few moments later, he was staring out the window where the sunlight was coming from. For the first time I comprehended the reality that this was a murder trial, I was a juror chosen to decide a man's guilt or innocence, and now that man knew my name and quite a bit else about me.

The panel was sworn in, two alternates were chosen and the trial finally got under way. At last we were going to find out what the pale young man had done. I'd been especially curious after hearing about the tabloid article referring to the defendant as "the Zen monster." I had tried to track the article even though this was against the rules, but when I mentioned the name of the magazine to a librarian friend on campus, she stifled a laugh and suggested I try checking the dumpsters behind supermarkets.

Judge Davis began by telling us that since the defendant was pleading not guilty by reason of insanity, the trial had to be divided into two parts. First was the "guilt phase," where we had to determine whether or not the defendant actually committed the crime. If we found him guilty, we would then move to the "sanity phase," in which the defendant would try to prove that although he did commit the crime, he was insane at the time. The judge did not explain why we couldn't do these two things simultaneously; it seemed like an inefficient way to go about it, and I began to wonder how long I was going to be stuck in this courtroom.

The prosecutor gave his opening arguments first. In his gentle drawl, with almost a hint of sadness in his voice, he told us that the defendant, Philip Weber, was a college drop-out who felt bored and unsatisfied with his life. He wandered for several years trying to "find himself" with drugs and mysticism, eventually joining the Los Angeles Zen Foundation, a Buddhist church in Pacific Palisades. He was attracted to this religion because it offered "enlightenment," a blinding flash of insight that turns anyone who has it into a spiritual master.

"Mr. Weber believed," the prosecutor said, making a noticeable effort to sound matter-of-fact rather than sarcastic, "that if he was an enlightened Zen master, he would no longer have any nagging doubts or insecurities about anything, and spiritually advanced people would respect him and seek his advice and wisdom. In January of this year, during the foundation's annual intensive meditation retreat, Mr. Weber apparently decided his time had arrived. On the afternoon of January fourth, he suddenly started shouting that he was enlightened and that he had become a Buddha. When

Mr. Kazuo Okakura, the Zen master leading the retreat, asked Mr. Weber to demonstrate his 'enlightenment,' the young man jumped up, grabbed a stick out of the Zen master's hands and savagely beat him with it. There were eleven people in the church at the time, not counting Mr. Weber or Mr. Okakura, and all of them witnessed the assault. The blows crushed Mr. Okakura's skull and broke his neck, and he died several hours later in a hospital."

As Mr. Graham described the crime, several of the potential jurors stared incredulously at the defendant. He looked too frail to commit such a brutal murder. I also noticed a bit of a commotion in the back of the courtroom. I looked out and saw a group of Asian people surrounding an old couple, also Asian. The younger members of the group seemed to be translating for the old couple. I guessed that they were the parents of the murder victim.

"The evidence will show," Mr. Graham concluded, pointing at the defendant and looking straight at him, "that Mr. Weber intentionally killed Mr. Okakura in order to demonstrate his spiritual strength to the rest of the world, and in order to eliminate the possiblity that Mr. Okakura might challenge the validity of his self-declared 'enlightenment.' When you've heard the evidence, I believe you will find you have no choice but to find the defendant guilty."

The prosecutor returned to his seat and the judge ordered the defense to make its opening statement.

Ms. Doppelt stood up and requested a private conference. Judge Davis reluctantly consented, and the court custodian led the jury out to the jury room so that we would not overhear what was said. When we returned to the courtroom I could see that Ms. Doppelt was unhappy about something. When the judge once again invited her to make her opening remarks, she faced us and said, "Members of the jury, I am only allowed to introduce evidence of mental illness during the 'sanity phase' of the trial. So you in the jury will be forced to go through the process of declaring Philip guilty of murder before I have a chance to properly defend him. I can only hope that when this part of the trial is over, you will be willing to try to hear the evidence of insanity with open minds. Thank you." The judge raised one of his massive eyebrows and looked prepared to rebuke her, but just as quickly his eyebrow settled back again. The defendant noticed this and laughed quietly.

As we filed out of the courtroom for the morning break the juror who read gas meters, whose name was Gary, asked me, "Sounds pretty weird, huh? Hey, I could be a Zen master—I have a baseball bat in my truck! Ha ha . . ." When he laughed I noticed that he had badly neglected teeth.

We'd been told at least a dozen times not to discuss the trial at all until the deliberations started; I smiled and tried politely to drift away from him, but he followed me to the water fountain and asked if I knew anything about Buddhism. I said I didn't, but that I assumed it would be explained more carefully later on in the trial.

"Yeah, I hope so," he muttered. "Maybe they'll have a demonstration and get some guy to walk on coals or something!" He laughed again at his own comment.

I remembered from his voir dire that Gary was in his forties, but he looked twenty years older, probably from working in the sun. It was hard to believe we were so close in age. He had a round, protruding belly over skinny legs and a completely flat behind. I noticed this only because he was always tugging at his pants, as if he was used to having to keep pulling them up. He asked if I followed sports at all.

When I answered that I didn't, he told me that, the night before, the Dodgers had suffered an embarrassing defeat.

"Against a shitty team, too," he complained. "It doesn't make sense, you know? A great team plays a shitty team, there shouldn't be any question. But when you get a shitty team against a good team, it rubs off and everybody plays shitty."

Relieved that he had at least changed the subject, I said that the same thing often happens in music. You can hire a terrific performer, but make him play with a weak orchestra and you'd be surprised how badly he'll play sometimes.

"Yeah," he said, nodding. "You know, my parents made me take piano when I was a kid for a few weeks. Man! Did I hate that— I made 'em let me quit. But now I have a kid, and my wife wants to make him take piano lessons. You're into music—what do you think? Should kids take piano because it's good for 'em, or do you think it's a waste of time if they don't seem interested? I mean, my kid's not begging for piano lessons."

I don't think anyone knows the answer to this question, so I said that it depended on the child; some seem to get a lot out of music lessons, some don't. You can't tell until they've tried it.

Maria-Teresa was standing close enough to overhear our conversation. She drifted over and commented that her mother, who had always liked the sound of the accordion, made her take lessons on it for nearly a year. The lessons ended when the family acquired a new puppy who chewed the accordion apart and buried the biggest pieces in the backyard. "My mother had a fit." Maria-Teresa laughed. "But I snuck him treats for a month after that. I hated that accordion." She had a beautiful smile.

"Do you ever wish you'd stuck with it, though?" I asked her.

She looked at me suspiciously and asked, "Have you heard an accordion lately?" That was her answer; then she excused herself to go outside for a cigarette. I laughed, but she'd already left. It took me a few seconds to realize she was being humorous.

Maria-Teresa's story reminded me of the night Wolfgang Bruggen, one of Germany's most influential financiers and statesmen after the war, made my mother and me the guests of honor at one of his elaborate dinner parties. As usual I felt uncomfortable through most of the dinner; the other guests and even my distinguished host seemed uncertain whether to speak to me as a child or as an adult, and in such august company I hardly dared initiate conversation on my own. Eventually, as almost always happened at those events, the group settled into eulogizing me rather than speaking with me.

To make matters worse, Herr Bruggen's eighteen-year-old son (I was fifteen) sat next to me with a pinched expression on his face, and avoided even looking at me. Just before the dessert course, Herr Bruggen brought all conversation to a halt with a wave of his hand, gestured in my direction and announced, "I would like you all to consider this: six hours a day, practically since the day he was born! And he never once had to be told to practice. Think of what each of us could have done with that kind of spirit! Think of it!" Having said this, he glanced pointedly at his son, then invited us to try the caramel custard.

After dinner, as the adults shifted over to the living room to smoke and sip brandy, Herr Bruggen ordered his son to give me a tour of the estate's flower and herb garden. Once outside, the young man dutifully but joylessly identified the various shrubs and plants until I finally asked him, "Do you like to grow things?"

"I've never planted a thing in my life," he answered.

"Me neither. I'm not big on flowers," I said, hoping to impress the older boy. Because of the difference in our ages, and perhaps because I sensed he didn't like me, I craved his approval. A kind word from him—or better yet, a virile gesture such as confiding in me a forbidden exploit or asking if I wanted to see his car—would have meant more to me than all of his father's accolades. Instead he squinted at me and muttered, "My father really enjoys doing this, you know. He gets somebody like you to come over to the house, he talks about how great you are, and it's supposed to make me want to go out and do important things. But do you know what would happen to me if I said I wanted to be an artist or a musician? Christ, I'd be disowned in a minute. These dinner parties are pure bullshit, is what they are."

Then, as if to make the point that he wasn't going to be forced to admire me, he went right back to identifying shrubs. This incident, like Maria-Teresa's story about her mother and the accordion lessons, makes me wonder how nature could have designed human beings to be so eager to make children, yet so uncertain about how to raise them. When do you let children follow their own instincts, and when do you push them to do what you wish you had done yourself?

11

The state's first witness, Benjamin Frederick Ellis, was a tall, thin man wearing a suit that looked as if it must have been sold in only three sizes—small, medium or large. He made his way toward the front of the room, holding his arms stiffly at his sides, seeming very self-conscious. He looked only about forty years old, but he was completely bald. As he walked past the jury box, I saw that his hair had not fallen out but had been shaved.

I saw Ellis glance angrily at the accused murderer on his way up to the stand. The defendant smiled and nodded enigmatically; I couldn't tell if he was putting on a "spiritual master" act by pretending to forgive his accuser with a pious smile or was truly off in a fantasy world of his own. Mr. Ellis took the oath and then sat down, sitting bolt upright with his hands folded symmetrically on his lap. I've noticed that Americans who become interested in Eastern mysticism always have to find ways to let you know it; they sit on the floor with their legs crossed even when there are chairs available, with their spines unnaturally erect, like West Point cadets. Mr. Graham stepped up to the witness stand, resting one foot on the platform and draping his right arm across the railing. He seemed to be trying by example to make the witness relax.

Mr. Ellis introduced himself as the senior resident monk at the Los Angeles Zen Foundation church, which explained the shaved head. He nervously described what happened on the day of the murder. The members of their church were conducting an "intensive meditation retreat." According to tradition, for one week they held to a rigorous daily schedule of getting up at four o'clock in the morning, chanting in Japanese, performing hundreds of full prostrations in front of an image of the Buddha, and sitting absolutely still for up to sixteen hours a day in meditation. They went to bed at eleven o'clock at night, but many of the students, Ellis explained, only pretended to do so; to show their determination, they would sneak back down to the meditation hall in the darkness and continue their efforts. The purpose of the meditation, he explained, was to try to find a solution to a seemingly irrational puzzle that the Zen master had privately assigned to each student. You could solve the puzzle only if you had a transformational insight, which they called "enlightenment."

"On the fourth day of the retreat," Mr. Ellis told us, "Philip started . . . um, breathing loud. This was in the morning, when we were sitting. Everybody thought he was just making a big push to concentrate, so no one bothered him about it."

After a lunch eaten in complete silence—talking was forbidden for the entire week—they again began sitting in consecutive fifty-minute periods. I was wondering, and I'm sure all of the other jurors must have been as well, how can anyone actually do this? The thought of having to sit cross-legged on the floor for even half an hour without budging, concentrating on a puzzle, struck me as being almost unimaginable.

And then to do this for an hour at a time, sixteen or more hours a day—does it feel good to these people? Or is it a form of penance, like flogging yourself or saying thousands of Hail Marys, a test of endurance that gradually makes you feel euphoric? Then I realized, with a sense of irony, that I probably knew more about it than I gave myself credit for, because I had practiced the cello six or more hours a day for nearly thirty years straight, which many people would consider an unbearable schedule.

Mr. Ellis told us that during the first hour of meditation after lunch, Philip started crying quietly to himself. But—incredibly, it seemed to me—no one disturbed him. Ellis said that since Philip didn't fall down or get up and seemed otherwise in control of himself, they thought he'd be all right.

"During the second hour," the monk recalled, describing all of this as if it were perfectly ordinary, "Philip looked OK. His breathing was quiet. During the walking period—we walk around every hour or so to stretch and break up the monotony—he was walking kind of funny; his steps were real light—you know, like he was walking on a mattress? Then, during the third hour, he started smiling to himself. Then it turned to giggling. This was at around three o'clock. Okakura signaled for him to be quiet, and that's when Philip jumped up and started yelling."

"Do you remember exactly what he said?" Mr. Graham asked.

"Yes. He said, 'I got it! I got my koan! I'm a Buddha! I always was a Buddha!' " Mr. Ellis glanced again at the defendant, who was nodding gently, as if he were listening to a story about someone else.

Mr. Ellis continued, "So Okakura stood right in front of

him and said, 'Show me the answer to your koan!' That's the Japanese word for the puzzle you're supposed to work on. Philip looked at him for a second, then grabbed the stick that Okakura always carried out of his hands, and . . . he hit him in the face with it. Extremely hard. It was so shocking—all of us were sort of paralyzed for a second. It was like it wasn't real, it was so . . . so unbelievable. Okakura fell down and Philip kept hitting him. There was blood . . . there was so much blood everywhere, and you could see his skull was . . . caved in . . . I . . . I can't really describe . . ." The witness closed his eyes and pinched the bridge of his nose with his fingers. "You'd have to know . . . what a wonderful man this was. . . ." he said, struggling to control himself. "Mr. Okakura was so wonderful . . . he was an inspiration to so many people. . . ."

I heard some noise out in the gallery and saw that the old Japanese woman was crying. Two young women were comforting her. Her husband sat stoically, staring straight ahead at the witness. His eyes looked moist, but he didn't dab them or even budge. At this moment I regretted that I had decided to participate in the trial. The sight of that old couple, having to hear about the brutal death of their son through a whispered translation, was almost too sad to bear. Meanwhile the defendant had a strangely compassionate expression on his face; he was looking at the witness as if he felt sorry for him for having to remember something so awful. He didn't appear to feel any responsibility or connection to what was being said.

After pausing to allow the witness to pull himself together, Mr. Graham asked gently, "What happened next, Mr. Ellis?"

"I jumped up and tackled him to the ground. By then he had hit Okakura four or five times. I kept holding Philip down, and Louise, one of the other members, ran into the kitchen to call the police."

Mr. Graham asked the clerk to bring exhibit number one into the courtroom. The clerk left the room and returned in a moment with a heavy oak pole, about four feet long and flattened at one end like an oar. There were dark stains at the flat end, and I felt queasy as I looked at it.

"Was this the stick that Philip Weber used to kill Mr. Okakura?"

"Yes."

Mr. Graham brought the stick over to the jury box and asked each of us to hold it to get a sense of how heavy it was. And it was heavy. Touching it was a genuinely nauseating experience.

After he'd returned the stick to the custodian, Mr. Graham resumed his examination of the witness. "Mr. Ellis, after you had tackled him to the ground, what was Philip like while you were holding him down? Was he struggling? Was he talking to you?"

An expression of disgust passed over the witness's face as he looked again at the defendant, who appeared to be listening closely.

"He was telling me, very matter-of-fact-like, that he was enlightened, and that now he was the Zen master. That if I wanted, I could be his first student."

The defendant looked as if he was about to stand up and say something, but Ms. Doppelt whispered something to him in time to prevent it. A detached, bland look returned to his face, which made me wonder if the public defender was actually encouraging him to look insane.

• • •

When we broke for lunch I decided to walk down the street to an Italian restaurant I'd seen that morning. Though it was packed, the hostess was able to seat me right away at the last open table. Not two minutes after I sat down, Maria-Teresa walked in. She had worn a simple black dress to court that day, and looked stunning in it. I saw the hostess explaining to her that there would probably be a ten-minute wait. Maria-Teresa frowned and glanced at her watch, then looked up and happened to see me.

Out of sheer nervous habit I looked down at my menu and pretended I hadn't seen her, but then it occurred to me how foolish that was—not only because it was unfriendly, but because I would have been thrilled if she joined me. When I looked back up, though, she was already turning to leave the restaurant. More out of anger with myself than anything else, I called out her name, pretended to have just noticed her, and invited her to share my table. She told me later that this gesture, along with what she'd heard about me during the voir dire, gave her the impression that I must be an easygoing but quietly confident man. She was right about my being quiet.

At first we made small talk about the voir dire and some of the people who were dismissed. She was so attractive that I was afraid of appearing to stare at her. I was used to being able to watch women for long stretches of time—students of mine playing the cello during lessons—without there being any self-consciousness about it. Sometimes I would get a bit lost in watching them play rather than listening.

So I spent a good deal of the hour with Maria-Teresa reminding myself not to let my eyes get stuck on either her magnificent face or her chest, which her dress did not entirely cover. She said she was enjoying getting away from her job for a while because "dispatching isn't what it's cracked up to be," to which I responded that I wasn't aware it had a favorable reputation.

"I was joking. Christ!" she said, laughing out loud.

She was not an intellectual by any means, but she wasn't dumb. Her appearance certainly added to the impression that she was worldly—the shadows under her eyes, the black dress and that smoky voice. "So you're a cello player, right? I should try to learn something about classical music. When I hear it I imagine guys in starched collars who all look like Freud standing around in a castle with their monocles on, clicking their heels and bowing. You know what I mean?"

"*All* classical music makes you think of that?" I asked her.

"Mm, not all of it. I have one classical tape that I like, come to think of it. The sound track to *Amadeus.* I got it after seeing the movie. I'll bet that makes you sick, huh?"

Musical ignorance usually depresses me, but her conversation was so impossibly trite it was charming. At least she could identify the sound track as classical music; hordes of people exist out there who think that the music was written for the film. These are the same people who refer to Bach's monumental toccata for organ as the theme song from *Rollerball,* or who giggle when they hear the *William Tell* overture played in a concert hall.

"Maybe you could tell me some other good composers to listen to," she said. "I want to hear more, but I don't know where to start."

I asked her which of the Mozart pieces she liked especially. She confessed that she hadn't listened to the tape carefully enough to recall a specific song. "Which makes me think of a question," she said, drowning her salad with French dressing. "You know classical music inside and out, right? So what's your favorite piece? Of all those symphonies and sonatas, which do you think is the best?"

"That's an impossible question! There's so much of it, and so much of it is indescribably beautiful. Just the music for cello alone—"

"OK, so let's whittle it down. What's your favorite cello piece?"

"Even that isn't fair! You can't compare, say, the baroque masterpieces with the romantic ones because they're entirely different kinds of music."

"Oh, all right, all right, what's *one* of your favorites, then? It doesn't have to be your absolute favorite. Is Mozart up there on your list?"

"Oh, of course. He'd be up there on any list. But the composer whose work I personally enjoy most is Bach—Johann Sebastian, that is, not his sons. Do you like him?"

"He's one of those guys with a wig, right?"

"Right."

"Well, I've probably heard some, but I couldn't hum it for you. Let me ask you something, though. Certain kinds of music charge you up, other kinds make you feel depressed, and some make you feel really calm. What's the feeling you get from Bach? Sometimes if I'm switching stations on the radio I hit a classical station, and most of it sounds so . . . so dry, I guess, that I wonder. Do you really get turned on by that stuff, or is it more of a cultural-appreciation thing—you know, something that you do because it's good for you? It's a stupid question, I suppose."

"No, it isn't at all. But it's a hard thing to put into words. When you ask what I feel like when I hear music, my first instinct would be to answer by playing something rather than saying anything about it. To me it 'feels' just like it sounds. But I think I can give you an example. My teacher in Germany had said he wanted a memorial concert at his favorite church instead of a traditional funeral service. Since he didn't say what he wanted played, the executor of his estate asked me to choose the program. Obviously it couldn't be cheerful music, but at the same time you wouldn't want something bleak or depressing. I chose a few choral preludes by Bach, finishing up with one called *Wenn wir in höchsten Nöthen sein.* It means 'When in the hour of utmost need.' Bach wrote it just a few weeks before he died, after an eye operation that didn't work. Since he couldn't see at all, he had to dictate the piece to his son-in-law. He wrote it knowing he was dying; the troubles of the world couldn't affect him anymore. There isn't a trace of suffering in the music; his mind heard only perfection and harmony. My teacher loved Bach, and had just passed out of a hard life, so I thought that would be just right."

To my surprise and mortification, I felt my throat start to tighten, and realized I had to change the subject before making a fool of myself in front of Maria-Teresa.

Before we left the restaurant I promised to lend her a tape of music that I thought she might like if she enjoyed the *Amadeus* sound track. When the check came I felt a pang of indecision; force of habit suggested that I offer to pay for both of us, but I was afraid that the circumstances might make this seem inappropriate. In the end I didn't have to decide because Maria-Teresa picked up the bill and asked if I would mind if we put it on her credit card, since she had forgotten to bring cash with her. I said I didn't mind, and gave her the correct change for my portion of the bill.

We walked together back to the courthouse, talking about

the drought. Living in Southern California gives you so much material for small talk; you have your choice among brush-fires, mud slides, earthquakes, smog alerts, droughts and freeway shootings, and those are only the obvious ones. Maria-Teresa said that she didn't have a garden, but coveted long showers and couldn't seem to keep within her monthly water ration. "And that's with only me living in the house most of the time," she added. This comment surprised me, and once again I could feel my cheeks redden, because I knew from her voir dire that she was married.

12

In the first cross-examination of the trial the defense attorney seemed determined not to let us forget how bizarre the activities of the Zen retreat were.

"Mr. Ellis," Ms. Doppelt began, "I'd like to start by asking about the stick." There was an edge to her voice, as if she were questioning an anxious college student about a fatal hazing accident. "Could you tell us something about it? Why did Mr. Okakura have it in his hands that day?"

The witness fidgeted a bit and answered that the stick was called a kyosaku, and was a traditional object used by nearly all Zen teachers.

"And how is it used?" the lawyer asked, using her finger to return a stray lock of hair to its proper place behind her ear.

"Zen teachers use it, um . . . to try to help you, if you're getting drowsy, or if your mind is wandering."

"OK—but how is it used?" she prodded. "Isn't it true the teacher hits you with it?"

The monk fidgeted again in his chair. "Yeah, on the back. But he doesn't do it for no reason—it's done out of kindness, to help you."

"Kindness?" she asked sarcastically. "How hard does he apply this kindness usually?"

"Not hard. It's like a slap—it's bracing. You look forward to it, especially if your back is aching from sitting for a long time."

"Did Mr. Okakura ever use the stick on Philip?"

"Yes. He used it on everyone."

A knowing look passed over Ms. Doppelt's face. "Didn't he use it on Philip," she asked in a slightly louder voice than before, "just before Philip went hysterical that afternoon?"

"Well, not right before . . . It was, oh . . . several minutes at least."

Ms. Doppelt nodded but looked unconvinced. "Mr. Ellis," she said acidly, "you didn't tell us about that in your testimony earlier."

"Yes, I did!" he protested. "I said Mr. Okakura signaled Philip to be quiet! A slap with the kyosaku is the signal we always use. Everybody in Zen knows about it; it didn't come out of nowhere."

"I see," Ms. Doppelt said. "Mr. Okakura hit him with the stick to make him quiet down. A few minutes after that, Philip suddenly started screaming that he was a Buddha and that he'd solved his puzzle. Did it occur to you at all—at any point during all this—that maybe this young man was in trouble?"

The monk looked upset by the question, shaking his head angrily and answering, "It might seem that way, but the thing is . . . crying, laughing, even hallucinating happen a lot during these retreats. He was acting strangely, but not so strangely that any of us could have seen he would do something like what he did."

"Mr. Ellis," the lawyer asked with a look of incredulity on

her face, "aren't you aware that inappropriate laughing, crying and hallucinating are also not uncommon during psychotic episodes?"

"I'm not an expert on that, no." The witness brushed his hands across his thigh. He appeared to be trying to press out a wrinkle in his pants.

"I'm aware of that, Mr. Ellis, but for heaven's sake . . . All right, let's move on to the puzzle, then—the one that Mr. Okakura assigned to Philip. Could you tell us what that puzzle was?"

The monk actually blushed, then answered, "It's hard to do it out of context like this. Koans aren't logical, so sometimes they seem . . . you would think they make no sense at all, or sound strange. They're meant to make you see the limitations of your reason."

The lawyer nodded but did not say anything. The witness coughed self-consciously but eventually realized he was not off the hook, and had to continue: "The koan Philip had is very well known. It's been used for over a thousand years. It goes, 'If you meet the Buddha in the road and he stands in your way, kill him.' "

The defense attorney's face suddenly changed to one of great puzzlement, and she glanced over at us, as if to see if we shared her confusion.

"That does sound strange, Mr. Ellis. Can you tell us the correct interpretation of the advice, 'Kill the Buddha in the road'?"

"No. I haven't passed that koan yet."

Then Ms. Doppelt asked the monk if it was true that according to Zen philosophy, a Zen master is considered a living Buddha. The monk said yes, that was true, and I thought I saw her fight back a hint of a smile. She clasped her hands behind her back, nodded significantly and reviewed the information aloud.

"So your testimony is that Mr. Okakura was a living Buddha, correct?"

"Correct."

"And Philip was given a puzzle that says if you meet a Buddha you should kill him, correct?"

"Yes, that's correct."

"When Philip started shouting that he knew the answer to the puzzle, Mr. Okakura ordered him to show it, to demonstrate it for everyone. Is that correct?"

"Yes."

"That's very interesting."

She walked slowly back to her seat next to the defendant, creating a dramatic pause in the testimony, then turned around, glanced at us and said, "The defense has no further questions, Your Honor."

I remembered the time I had a music-theory student who occasionally complained of depression but who otherwise seemed normal and well adjusted. During the school year a group of acquaintances repeatedly urged him to attend what they described as a "casual chat session for Christians." He finally gave in, at first saying that he was interested in it only as a social activity but within a few months becoming seriously involved in their organization. Once he had become a full-fledged member he was expected to proselytize, and he even tried to get me to attend one of their meetings. Whenever he mentioned the Lord Jesus Christ, which was almost constantly, even during lessons, his face took on a relentless expression of happiness. He never missed an opportunity to remind me that since accepting the Lord Jesus Christ into his heart he was happy all the time, no longer saw the need to use profanity and had learned never to hold grudges or think negative thoughts. Most important (judging from the number of times he repeated it to me) was that he had "found out who he really was," although he never was more specific than that. When I found out he was pressuring some of my other students to join, in particular an exchange student from China who could barely speak English well enough to understand what he was talking about, I lost my composure and told him to keep his missionary activities out of my classroom. He dropped my course immediately and filed a grievance against me, but it didn't come to anything and I never saw him again. I don't even know if he graduated.

From what we'd heard in court that day, Zen sounded something like my student's sect. Enlightenment, salvation, finding your "true self"—it all sounded too grandiose, hopeful and vague at the same time to be believed. I couldn't understand how anyone could walk into a building, see a bunch of shaven-headed Caucasians dressed in robes, hear them chant in Japanese and not want to tiptoe as quickly as possible back outside to safety.

13

Things went both well and badly during Kyung-hee's second lesson. No sooner had the boy and his mother gotten through the door than Mrs. Kim thrust the exercise book I'd given Kyung-hee in front of me, made an unpleasant face and said, "Too easy! Kyung-hee already good, why you want him do this?"

"Because, Mrs. Kim, it's necessary if he wants to become great. He's good now, but he'll never be great if he doesn't pay attention to the basics."

"Eh?" she grunted, frowning at me as if I were the one with the language problem. "This too easy," she repeated in a shrill voice, waving her plump little hand dismissively and planting herself on the couch in the studio. She crossed her arms in front of her and glared at me.

No wonder Kyung-hee never says anything. What child would dare express himself around a parent like that? For the first time, I felt sympathetic toward the boy rather than just annoyed by him. As he rosined his bow I tuned his cello for him, and saw that on the back of his cello he had placed a tiny sticker with an Asian character written on it. "What's this?"

I asked him. He looked at me from behind the thick lenses that made his eyes look the size of nectarines.

"That means cat," he said in a tiny voice.

"Cat, cat," Mrs. Kim echoed. "Always cat!" She finished her thought in Korean, but Kyung-hee didn't appear to be paying any attention to her.

"Do you like cats?" I asked partially to defy his mother.

He nodded. "Cats can see at night."

"Yes, that's true. And they're excellent hunters. Have you ever seen one catch a mouse?"

He shook his head, looking at me expectantly. At least he was looking at me.

"Well, they creep up, very silently, until they're very close to their prey. Then they freeze, just like a statue, and wait for exactly the right moment, and then . . ." I mimed the action of hunching up motionless, then bursting out of hiding. "They jump, just like they were shot out of a gun! It's pretty exciting."

He actually smiled and I saw his teeth for the first time. I felt as if I'd just caught a glimpse of the Holy Grail. Not wanting to lose the momentum, I picked up my bow and said, "You know, that's exactly the kind of feeling you want to have when you begin a great piece. Watch me."

I drew the bow and held it over the strings and froze, gathering energy for the first note. Then I let go and dug into it—high C on the A string, then tumbling down to the low C string at the bottom. It was the initial phrase of the third Bach suite. "You see?" I asked, hoping he would figure out that even a simple line could lead one to a world of musical images and emotions, "That last C was the mouse! I burst out of the woods, chased it down and caught it! Can you try?"

He froze like a little kitten, with an unintentionally comical look of determination on his face. Then he pounced, unfortunately hitting the thin A string so hard that it snapped. His face fell as if he had been shot; he went pale and his body turned stiff, as if he were going into shock.

"Aiyo," his mother yelped, and then bolted up, leaned over him and scolded him, repeating the same phrase in Korean over and over. He hung his head and seemed to tune out; it was as if he were trying to make his body as small and unobtrusive as possible, and then make his soul disappear. Mrs. Kim shook her head in frustration and said to him in English, for my benefit, "You don't listen to teacher! You don't do like teacher do! How we going to pay for that if you breaking it? Daddy very angry when he gets home."

I know that it's best not to interfere with students and their parents, but I could not restrain myself. "Mrs. Kim," I said, struggling to keep my voice under control, "your son is a cellist—an extremely talented cellist, and he may one day be a great and famous cellist. But he will never be anything if you don't let him make mistakes. Cellists break strings—it happens all the time. There's no way to avoid it. It isn't your son's fault—I asked him to play that way to try to help him!"

I couldn't tell whether Mrs. Kim was furious with me or stricken with embarrassment. She walked stiffly back toward the couch and sat down slowly, fixing her eyes somewhere in the middle of the floor.

The rest of the lesson was a disaster. Kyung-hee had totally withdrawn; he didn't even answer yes or no to my questions, merely shrugged. On the other hand, when he played his exercises for me I could see he'd made good progress.

Which left me even more confused than before over what to do about him.

• • •

The next state's witness was the policeman who had first arrived at the scene and taken Philip Weber into custody. He was a young man, with a regulation mustache, of course, and all business. He never smiled, never paused to think about his answers or choice of words, didn't look at anyone but the attorney examining him, and said "sir" in almost all of his responses to the prosecutor's questions. Still, his testimony, in spite of his formulaic attempts to make it sound like objective fact and nothing more, let you know that he thought Philip Weber was a self-absorbed deviant who knew exactly what he was doing that day.

"Did Mr. Weber seem in control of himself when you arrested him?" the prosecutor asked.

"Yes, sir, he was completely in control. The suspect did not resist arrest. He was not agitated."

"Did he speak to you at all after you had read him his rights?"

"Yes, sir. The suspect spoke quite a bit."

"What did he talk about?"

"The suspect talked about his philosophy. It all sounded like gibberish to me. He was saying that everything was an illusion, but then he asked if we could adjust the handcuffs because they were uncomfortable. Also, in the car on the way to the station, the suspect told me to avoid a certain street because of construction. He said we would be delayed."

"Was he right, officer?"

"Yes, sir. We were delayed several minutes."

I thought I saw the policeman's eyes dart uncomfortably as he said this; I think he was a little embarrassed.

The state's last witness was the homicide detective who

had interviewed Philip Weber just after he was arrested. He was more of a bureaucrat than the officer had been; he didn't need to use paramilitary terminology, nor did he sport a regulation mustache. He was black and seemed like a reasonable man, and I noticed that he looked at the defendant several times without any apparent malice or eagerness to see the young man punished. I got the impression that this had been a relatively trouble-free case for him.

"Did Mr. Weber make a confession, Detective Wright?" Mr. Graham asked.

"Yes, he did."

"Had you read him his Miranda rights?"

"Yes."

"And what did he tell you?"

"Well, he was very cooperative. He acknowledged right off that he'd killed the man, and when I asked him, he said he didn't feel any remorse over it. He said that the killing was something between Zen masters, that us ordinary folks just wouldn't get it, and there wasn't much point in trying to explain it. He seemed to feel that the victim—the Japanese man—understood and wouldn't have minded. Philip claimed that killing the Japanese man was really the best way to put the victim's philosophy into action."

"Did Mr. Weber say what that philosophy was?"

Detective Wright laughed and said, "Well, he tried to explain it to me, but I'm afraid it went over my head, me being just an ordinary guy, you know. It's all in my report—you might be better off reading it straight from there than relying on my memory. Overall, Philip seemed to be saying that the whole Zen thing is about confidence. That if you have complete confidence in yourself, anything you do is all right—that it's perfect, in fact. It all sounds great—all these cults sound great at first—until you see what they lead people to do."

During the breaks I tried not to talk about the case, but it was difficult. Gary, the meter man, in particular, evidently couldn't bear to remain silent. He made it amply clear that he thought the whole thing sounded crazy; I did too, but hearing Gary talk you'd have thought the murder had taken place in a circus fun house. I actually heard him snort a few times during the witnesses' testimony, as if he were squelching laughter; he told me that the image of a group of bald priests hitting each other with sticks struck him as being almost too comical to believe.

Whenever I could I found a chance to say a few words to Maria-Teresa, and a few times she initiated conversations with me. To my surprise, she and I were the only ones who didn't follow the general pattern of the men talking to other men and the women talking to other women. After being at the university for so many years, where faculty and students of the two sexes mix regularly, this pattern seemed almost quaint. The only other exception I noticed was that Rose, the secretary, and Dwight, who worked at the defense industry plant, occasionally talked. But that seemed to be because they were the only two blacks on the jury.

After the detective's testimony the state rested and Judge Davis invited the defense to call witnesses. When Ms. Doppelt declined the opportunity, saying that the witnesses for the defense would have nothing to say if they couldn't discuss Mr. Weber's mental condition, the judge raised his considerable eyebrow once again, then shrugged and instructed the lawyers to make their closing arguments. I knew that public defenders were overworked and underpaid, but I always assumed they had to possess at least a certain degree of competence to represent clients in trials, particularly murder trials. Ms. Doppelt, however, hardly seemed to be putting up much of a fight.

Mr. Graham went first. He approached us in his usual relaxed manner and briefly reviewed the testimony. He emphasized that the witnesses all described the crime in unrefuted testimony, leaving no room for doubt that the defendant intentionally killed Mr. Okakura.

Ms. Doppelt, strangely enough, didn't even make a closing argument, which seemed shocking to me. With the evidence part of the trial over, the judge then gave us brief instructions about how to apply the law to the evidence and come up with a verdict. He reminded us that the crime of second-degree murder required that it be an intentional killing—not accidental—but did not require that Weber planned or thought about the crime beforehand at all. Even if the killing was entirely impulsive, it still counted as murder if the defendant possessed the intent to kill when he swung the stick. The custodian led us to our deliberating room, and we each chose a seat around a long oak table. I took a chair near a far corner, and Maria-Teresa sat down next to me.

Dwight Anderson was the last person in the room. He took the one remaining chair, which everyone had avoided because it was located at the head of the table. No one wanted to be foreman. Dwight, who was heavyset and had an air of military discipline about him, didn't seem to mind. When he sat down, everyone naturally looked in his direction.

"As I understand it," he said, "the first order of business is to appoint a jury foreman. Does anybody want to volunteer?"

No one raised a hand.

"Has anybody here ever done jury duty before?" he asked.

The older Jewish lady, who was a retired practical nurse, said she had served on a jury years ago. Her accent made her sound a bit like my mother.

"That makes you the most experienced, then," Dwight said. "I nominate you. Anyone want to second that?"

A few people murmured their approval. The tiny nominee accepted with a shrug, but asked Dwight, "What about you, mister? You seem like you'd be better at it than me. I nominate you."

He nodded pleasantly and asked for any other nominations or volunteers. No one spoke up, so he suggested we vote. He handed out some paper and pencils that the clerk had left for us, then said, "My name is Dwight Anderson. And your name is—ma'am?"

"Ruth Friedman."

I figured that Dwight was going to be chosen because he was so obviously suited for it, so I voted for Mrs. Friedman as a kindness.

Either six other people had soft hearts like me or a majority of our group didn't want to be led by a black man, because Mrs. Friedman won the vote seven to five. She looked surprised, but seemed resigned to it and said, "OK, so let's get it over with." She told us that in her other trial the jury cast a secret ballot first, and then reviewed the evidence as a group before voting again. So more slips of paper were passed out and we were instructed to write either "guilty" or "not guilty" on them.

Just before we started, the housewife with the pharmacist husband, Mathilda Jencks, raised her hand and asked, "But what if a juror is undecided? What do you write then?" There was something about her—an anxiety in her voice, a confused look—that made me think she was going to be a pain.

"It's good you asked," Mrs. Friedman responded. "If you're undecided, that's what you should write."

We all scribbled away and handed our slips to Mrs. Friedman to count. I'd written "guilty" because there really was no choice. I wondered, though, if it would get more complicated during the second phase of the trial. When Mrs. Friedman had counted them all, she grinned. "Eleven guilty, one undecided."

I think everyone tried not to look at Mathilda, but she sighed and said in an exasperated tone, "Well, so much for the secret ballot."

"Let's not worry about it," Mrs. Friedman said, "there's no rules about how this has to go, so . . . in the other trial I was in we reviewed the evidence; everybody did it together, we went over all the main points. That was a complicated trial. This one, it's not so complicated. . . . Who wants to start? Mathilda, you want to tell us what you're thinking?"

"I don't see the direction we're heading in here . . ." Mathilda said nervously. "I've just heard the evidence myself, and it's not obvious to me that everything is out in the open here."

An embarrassed silence followed. My guess is that everybody was thinking what I was thinking, which was Uh-oh. Mrs. Jencks appeared to be having difficulty either thinking or expressing herself clearly. The responsibility lay with our foreperson to break the silence. She shrugged and asked,

"Well, do you want us to go over the evidence? What would make you comfortable?"

"Frankly, right now I'm feeling a little pressured! I've been painted into a corner that I didn't necessarily want to be in."

"There's no reason, dear. There's no hurry here, is there? You take all the time you want." It was nice of Mrs. Friedman to say that, but the truth was, we couldn't do anything until Mathilda decided she was ready to talk.

We all sat quietly staring at the table, until Mathilda said, "I'm not saying he isn't guilty. I'm just saying I don't think he's been *proven* guilty. I mean, they never went into the question of what kind of man he was, I mean the leader of their cult, the Japanese man who was killed. What if he was someone like that . . . what was his name? Tom Jones? The one who made all those poor women and children drink that awful poison in Guyana? If somebody had killed that monster before he did his evil things, would we call that murder? Or Hitler?"

The comparisons were so out of line that no one seemed to want to try to tangle with her. At last Mrs. Jencks, looking even more exasperated than before, shook her head and blurted out, "Well, if you're all so sure he's guilty, I guess I must be missing something. Whatever you say—if you say guilty, that's fine."

A more idealistic group might have encouraged her to stand by her sense of doubt for at least a few minutes more, but we accepted her surrender without hesitation.

"Good—it's unanimous, then," Mrs. Friedman confirmed. "Shall we let the judge know we have a verdict?"

We nodded, hoping to get back into the courtroom before Mrs. Jencks had any second thoughts. As we found our seats in the jury box, I noticed that the defendant was looking closely at each of us. When his eyes met mine I started to look away out of habit, but then thought, Why not look back if he's going to stare at me? So I returned his gaze, feeling a bit queasy again, as when I'd held the murder weapon. His face looked like a baby's; he was utterly relaxed, and stared at me with benign curiosity. After a few seconds he lost interest in me and looked at Maria-Teresa. She actually smiled at him, and he smiled back.

When the time came, Mrs. Friedman stood up and handed the verdict forms to the bailiff, who passed them to the judge, who then gave them to the clerk. After this oddly calming ritual, the clerk faced the courtroom and read in an even voice, "We the jury find the defendant guilty of the charge of second-degree murder." The pale young man sat with his back straight and his eyes closed, and showed no reaction. Neither of the lawyers looked at all surprised. It was only when I noticed the group of relatives of the murdered man whispering to one another and nodding with satisfaction that I was reminded that we weren't deciding whether to fine someone for parking illegally. Their response was controlled, though; they certainly knew that the killer could still be found insane and therefore acquitted in the second half of the trial.

Again I looked at the defendant. It was still almost impossible to imagine him committing the crime. He looked so passive and resigned. He had just gone halfway toward spending a long time, maybe the rest of his life, in jail, and he didn't seem affected at all. It was a maddening, incongruous sight, and I didn't know what to make of it. Was he faking? Was he really out of his mind? Or did he really undergo some sort of drastic transformation as a result of all the concentration and riddles?

14

I once saw a documentary about India that focused briefly on mystics. One man was shown standing barefoot on a frigid, snowy mountaintop, wearing only a thin muslin cloth. He stood there, stock-still, all day, every day. He hadn't spoken for over ten years. At night local villagers would bring him rice and vegetables to eat. What could he be thinking about, staring straight ahead like that all day? It does seem that a human being would have to possess a substantially different way of looking at things to be able to endure such a discipline.

The documentary also discussed another man whose guru had died and who vowed to stand in prayer at his teacher's gravesite until the guru gave him a sign that it was all right to stop praying. The local villagers helped build the man a sling from a tree so that he could even sleep standing up. At the time the documentary was shot he had been standing for three years. Two questions came to my mind: you would think that after only a few days, exhaustion and sheer boredom would have caused this fellow to imagine that the teacher was giving him signs. I know that I would interpret every tweet of a bird, every barking dog or police siren as a sign to go home and lie down. My other question was Why did the local people seem so willing to go along with this? In fact, they were largely responsible for making it possible, both for the bereaved student and the stoic old man in the muslin drape. They fed these mystics and seemed to worship them. Why did they find this sort of behavior inspiring and holy, whereas we . . . I tried to imagine a man wearing only a bedsheet planting himself in the center divider on the Santa Monica Freeway, staring straight into the smog and not speaking and being fed by pious locals. He would have been carted away in a matter of hours.

I've never had any interest in mysticism, of either the Eastern or Western variety. Maybe it's just because I don't know much about it, but it all seems half-baked to me. Maybe if you starve yourself and don't talk or move for a long time you do go into some kind of trance, but what would the point of that be? Sleeping is an even better trance because you disappear completely for a few hours. We all do that every night, so why try so hard to do it in the daytime? Is it enjoyable for those people? Then there's the fact that we all die anyway; no matter what we do, we're all going to experience the ultimate trance, so what's the rush to imitate it? It seems so unnecessary; you don't see animals forcing themselves into unnatural postures and then trying not to move for hours. The closest parallel might be a flamingo standing on one leg without moving, but a flamingo is built to do that. Human beings are primates, and primates weren't designed to tie themselves up into knots and hold still.

Someone once told me that I should try meditation—that I would be good at it because of my ability to concentrate for hours a day practicing the cello. I read a book on the subject and even tried it a few times, but couldn't find any similarity at all. When you are playing music, you have a clear goal: to organize and produce sounds in such a way that they express shades of emotion. By practicing, you struggle throughout your life to make your communications more direct and concise, so that a person hearing you play receives emotional impressions in as pure a form as possible. Meditation, on the other hand, seems to be a kind of free-floating concentration, where you fix your mind on either nothing at all or on a repetitious chant or irrational puzzle—concentration for the sake of concentration. What do you do with it? How would you measure your progress, and how could you be sure you weren't fooling yourself about your abilities? I couldn't see any purpose to it, so I gave up after a few attempts.

I take after my father in this regard; he treated Judaism as a form of culture rather than as a religion. He believed that by observing the holidays, learning Jewish history and studying the Talmud, one gained an intellectual understanding of the tradition that helped give one a good starting point, but not an end point, for the development of personal morality. He felt that people had to adapt to changing times, and that strict religious dogma was unnatural. He and my mother argued over this frequently; my mother would accuse him of just telling himself what he wanted to hear, and my father would respond by saying, "*Ja,* and so? The rabbi says what he wants to hear, and you want to listen! What makes *your* judgment so good?"

Von Kempen was a deeply religious man, but not in the sense of contemplation of the supernatural or the promise of an afterlife; he simply couldn't get over his sense of awe and wonder that something as magnificent and beautiful as music could be channeled through such flawed creatures as human beings. Every time he encountered music he opened his mind to it with the humility and gratitude of someone receiving a gift he could not possibly deserve. Toward the end of his life that attitude grew to embrace such ordinary phenomena as the changing light of the seasons, the sounds of migrating birds or the taste of fine tobacco. The only thing I could see that he felt no particular sense of gratitude for was politics. He had the newspaper delivered to his home every day, but would not even glance at it until Frau Schmidt, his housekeeper, had first thrown away all of it except for the art, science and food sections.

Judge Davis had a huge head. At first I hadn't realized it because the rest of him was so big as well, but when either of the lawyers approached the bench you could compare more easily. His head looked like one of those heroic Roman busts of Caligula or Nero or Brutus that at first look life-sized, but gradually you see as you get closer that they are really about half again as big. During lulls in the trial, I enjoyed picturing him with a little crown of olive leaves on top of his head, presiding over events at a marble coliseum. After we'd brought in the guilty verdict, he swiveled his massive chair around to face us, taking a quick moment, I noticed, to arrange his robes so that they spread out evenly on either side of him. He resembled an already large bird puffing out its feathers to look even more impressive.

The judge reminded us that since we had brought in a verdict of guilty during this first part of the trial, we would now move on to what was known as the "sanity phase." He explained in his deep but monotonous voice that in the part we had just completed the burden of proof was on the state. Now, he said, everything was reversed: the defense had the burden of proof.

"From this point on," he droned, "there is no question of whether or not the defendant committed the act of murder. You are only to consider evidence relating to the question of whether or not he was sane at the time he killed the victim. The defendant claims," he continued, and from the way the corners of his mouth suddenly drooped you got the impression that he did not put much stock in the claim, "that at the time of the crime he suffered from a mental disorder, and as the result of his disorder did not form an intent to kill. He and his attorney, Ms. Doppelt, are seeking an acquittal by reason of insanity. The burden of proof rests with them now; the defense must clearly demonstrate evidence of this mental disorder, and prove by a preponderance of evidence that Mr. Weber was insane at the time of the crime—that he did not understand what he was doing when he killed Mr. Okakura. The state, represented by Mr. Graham, does not need to prove anything this time around. If, by the end of the trial, there is any doubt in your mind that Mr. Weber was insane, you are compelled by law to bring in a verdict of guilty."

Ms. Doppelt brushed her hair behind her ear again and sighed angrily; I gathered that she felt the judge's instructions showed bias against her client. Certainly I got the impression that Judge Davis would have been pleased to finish the trial right there with a conviction and dispense with the sanity phase altogether.

That day I had brought a book with me to court; I planned to read it during our breaks in the hope that it might discourage Gary, the tiresome meter reader, from cornering me and talking about himself. He seemed genuinely uncomfortable with silence; during the trial he was fine because someone was always talking, and if someone else was talking during the breaks he would happily listen without interrupting. But if a lull in conversation appeared for more than a few seconds, he would fidget, look around and make an irritating sound by sucking air between his teeth, and if anyone looked up and made eye contact with him, he would start talking to that person. But if no one looked up, he would start talking to me.

The book I had brought was a new work about the interpretation of early music, and began with a question: Do you do greater justice to the old composers by striving for an authentic re-creation of the way their music was performed when it was written or by incorporating modern sensibilities and musical tastes in order to give an honest contemporary performance? With all the recent developments in "authentic" or "period" instruments and musical scholarship in the last few decades, the issue has inspired a lively, ongoing debate. On the one hand, you have people who feel that playing early music with modern instruments, phrasing and tone color is like taking Rembrandt's paintings and painting over them with the bright palette of Matisse, an obscene distortion. On the other hand, you have people who insist that modern instruments, phrasing and tone color represent advances over the earlier versions, and to withhold them would be like practicing dentistry with turn-of-the-century drills, a waste of hard-won knowledge.

During the break just before the second phase of the trial began I saw Gary beginning to fidget and heard him making sucking sounds through his teeth, so I took this as my cue, opened the book and started to read. It worked; Gary hovered near me for a bit, coughed a few times, then caught Roy, the retired plant manager, on his way out of the men's room and started asking him about worker's-compensation lawsuits. Maria-Teresa was out having a cigarette while all the other women were clustered on the far side of the room, looking at pictures of Jesusita's first grandchild. Just as I started to relax and concentrate on the book, Mrs. Friedman wandered away from the ladies' group, sat down next to me, tapped me on the shoulder and informed me that ever since the prosecutor mentioned one of my records she'd been looking for it.

"It wasn't easy to find, you know," she said. "You ought to talk to your record company about that. I had to go all over town. You know how much it costs now?"

"No, how much?"

"Seventeen dollars to order it!" She looked at me as if she expected a response. "But it was worth it!" she said at last. "You're terrific, really. My brother is an oboist with the Boston Symphony, so I hear a lot of music."

I thanked her and asked about her brother, since I know so many of the musicians in that orchestra, but the name didn't sound familiar. It turned out that her brother had studied with Hans Barreiss, about whom I had heard quite a bit from von Kempen. They had played together many times before the war. When I mentioned the connection, though, Mrs. Friedman visibly stiffened. "Johannes von Kempen was your teacher?" she asked coolly.

"Yes," I answered, immediately regretting that I'd brought it up. I tried to pretend not to notice her change in attitude, hoping that we could move gracefully on to another subject, but she sighed and shook her head sadly. "Your name . . . That's a Jewish name, isn't it?"

"Yes."

"You were born here, though? Not in Europe?"

"Right. I was born in Poughkeepsie."

"But what about your parents? They must be from over there to give you that first name, no?"

"Yes, they're both from Germany."

"So how could they let you study with him?"

"They knew that von Kempen had nothing against Jews. The treatment he received after the war was a terrible mistake."

"Did your parents live in Europe during the war?" she asked me.

"No, they left before that."

"Then they don't know and you don't know what's a terrible mistake. Let me tell you, Herrigel, von Karajan, your teacher—all of them . . . Every concert they gave those years was a mistake. Every note they played hurt us. I know, I lived there."

There wasn't any point in debating with her. I suggested that since they were all dead now, she and I needn't spoil our acquaintance by arguing over questions that no one can answer with certainty.

"I'm not arguing with you, I'm just saying, that's all. It wasn't right what they did, and it isn't right to forget. That's all I'm saying." I was afraid she might go on, but thankfully she seemed satisfied at having made her point. I worried, however, about having to deal with the tension between us for the duration of the trial.

All that morning I had wanted to ask Maria-Teresa how she liked the Saint-Saëns recording I'd lent her on Friday, but by the time she returned from having her cigarette I didn't feel like discussing music anymore. I couldn't concentrate on my book, either, so I found a window in the hallway and watched some construction workers laying asphalt across the street. Sure enough, Gary found me there and started talking. The Dodgers had lost two more games over the weekend and he was inconsolable. I tried to seem interested, but failed. I was still upset from my exchange with Mrs. Friedman, and cut him off in mid-sentence to excuse myself for a trip to the men's room. I said I had a headache and needed to take some aspirin. He asked if I had ever tried ibuprofen; he had some in his truck, he said, and would have been happy to run down and get it for me except that it was parked in the far lot. "I could probably find a pharmacy outside, though, if you want some? I'm telling you, if you try it, you won't waste your time with aspirin anymore." I thanked him but said that aspirin had always worked adequately for me.

At last we were called back in, and the new trial got under way. Sounding irritable, Judge Davis ordered the defense to make its opening statement. Ms. Doppelt practically leaped out of her chair, as if she had been held prisoner for some time and had at last been released.

She began by saying we all must have wondered what kind of defense lawyer she was to have done so little for her client during his trial for murder. She reminded us that the odd bifurcated trial system now used for the insanity defense put her and her client in an impossible bind; for the first part of the trial it had been impossible for her to defend her client because the very reason for his innocence—his insanity—could not be mentioned as evidence at all. "But so be it," she said, looking hard at each of us, "I'm counting on you to put the first part of the trial behind you and hear the new evidence with open minds."

She took a sharp breath and walked over to the defense table. She touched her client gently on the shoulder and the pale young man smiled up at her calmly. Several of the Japanese people in the gallery rustled in their seats disapprovingly. The defendant looked utterly content, in spite of having recently been declared guilty of murder. It was an unsettling sight; if he was insane I suppose he should have been pitied, but my reaction to his oblivious demeanor was to feel disgusted. Ms. Doppelt appeared to sense that the human-touch approach was backfiring, and briskly returning to her spot right in front of us, she began telling us about her client's life before his fateful decision to study Zen Buddhism. Philip Weber's mother was first hospitalized for what proved to be chronic mental illness when Philip was only three years old. His father's business required extensive travel, so the boy was raised mostly by nannies and had to change schools every other year because of job relocations. He had lived in San Jose, Riverside, San Diego, Sacramento, Los Angeles and Davis before he finished high school and left home for college.

Philip's grades and IQ tests from elementary school indicated that he was an exceptionally bright child, and the teachers' comments on his report cards from this time suggested that, considering his disruptive home life, he was a well-adjusted boy. But he started having trouble in school beginning in the eighth grade; his marks went from being extremely high to near failing by the eleventh grade, and reports from his teachers indicated that he was becoming withdrawn and apathetic.

"This situation," Ms. Doppelt suggested, "might have been dealt with more properly if he had stayed in one place for any length of time, but since his father withdrew him from school to move so often, Philip's problems went ignored. None of his teachers developed enough of a relationship with him to see how quickly he was deteriorating, so none of them recommended that he see a social worker or doctor. Moreover, Philip's relationship with his father became so tense and distant that the elder Mr. Weber also did not think to send his son to someone for counseling. He thought his son was just going through 'a rebellious phase.'

"In spite of his poor grades and miserable home life, Philip tested very high on the SAT exams and was accepted at the University of California at Santa Cruz. He went there for only one semester, failed all of his courses and dropped out. He came home, but could not get along with his father at all. In fact, his father was so disgusted by his son's performance at college that he kicked him out of the house.

"After that Philip lived and worked in the Santa Cruz area for a year. He developed an interest in religion, and joined a Unitarian church in Santa Cruz. He was enthusiastic at first, but became disillusioned quickly. He was searching to find himself, but the church members, as he put it in a letter to his mother, 'just sit around and and organize bake sales—there's nothing spiritual about it at all, and they beat around the bush on everything. You might as well be an atheist.' He took up with the Church of Scientology for a while, and even traveled to Los Angeles to work at the Scientology headquarters building here, but apparently had a falling out with other members of that group and left after only a few weeks. He moved into an apartment and found a job, then began visiting the Los Angeles Zen Foundation. Zen Buddhism appealed to him because of its promise of absolute spiritual enlightenment, so he attended morning and evening meditation sessions there for six months. After that period he moved into the building as a resident to practice Zen full time, earning his room and board by working in the organization's kitchen."

Ms. Doppelt reminded us that the witness from the Zen Foundation had described Philip as being obsessive and self-absorbed, as if he were in his own little world, and that Philip had put all his hopes on the winter retreat, when Mr. Okakura would finally return to Los Angeles and lead the group through an intensive session. She reviewed the harsh schedule of the retreat, the hours of sitting cross-legged without moving a muscle, the corporal discipline with the heavy pole, and the goal of solving riddles that are, as she understood it, designed to be irrational.

"The evidence will show," she said, "that the witness you heard from last week had mentioned only part of the puzzle. I'd like to read the complete puzzle to you now."

She picked up a book from her cluttered desk and opened it to a page marked with a torn strip of yellow legal paper. She read:

> "The Zen master Lin-chi was once asked by a monk, 'What would you do if you were going somewhere, and you suddenly met the Buddha in the road?' Lin-chi answered, 'If you meet the Buddha in the road and he stands in your way, kill him! If you meet the great Zen teachers of the past, kill them! If you meet your parents, kill them! That is the only way to be free!' "

A murmur rose up from the courtroom. The full puzzle sounded horrifying. Ms. Doppelt frowned at us and said, "Philip was repeatedly told by the Zen master, and by the other Zen students, that his one goal, the whole reason for attending that retreat and enduring its painful schedule, should be to solve this riddle. Only by solving it could he become enlightened. You all know what that led to."

Ms. Doppelt put her hands in her pockets, and then took them back out again. Even though she was young, thin and probably in good shape, she was not a physically graceful person. The sloppy-looking, overweight prosecutor moved with more ease than she did. Just to see him walk across the room made you feel comfortable, whereas her movements made you feel wary.

"To sum up," Ms. Doppelt announced, "evidence will show that Mr. Weber suffers from chronic schizophrenia, a severe mental illness." She looked at each one of us, trying to make personal contact with individual members of the jury. I respected her effort; I could tell she was trying her best to defend her client, but her technique was rough around the edges. Looking at us the way she did was a little off-putting; it was as if she assumed we wouldn't pay attention unless she kept a close eye on us. Her youthfulness when compared with the average age of the jurors also made this attitude seem awkward.

"The extreme stress of the meditation retreat, with its brutal discipline and humiliating rituals, and the confusing moral environment favored by the Zen religion, aggravated Mr. Weber's preexisting mental illness and—to put it bluntly—drove him out of his mind. He became utterly disoriented and experienced his first acute psychotic episode. He lost the ability to distinguish between symbolic gestures and real ones, and killed a man thinking that in fact he was only answering a question. An expert witness in the field of psychiatry will testify that my client had no proper understanding of what he was doing at the time, and still does not. You couldn't find a better illustration of the legal definition of insanity."

Ms. Doppelt walked purposefully back to her desk, arranged some papers on it and sat down. In general, I found that I agreed with what she was saying, but didn't like the way she said it. I felt myself resisting her arguments for the same reason that I don't like buying from aggressive salesmen. I don't like being talked into things by ungraceful people.

The prosecutor, Mr. Graham, couldn't have been more unlike her. Standing up behind his desk and smiling gently—he didn't need to walk over and stand right in front of us—he said in his pleasing drawl, "I guess the only thing I can say at this point is that the better you understand the legal concept of insanity, the guiltier Philip Weber seems. If he's going to be acquitted, Mr. Weber has to prove that because of a mental disease or defect he had no idea what he was doing when he killed his teacher. The evidence will show, though, that Philip Weber *did* know what he was doing. So," he said, patting his belly with his hand, "I move we have lunch as soon as possible so our stomachs don't drown out the testimony."

Judge Davis appeared pleased by the prosecutor's brief statement. The corners of his mouth rose up into not quite a smile, but high enough so that for the first time he no longer appeared to have just swallowed a bad piece of fish. He seconded the prosecutor's motion and adjourned the court until two o'clock. I thought I saw another scowl pass over Ms. Doppelt's face; I'm sure she didn't enjoy seeing the kind of old-boy rapport the prosecutor and the judge had with each other. At that moment I felt a bit sorry for her, surrounded by her piles of notes and having to defend this unpleasant, destructive young man. Unlike Mr. Graham, she had no charm at all. I made a mental note to myself to try, out of fairness, not to hold it against her.

15

I asked Maria-Teresa to join me for lunch again, but she had already made plans to eat with Jesusita and Rose. I found a little sandwich shop nearby and ate at the counter, something I hadn't done for a long time. My debate with Mrs. Friedman was still on my mind.

Von Kempen and Casals were the two great cellists of their generation. During the war, Casals, who was Catalonian, fled to southern France, where he was frequently harassed by the Nazis. For a while no one had any news of him and a rumor spread that he had been killed for refusing to go to Germany to play for Hitler. He had in fact refused just such an invitation, and was nearly arrested, but his life was spared by a German officer who apparently was moved by his integrity. Von Kempen was distantly related to the Bavarian royal family, and since the early 1920s had been the director of the Munich symphony orchestra. He loathed the Nazis, and helped several Jewish members of the symphony escape to France and Switzerland, but felt he himself had to stay behind with the orchestra. "Munich was my home," he once wrote me, "and the symphony was my life. That orchestra had been an important part of the German musical tradition for over two hundred years—how could I leave it to those degenerates? They had to fall—they were doomed, those men. No regime like that could last, I truly believed in my heart. I felt an obligation to see the orchestra through those dark times."

Von Kempen's prediction about the Nazis proved correct, but after the war he, along with several other prominent German conductors and musicians, was accused of being sympathetic to the Nazis. Some of these men, like von Karajan, tried to continue performing internationally after the war but were booed and in some cases banned on stages around the world, including the United States. Von Kempen was a deeply sensitive man, and could not bear the thought of being the catalyst of such bitterness, so he resigned from the symphony in 1946 and never again gave a public concert as a cellist. He chose Ederstausee as his place of retirement and thereafter practiced for his own enjoyment and taught quietly at home.

For a while, talented cellists quietly slipped in and out of Ederstausee to study with him, but their numbers soon dwindled. His voluntary withdrawal from the stage, which he had intended as a gesture of respect toward those who had suffered because of German nationalism, came to be interpreted as an admission of guilt. Also, he suffered by comparison with Casals, who had vehemently resisted fascism from the very beginning and who also silenced his cello after the war, but for different reasons: Casals announced that he would not perform on stage again until Franco was ousted from Spain. As for von Kempen, when I first met him in 1965, he had fallen into almost complete obscurity, and I was the first significant student he'd had in thirteen years.

Ironically, it was Casals's idea to send me to him. Like every other young cellist, I had hoped to study with Casals, but he was busy with his many humanitarian projects and unwilling to take on someone as young as I was. He agreed to hear me play when I was eleven, however, so my mother and I flew down to Puerto Rico, where he spent the winters toward the end of his life. Of course, Mother and I hoped that he would change his mind.

After I played for him he said to my mother in his delightful accent, "Take your dear boy to Kassel, madam. Have him play for von Kempen. You won't regret it."

My mother, who knew all about the collaborator controversy, was shocked. She made a long protest, but Casals, after waiting politely for her to finish, argued that it would be an ideal arrangement. "Johannes von Kempen is one of the greatest cellists who ever lived," the maestro said, "and he has been thrown away like refuse, another casualty of the Nazi madness. Whether you blame him or not, he has paid a dear price. I can hear in your son's playing a closeness to von Kempen already; musically, he would be the right choice as teacher. Furthermore, he could devote himself entirely to your son. It would be the last great gesture of his life—especially considering your heritage. Trust me, it is an opportunity too precious to ignore."

One of many remarkable things about Casals was that he seemed incapable of misjudging situations, musical, political or otherwise. Von Kempen even believed that Casals possessed the ability to see into the future. True or not, Casals's hunch that the old German and I would make a good combination proved true.

When Mother and I visited von Kempen the first time in Ederstausee, we tried ringing the doorbell to his house but it didn't work. We had to pound several times on the door before getting the attention of Frau Schmidt, his severe-looking housekeeper, who led us up a flimsy staircase to Herr Professor's study. Von Kempen sat slumped on a partially collapsed sofa in a dark room. He wore a baggy, dark wool suit and old but recently polished shoes. My mother squeezed my hand and gestured with her eyes for me to look upward; there were spiderwebs all over the ceiling. The old man must have noticed where we were looking because he hastened to explain that the older he got, the more he hated to kill any living creature or destroy its home, so he had asked the housekeeper to leave the webs alone. Frau Schmidt shook her head in dismay and left us.

Von Kempen stood painfully to greet us, kissing my mother's hand, then sank back onto the sofa. He spoke only German, but since my parents frequently spoke it at home, I was able to understand most of what he said. He asked me what I would like to play for him, but he had to repeat himself several times; I could barely understand his Bavarian accent, and also his speech contained the sort of elevated, archaic expressions that one finds today only in Thomas Mann novels. I chose the Bach suite in C minor.

Bach, there can be no doubt, brought classical music to perfection. He expressed his musical ideas with devastating precision and understatement. Each piece is like a finely cut diamond: clear, simple and almost mathematical in appearance, but underneath the surface what complexity and structural integrity! The possibilities for interpretation are limitless; just as there are countless ways to project light through a diamond, no two performances of Bach can be the same because each musician's unique personality has its own spectrum of feelings that can be conveyed freely through Bach's inventions. If two very different performers play the same Liszt piece, for example, you will still hear primarily

Liszt. But Bach's musical personality was so expansive, so beautifully transparent, that when you interpret him, his ideas become your ideas, and you feel that he must have known you to have written a piece so close to your own heart.

As I played, the old German master slowly straightened up in his sofa. By the end of the suite he sat ramrod straight, like a Prussian general, his face rigid with concentration. At last he stood up and walked over to my mother. "*Meine liebe Frau Sundheimer*," he said, bowing impeccably and kissing her hand out of joy and gratitude. Then he kissed mine.

His formality embarrassed me. He asked to speak to my mother privately and had Frau Schmidt take me for a stroll in the back garden. I resented the fact that I wasn't part of the negotiations. Later that afternoon, when Mother and I returned to our little pension in town, I told her I didn't want to be "that old German guy's" student. She asked me to meet with him once more before making a decision.

The next day we went to his house, and instead of asking me to play right away, von Kempen invited us to join him for a picnic. Frau Schmidt drove us, with my cello in the expansive trunk, to an ancient little church in Kassel about twenty miles away, where under a sprawling elm tree we had a delicious basket lunch of potato dumplings and boiled sandwich meats. Then we went into the church. He told me that Father Bach himself had visited this very church to test their new organ. A young rector greeted us and led us to the organ, where von Kempen sat down and played a Bach cantata. He gestured for me to sit next to him on the bench.

When he had finished playing, von Kempen said, "Father Bach sat in this very spot more than two hundred years ago. The original organ is gone, but the echoes of his playing are captured in these walls, these pews, these window panes. His spirit lives in this building." He paused to look at me, and held me under his spell for a few long seconds. "Would you like to play your cello now, Herr Sundheimer?"

I felt intoxicated. I took my instrument out of its case and played my heart out. The church had marvelous acoustics; the whole building seemed to have become a giant cello, and I was sitting inside it, feeling it vibrate all around me. It excited me beyond description to think that Bach had sat in this very room, had breathed the same air, and here I was, breathing life into the voices he heard in his mind, those perfect voices. When I finished, von Kempen bowed deeply to me and kissed my hand again. This time I didn't feel embarrassed at all.

16

The first witness for the defense was a psychiatrist, Dr. Jeremy Libertson. He must have been in his late thirties, but looked much younger. He had thin blond hair, a neatly trimmed beard and an angelic face. If it weren't for his briefcase and professional-looking glasses I would have mistaken him for a college student. He even wore a collegiate-looking sport jacket over his narrow shoulders. He was a research psychiatrist at the Pasadena Neurological Institute, and bristled with Ivy League credentials. Like me, he had apparently been something of a wunderkind; he had finished medical school when he was only twenty years old. After a lengthy recitation of his qualifications, he told us that he specialized in the study and treatment of schizophrenia.

Dr. Libertson testified that he had met with Philip Weber on twelve separate occasions since his arrest for murder, and had administered a large number of psychological tests to him, which he named and attempted to explain to us in great detail. I found it difficult to keep track of that part of his testimony. When he finished reviewing the tests for us, Ms. Doppelt asked him, "And were you able to make a conclusive diagnosis?"

Dr. Libertson smiled warily. "Until we can positively identify the chemical and neurobiological components of all thoughts and feelings, no psychiatric diagnosis will ever be *absolutely* conclusive. Fortunately for the purposes of the trial, this was not a difficult case to evaluate. Mr. Weber's symptoms, behavior and case history are all perfectly consistent with those of a specific mental disorder."

"And what is that?"

"A progressive illness known as chronic undifferentiated schizophrenia."

Ms. Doppelt asked the doctor to try to explain, in layman's terms, what that term meant. He folded his hands eagerly on the railing in front of him and slid up to the edge of his seat. You could tell that the subject excited him.

"Most of us are comfortable with people depending on how predictable they are," he began. "Schizophrenia is a disease that makes its victims seem unpredictable. If you observe the disease carefully, however, you realize that the symptoms aren't so unpredictable, after all. But the average person doesn't know enough about schizophrenia to notice."

Dr. Libertson said that, first of all, it was significant for Mr. Weber that his mother had been diagnosed as a schizophrenic; apparently the disease has a genetic component. He read aloud from several documents relating to the mother's medical history, then returned to the disease itself. "Almost all schizophrenics begin to show symptoms in their adolescence," he explained. "But it's kind of like what they said when Calvin Coolidge died: 'How could they tell?' " He laughed and seemed to expect a response, but it took a few seconds to figure out the meaning of the punch line, which was that teenagers and lunatics are hard to tell apart.

"For most of us," Dr. Libertson said, wincing as if he were speaking from experience, "adolescence is a horrible, confusing time. We are trying out new roles, breaking away from our family and attempting to discover our 'true selves,' whatever that means. We struggle with the question 'Who am I?' and why it is that we can act one way with our friends and another way with our parents. Which way is the real you? It's terribly stressful. Luckily, most of us settle down and become comfortable with ourselves in our twenties." He nodded as if relieved to get this part of the testimony over with.

He told us that schizophrenics, sadly enough, don't get comfortable with themselves as they get older. Their sense of confusion only becomes more intense as they reach adulthood. They observe themselves with such frightening intensity that, in the glare of all this self-awareness, they lose all spontaneity. The doctor told us to imagine having a bad case of stage fright, and having it nearly all the time.

Naturally I found this image absolutely chilling. I had experienced moments like those he was describing in some of my last concerts, where I observed myself with grotesque self-consciousness; my fingers on the strings felt and looked like clumsy sausages, the bow in my hand seemed as heavy as an oar, and I became terrified that I might go blank and lose my place in the music. Panic and anger and despair all mixed together. I could easily believe that someone who felt that way all the time, day after day, would fall apart.

Dr. Libertson told us that as the disease worsens, the patient's thoughts, feelings and actions get mixed up. He may be thinking of something very positive while at the same time feeling crushed with sadness. Some patients lose control over their thoughts, and actually think they are hearing voices or commands coming from outside them. This, he explained, is why so many schizophrenics are convinced they are acting upon orders from God, or the Devil, or the CIA. Most of these unfortunate people become withdrawn and terribly shy in order to compensate for what they feel is a lack of self-control. It is also why most of them are far from dangerous, the doctor emphasized; if anything, they tend to be nervous, frightened hermits. Occasionally, however, a schizophrenic will have what psychiatrists call a psychotic episode, an acute phase of psychosis. Then the symptoms become so overwhelming that the patient really does lose control of himself.

Ms. Doppelt asked if Philip Weber had been psychotic when he killed the Zen master.

The doctor nodded vigorously and tapped against the rail with his finger for emphasis. "Absolutely," he said. "And something to remember is that once he slipped into that state of mind there was nothing he could have done to pull himself out of it. Once a patient becomes psychotic, he or she loses all coherent sense of reality, and therefore of self-control." He shook his head and looked up at the ceiling, appearing to be searching for words. Then his face lit up and he leaned forward in his chair again. "You know," he said brightly, "it's kind of like what physicists say about 'black holes,' those collapsed stars floating around out there in space: if you get too close to one and get caught in its field of gravity, you can't escape. You have nowhere to go but down, nothing to do but fall. Nothing is strong enough or fast enough to get out, not even light. With a schizophrenic, once he becomes psychotic the part of him that you might think should 'know better'—the nice person his family and friends once knew—that person, that self, can't resist the forces that are throwing his mind into confusion. He's being tossed around with nothing to hold on to, and everything around him becomes a jumbled mess." The doctor looked at the defendant, who was calmly jotting down notes on one of Ms. Doppelt's yellow legal pads, then turned to face us in the jury box. "Those of us who are healthy should all be grateful we don't know what that feels like."

The "black hole" analogy really struck home with me; I'd finished the astronomy book I bought in Santa Barbara, and black holes were discussed in it at some length. I got distracted from the doctor's testimony playing with that analogy because there were ways that it could be expanded upon. Physicists say there may be only one way to escape from a black hole, and that is by falling right through it and popping out into a separate universe. You may be the same as before, but everything around you will be changed. Because of what Philip Weber had done during his psychotic phase, I was thinking that even if he could be successfully treated, his life would be forever changed. All of us—the rest of the world, to him—saw him differently after that. He was a killer, someone who had taken another man's life. He really was living in a parallel universe; with treatment he might even become a reasonably healthy man, but he would certainly never be perceived as one. For the first time I felt a kind of pity for this young man, who was beginning to look more pathetic than evil to me.

When I turned my attention back to Dr. Libertson, he was saying that during his psychotic episode at the church Philip Weber suddenly found himself swept up in a euphoric delirium, and in that delirium imagined that the correct answer to the puzzle "Kill the Buddha in the road" was to attack the Zen master with his staff.

The testimony became particularly interesting, I thought,

when the doctor talked about some of the kinds of situations that can trigger these psychotic episodes. He said that sometimes they occur without any apparent reason, but nine times out of ten they can be traced to an emotionally stressful situation, like a visit to one's parents' home, or having to ride a public bus and risk being stared at, or having to take part in any social situation that would make one feel more self-conscious than usual.

Ms. Doppelt asked if the doctor thought that the Zen retreat could have triggered Weber's psychotic episode, and the psychiatrist actually laughed out loud. He shook his head with an almost bitter expression on his face and said, "Ms. Doppelt, I find it hard to believe that even you or I could participate in an activity like that without some sort of breakdown. As a matter of fact, it is my opinion that this is precisely what most so-called religious experiences are: episodes of nervous exhaustion brought on by sensory deprivation, extreme fervor—"

"Objection," Mr. Graham interrupted. "The doctor's opinion concerning normal religious experience isn't relevant, your Honor. It biases the jury against the religion that Mr. Weber chose to adopt."

"Sustained."

Dr. Libertson didn't seem upset. He shrugged and continued pretty much where he had left off. He said it was quite common for exhausted people to experience mild hallucinations and interpret those hallucinations as evidence of deep insight, visions of God or divine commands. There was no doubt in his mind, he said strongly, that the retreat had triggered Mr. Weber's psychosis. "Frankly," he added, "from my point of view the activities of this retreat . . . Put it this way: it would take an evil genius to create an atmosphere more likely to produce psychosis in a schizophrenic patient."

"Could you be specific, Doctor?" Ms. Doppelt asked. "What specifically about this retreat do you think caused Mr. Weber to become psychotic?"

"Well, just about everything," the doctor mused, tugging at his compact beard and frowning. "But, yes, I can be more specific. First of all, there are the hours and hours a day of meditating, all the time sitting cross-legged without moving, with no talking or moving about allowed. That's sensory deprivation, which leads to disorganized thinking and delusions in *anyone* if it goes on long enough, but in a much shorter time with schizophrenics. Then the participants in the retreat are allowed only four or five hours of sleep a night; they are awakened at four in the morning and have to rush around in complete silence to get to the meditation hall, where they must do a series of one hundred full prostrations in front of an image of the Buddha before settling into their meditation. Sleep deprivation and repetitive motor activities also lead to disorganized thinking, along with increased receptivity to hypnotic suggestion. Then there are those puzzles that they're supposed to be concentrating on all day and night. I'm told that Zen students are led to believe that solving these puzzles will bring them profound insights into the 'true nature' of the universe, which presumably contain the answers to all their questions about the meaning of life and so on. These puzzles, I'm told, make no sense whatsoever, and apparently that is their point. As I think I mentioned, disorganized thinking practically defines schizophrenia. What could be more stressful for such a person than to engage in rigorous exercises that were purposely created to short-circuit our conventional notions of reality?"

The doctor told us about a fascinating case in England involving an extremely talented theater student at Oxford who was cast as a schizophrenic in one of the drama company's plays. One night, in the middle of an exhausting performing tour around England, he got into character and couldn't get out. He spent the rest of his life in a mental hospital. Obviously he was vulnerable to the disease, to begin with, but the exercise of having to pretend to be psychotic clearly pushed him over the edge.

"These Zen exercises," Dr. Libertson said emphatically, "are carried out in an atmosphere of severe discipline, allowing for no relaxation of one's will or self-control. What happens to a person who is terrified of losing his self-control, and who knows that he has very little of it in the first place?"

The doctor shook his head and an almost despairing expression came over his face. "Then there's the fact that the Zen master is considered a spiritual authority, whose clear, spiritual vision allows him to see through all of the illusions we ordinary people live under. Presumably he can see through any false pretenses, and since he claims to understand the nature of the universe, presumably he knows you better than you know yourself. How does someone with a deep fear of seeming shallow or false feel in the presence of such an authority? Terrified, I should think. Terrified of being discovered, of being positively identified as a spiritual and social failure. Add to this the tradition that allows the Zen master to strike students with a huge wooden pole as punishment for making unnecessary noise, and the situation becomes even more frightening. When Philip started to lose control over himself by crying, then laughing, and the master struck him with the pole, he quite simply became hysterical. That blow with the stick was . . . it was the point of no return for him. After that he had no sense of what he was doing."

The doctor inferred that since Zen masters have shaved heads and wear robes, and since Mr. Okakura was Asian like the Buddha, Philip probably thought that the master was some sort of apparition, a ghost of the Buddha, and acted according to the behavior described in the puzzle. This is where hypnotic suggestion plays a part, he said. Philip had repeated the puzzle to himself perhaps thousands of times over the four days of the retreat; in a situation of extreme psychological distress, it would have taken on such resonance in his mind that he felt it was coming from all around him—from the universe itself, or perhaps from God.

"In any case," the doctor summed up, "Philip believed at that moment, and still believes, that he did the right thing, the only thing he could do, and that he had the moral force of the entire universe behind him. That is why he seems to have no sense of remorse at all. His sense of reality is utterly inconsistent with our own agreed-upon reality."

Ms. Doppelt nodded smartly, took a few steps toward the counsel table, then stopped and half turned toward the stand. "Dr. Libertson, was Philip aware that he was killing a man when he swung that pole?"

"N—" the doctor checked himself for an instant, then continued. "Not in any practical sense. To him, what was happening that day had no substance or reality—it was all a kind of dream, or nightmare. He acted the way we might in our nightmares because, in light of his psychosis, he was no more in control of himself than we are in our dreams."

I hadn't decided whether I thought Philip Weber was insane when he committed his crime, but if he had really been in the state of mind Dr. Libertson was describing, it seemed plausible that he could have killed someone without understanding what he was doing. I knew from a very brief but unforgettable experience that it was possible to be wide awake but feel and act just as in a dream. It happened to me after that last recital in Chicago. I'd put the cello down on the floor of the stage and walked away. Once I'd made it behind the curtains a stagehand led me to the dressing room. My mother came into the room, and I remember being surprised at how calm she seemed. Someone delivered my cello to the room and my mother put it in its case for me, and it occurred to me that this was the first time I'd ever seen her touch the instrument. We left by the stage door and walked toward a waiting cab.

My mother was trying to put the cello in the front seat when all of a sudden, with an almost audible *whoosh,* I felt my normal sense of being present drain out of me. Just as in a dream, I saw myself walking down the sidewalk. Everyone I could see was staring at me, or so it seemed. They looked drained of their souls; they seemed to be marionettes sculpted out of pliable rubber. I must have stopped walking, because next I remember the marionettes standing in what appeared to be a perfect circle around me. The buildings stood in a larger concentric circle around us, with me at the dead center of it all. The composition of the scene, like that of a Persian miniature, seemed too symmetrical to be real. Then, as suddenly as it had arrived, the feeling of unreality disappeared. Things looked asymmetrical and mundane again, people looked less puppetlike and once again seemed to have souls, and I felt my sense of presence—of being an awake mind inside a real body—return to me. The whole episode probably lasted less than ten seconds—I had taken only four or five steps away from the cab—but for that time I was truly lost. If my body had decided to suddenly jump into the street or push someone into the traffic, I could no more have stopped myself than I could have willed my heart to stop beating or my stomach to cease digesting its food.

When it came time to cross-examine the doctor, Mr. Graham asked which of the psychological tests given to the defendant confirmed the diagnosis of schizophrenia. Dr. Libertson smiled, as if he had been waiting for the question, and answered that no test can absolutely confirm a diagnosis of schizophrenia; the disorder has to be inferred from behavior, and from responses to treatment.

"I see," Mr. Graham mused, waving a fly off the railing in front of the witness stand. "And what about insanity—is there any test that can confirm a diagnosis of insanity?"

"No. Insanity is a legal term, not a medical one. It's up to the court to decide if he was legally insane or not."

The prosecutor nodded politely and said in his soothing voice, "Yes. Thank you, I was just about to get to that. I'd like to read something aloud to the court. . . . Just a moment . . ." He went back to his desk and pulled a sheet of paper out of his briefcase. "Here it is. . . . This first quote is from a report published by the American Psychiatric Association. It says, 'The line between an irresistible impulse and an impulse not resisted is probably no sharper than the line between twilight and dusk.' Would you agree with that, Doctor?"

"In theory, yes," the doctor conceded.

"Ah. Thank you. This second quote is from another report on the insanity defense, published by the American Bar Association. This says, 'Experience confirms that there is still no accurate scientific basis for measuring one's capacity for self-control or for calibrating the impairment of such capacity. There is, in short, no objective basis for distinguishing between offenders who were undeterrable and those who were undeterred, between the impulse that was irresistible and the impulse not resisted, or between substantial impairment of capacity and some lesser impairment. . . . The question is unanswerable or, at best, can be answered only by moral guesses.' "

Mr. Graham looked at the doctor, again without seeming confrontational at all, and asked, "What about that? Does it sound right?"

Dr. Libertson did not look pleased at the way the testimony was going, but he kept his composure and answered, "I have no choice but to agree that there is no absolutely objective basis for telling the difference, no."

Mr. Graham nodded gently, then said, "So all of this means, doesn't it, Doctor, that in the absence of a conclusive medical diagnosis of insanity, it will be the jury's moral sense that decides, won't it?"

"Objection!" Ms. Doppelt cried out. "This line of reasoning is gratuitous. He's trying to invalidate the doctor's testimony by asking him legal-philosophy questions, not medical ones."

"Sustained. Mr. Graham, please."

The older lawyer bowed his head toward his female opponent in a gesture of penitence. "Dr. Libertson," he resumed, facing the doctor once again. "Isn't it true that many criminals who are not insane nevertheless have personality disorders that make them violently antisocial, and without any sense of remorse for what they do?"

"That's a different type of illness, but yes."

"Ah. The reason I mention this, Doctor, is that I want to remind the court that mental illness by itself does not automatically make a man legally insane."

"Objection," Ms. Doppelt protested. "The prosecutor is testifying, not questioning."

"Sustained."

I was intrigued by the quote about self-control—the one that suggested that trying to establish the boundary between an irresistible impulse and an impulse not resisted was like trying to determine when twilight ended and dusk began. We all think we can tell when someone is mentally ill or psychologically out of control; an inappropriate facial expression, a voice with an unnatural rhythm, a subtle awkwardness of movement—even the slightest cues give us an immediate sense of recognition. But maybe we aren't as good at identifying mental illness as we think. In a way I wished the defense attorney would let Philip Weber get up on the witness stand, because I felt I could tell a great deal from listening to him and watching him react. But Judge Davis had warned us that the defendant did not have to testify, and Ms. Doppelt had made a point of informing us that sometimes it serves justice better to let the evidence argue on behalf of the accused rather than the other way around.

17

Our day ended with the doctor's testimony. On the shuttle ride out to the parking lot I at last had an opportunity to ask Maria-Teresa how she liked the tape I'd given her.

"You want the polite answer or the rude one?" she asked.

"The honest one, I suppose."

"Saint-Saëns sucks," she said, grinning and lighting a cigarette.

"Do you mind not smoking in here?" Mrs. Friedman asked loudly, glancing at me as she spoke. She had not failed to notice the attention I'd been paying Maria-Teresa. I suppose I shouldn't have given it any thought, but I'm not used to being disapproved of.

"It wasn't really that bad," Maria-Teresa explained, tossing her cigarette out the window, "I mean, I'm sure it's incredible music and I'm just too thick to get it, but it just didn't hit me. All those instruments, all those fast notes, but it didn't mean anything; it was like hearing a whole crowd of people talking in another language."

"It didn't move you at all, then?"

"Well, again, I'm sure it's great music. . . ." She shrugged and looked at me apologetically. She was a philistine, all right, but what an inexplicably stimulating experience it was to have a beautiful woman tell me that Saint-Saëns sucks! I don't think I've had a conversation with someone unimpressed by classical music since I was six years old. What could I talk to her about? I wondered. Should I have been talking to her at all?

I told Maria-Teresa that I was surprised she could enjoy Mozart but remain unmoved by Saint-Saëns.

Her eyes lit up. "Yeah, but that's because I have some kind of image to associate with it, you know? When Amadeus is in bed sick, but that old guy is making him write the music even though he knows it's killing him, and you hear the music as he's writing it? I'll tell you one thing, Mozart gives great sound track, boy."

"Yes," I said, "but now, every time you hear Mozart, you'll visualize a bunch of actors acting out a scene that never really happened. That business about Salieri killing Mozart is pure nonsense, you know. Those Hollywood—"

"Those Hollywood phonies!" she teased, imitating my habit of fiddling with my tie. "Don't have an aneurism, OK? If I wanted the truth, I could always watch public television, but life is boring enough as it is. Don't take offense or anything, but for a guy who can't be much older than me, you kind of act like a character in a movie with subtitles! Come to think of it, we've been going about this totally the wrong way; I think you should borrow some of *my* tapes, instead of the other way around."

"Really? Do you think they'd cure me?"

"Does Imelda like shoes?" she rasped. "You better call up

that university you teach at and tell 'em you're quitting your job. I'll bring you something that'll make you want to take up guitar."

The shuttle dropped us off at the lot and we said good-night. My car was at the far end of the lot. Just as I reached it, I heard someone curse loudly, and I turned to see Maria-Teresa slapping the roof of her car. She must have slapped too hard, because then she started cursing even louder, all in that smoky voice of hers.

I went over to see what was wrong.

"I locked my fucking keys in my fucking car," she growled. I looked inside, and there they were, gently swinging from the motion of her slapping the car.

"Do you have another key?"

"Yeah, but it's at home. Shit! It's a good thing I dispatch ambulances and don't drive the fucking things! Can you imagine if I did this after putting some poor cardiac arrest in the back? Christ!"

When I asked if her husband could bring the key to her, she laughed. "What day is it today? Monday? He's probably in Indiana. Either that or Colorado."

I offered to drive her home to get her key and then drop her back off at the lot, but she said she didn't want me to have to go to the trouble, and that there was an easy bus she could take. I said that I really wouldn't mind, and added that this way she could lend me a tape right away. I said that if I was going to have to quit my teaching job after listening to her music, I would have to get started on the paperwork as early as possible. Finally she relented.

"Nice car," she said as I unlocked the door for her. It was an old Jaguar, not the flashy E-type but the old sedan, something I bought and had restored as soon as I could afford one. I told her that I fell in love with this model when I lived in Germany and saw them all the time on the autobahn. Naturally she asked why I had lived in Europe, and I told her a little bit about the years I had spent with von Kempen.

"Speaking of that," she said, "I remember the lawyer saying he listened to one of your records. Do you have a tape of it that you could lend me?"

"You didn't read the label?" I asked. "I was the soloist on the Saint-Saëns tape."

She clapped her hand over her mouth and slid down in the seat. "Oh, man, I'm so sorry!" she said, to my sheer delight. I was overjoyed that finally—*finally*—she was blushing rather than me.

"No need to apologize," I said. "I've had worse reviews than that, I can tell you."

"Well, what do I know, anyway. I blame society."

She directed me to her home, which at first looked like a dilapidated shack, but on closer inspection turned out to be a charming little bungalow that really only needed a new porch and a paint job.

Inside, the house was a mess. Maria-Teresa apologized, but said that when her husband was away she enjoyed not bothering to keep house. "You want a beer before we go back to the lot? I really appreciate your doing this for me."

"No, thanks. I'm not much of a beer drinker."

"What do you drink, just out of curiosity?"

"Wine, gin, scotch—whatever."

She rolled her eyes up into her head. "When you drink gin, do you drink it out of one of those Y-shaped glasses?"

"Sometimes, yes. Why?"

"I just want to know what I'm up against here—as far as picking out a record for you, I mean. It sounds to me like you've got some kind of premature aging thing that makes you want to listen only to music by dead guys. It must be far along by now. We'll have to start gradually—I don't want you to have a stroke or anything."

She walked over to a small table that was overflowing with cassette tapes. Most of them didn't appear to be in their boxes. The furniture in the house was all overstuffed and looked as if it came from Sears, and there were no bookshelves or books anywhere. "Actually," she said, fingering an earring, "I'll want to give this some thought. I can pick one for you later. You probably want to get going, huh?"

"I'm not in a hurry, but if you have things to do . . ."

"No, I don't have anything to do. You sure you don't want a beer while you're waiting, then? I'm gonna have one."

"In that case, yes, I'll join you."

She handed me a can of beer and told me to have a seat on the couch. I noticed it was covered with dog or cat hair, but I didn't see any pets. As she thumbed her way through the chaotic pile I looked more carefully around the room. The only personal touch I could see was a collection of tiny glass animals arranged on a ledge in front of a window and a wooden carving that spelled out the phrase OH SHIT! Everything else was strictly functional.

I felt uncomfortable but happy at the same time. There was something darkly satisfying about sitting in Maria-Teresa's messy house, drinking beer out of a can and listening to her caustic sense of humor. Also, her faux pas about my recording made me far more at ease around her than I might otherwise have been. I was still nervous, though. There was no avoiding the fact that I was sexually attracted to her, so what was I doing, letting her choose a rock-music tape for me? Was I leading her on?

I tried to put such thoughts out of my mind. What was I worrying about? Even if I were considering getting involved with a married woman, which I wasn't, it wouldn't be someone like Maria-Teresa. We had absolutely nothing in common, and she was married to a man who would probably knock me over the head with a railroad tie if he found out. Also, I had no reason to believe she was interested in me. We were the two youngest on the jury by at least ten years, so it was only natural that we would end up talking more to each other than to the others. Still, I couldn't quite explain to myself what I thought I was doing in her house.

"Ahhh, just the thing."

"You found what you were looking for?"

"Yep." She handed me an unmarked cassette. "I'm pretty sure this is it. Make sure and listen to all of it before you report back to me, even if you can only take it in doses."

"What sort of music is it? Is there a name for it?"

"I'm not gonna tell you. I don't want you to have any preconceived ideas. But I'll spare you one worry—it isn't me."

She flopped down into a chair and brushed her hand through her hair. "I know we aren't supposed to talk about the trial," she said, "but I'm curious—are we supposed to be able to remember all that stuff the psychiatrist was talking about?"

"I don't know. Maybe we're just supposed to get an overall impression from it. They certainly can't expect us to remember all that technical information."

"Yeah, like the business about going into a star hole and not being able to come out? What's that all about?"

"Oh, it's incredibly fascinating. There are all sorts of ways stars can die. I just read that some become black holes, some become white dwarfs and others turn into red giants."

She cast a sidelong glance at me. "Better be careful who overhears you when you talk like that."

"I know," I said, starting to feel a bit relaxed from the beer. "People think scientists must be boring, but they really have a sense of humor. For example, I read in a magazine that there are a group of physicists working on a theory that would unify all the different theories about where matter comes from, where it goes and all that, and you know what they call it?"

"No. What?"

"The Theory of Everything! Isn't that funny? That's the real name for it!" I laughed, but Maria-Teresa wasn't bowled over.

"That's like this girl that works where I do," she said. "She has an orange cat named OrangeCat and a parrot named Parrot. It goes over my head, I guess. Anyway, I didn't like that psychiatrist. I thought he came off as kind of a snob. He liked being up there where everybody had to listen to him, you could tell. I thought he was always trying to let us know how educated he was."

"He *was* kind of eager."

"Yeah. And the way he was always fussing with his little hands when he talked . . . I bet he's the kind of guy who's always arranging the things on his desk so all the edges are exactly even. A lot of doctors do that kind of stuff. I see it at work all the time."

"Well, I'm kind of like that myself, so . . ."

She screwed her face up in an expression of disappointment. "You? No! You're a musician! I thought musicians were supposed to be too spacey for that. I figured you'd wear socks that didn't match."

"No. Never. If I lose a button on a shirt and don't have an exact match, I throw the shirt away. It really bugs me if I see it in a mirror."

"That's wild."

"But that's not the worst of it," I said. I told her about how my sense of pitch was so strong that if even mechanical sounds were out of tune it annoyed me.

"What do you mean, mechanical sounds? You mean machines?"

"Right. If a blender is a little flat, or the neighbor's lawnmower is a little sharp, it's actually physically painful for me."

"Wow! So it would be torture for you to have to, say, go to a stock-car race, huh?" All of a sudden a huge grin spread across her face. When I asked her what was so funny she said, "I was just thinking how awful it would be if you had to spend a weekend with my husband! He's not happy without something gas-powered to play with. When he isn't driving a train he has to be either on his bike or a snowmobile or a jet ski—it just better be loud, or it's queer as far as he's concerned. And you get pissed off if a blender is out of tune! That's great! I guess you don't make margaritas at home much, huh?"

"Actually, I can. I found a blender that mixes at F-sharp."

"Bullshit!"

"No, I'm not joking—it's dead on."

When I got home I played Maria-Teresa's tape right away. As I figured it would be, the music was almost intolerable. It was a recording of a live concert, and listening to it forced me to visualize the scene: the lead singer, a woman in torn jeans and an oversized shirt, wailing about gloomy things onstage with a bunch of session musicians behind her, men with long hair, funny hats and skinny legs. I made myself listen to the whole thing, however, so that when I told Maria-Teresa that it sucked, I could do so from an informed point of view.

18

Kyung-hee looked as vacant as ever when he arrived for his third lesson. The novelty had worn off by then, and his tedious lack of personality distracted me more than ever. His mother insisted on paying me for the replacement string at the beginning of the lesson, in single dollar bills and quarters wrapped in an envelope that she handed to me formally, with both of her hands. I was sure this must have only reminded Kyung-hee of the dangers of trying to please both me and his mother. After only a few minutes of watching him bow listlessly through his drills I knew I couldn't stand a whole hour of it. Desperate to make him enjoy himself, so that I could at least enjoy *myself,* I told him to put down his cello and asked when his birthday was. "In October," he answered, blinking at me through his enormous glasses.

"Well, I'd like to get you an early birthday present."

This idea was inspired by something that had happened to me in Ederstausee, when I complained to von Kempen that I was getting bored with drills and wanted to play only music. I was just eleven years old.

"Ach, ja," the old man mused, nodding thoughtfully. I

remember his turning his head so I could see him in profile against the open windows facing his garden. He always kept the windows open, even in winter, so that he could hear the birds outside during lessons.

"I think the problem is to be found in your clothing," he said finally. "You have noticed, have you not, that I dress carefully for our lessons? Even when I practice I wear this suit, which was made for me before the war. Let us pay a visit to Herr Unterhalter, a tailor with whom I am acquainted."

He had Frau Schmidt drive us into the village to see the tailor, a man even older than himself, who bowed deeply from the waist as we entered his dark studio.

"The young master needs suitable clothes for his practice," von Kempen said. "It must be something he likes. Would you do us the kindness of allowing him to see your portfolio, along with the fabric samples?"

The tailor treated me like an adult to be respected; if he found this ceremony at all amusing, he didn't let it show. I looked through a catalog of suit patterns, but couldn't really tell the difference between them.

"Choose as you like, Herr Sundheimer. The suit must bring you pleasure. That is the only requirement," von Kempen said.

At last I blurted out in my halting German, "I . . . I want one like the one you wear, Maestro!" Herr Unterhalter looked quizzically at von Kempen, who merely nodded and assured me that the tailor could fulfill my request. To their credit, neither of the old gentlemen even cracked a smile.

Three days later the suit was ready. When Frau Schmidt brought it back from town, I couldn't wait to put it on. It was a dark formal suit with baggy pants, a stiff collar and a vest, and it came with a brief note from its maker: "My dear young maestro: I hope this will be to your satisfaction. I have tried to be faithful to the pattern and fabric of your dear teacher's outfit. Perhaps, if it is to your liking, you might convince your estimable Professor to allow me to make one like it for him. Thirty years is really too long to wear any suit, no matter how fine the quality."

"Young man," von Kempen advised me, ignoring the suggestion from Herr Unterhalter, "this suit is to be worn only for music, not simply for amusement. Take good care of it, and put it on with care. Comb your hair neatly, and look carefully in the mirror to be sure everything is in order, as any estimable gentleman might. Only then should you practice. I assure you, it will relieve the boredom you mentioned."

And it did. From that day on I couldn't wait to jump out of bed to get dressed, and when I wore the suit I felt majestic. I bowed to myself in the mirror. It lent an aura of formality to my practice sessions.

With this in mind, I asked Mrs. Kim's permission to take the two of them shopping for a suit for Kyung-hee. I insisted that this would be my treat—my way of repaying my own teacher for having done the same for me. At first she looked stunned, as if she couldn't decide whether to reason with me or simply take the boy and flee. At last she agreed, but with little enthusiasm. She had a way of making me feel permanently under suspicion that was highly irritating, but I kept telling myself I would probably be just as protective if I had a child of my own and was raising him in a foreign culture.

I told Kyung-hee what von Kempen had said to me: that he would find his exercises less tedious if he wore the right outfit, and that our mission this evening was to find the outfit.

"Wouldn't you like some clothes that you chose yourself?" He seemed to have to think about this for a while. At last he nodded, but without much conviction.

I took them to the mall near campus and we visited my favorite shop, which specializes in European-style men's clothing. I assumed that Kyung-hee would want a suit like mine, but he showed no interest at all in the patterns I guided him toward; in fact, he didn't seem to want anything in the store. Reluctantly I suggested we move on; we browsed through a few of the chic stores, most of them specializing in flashy clothes for teenagers, but Kyung-hee didn't respond to anything there either. We walked through the boys' department of Nordstrom's, but again nothing seemed to catch his eye. I started to think the idea was a mistake; maybe Kyung-hee just didn't get excited over clothes. But then, as we made our way through the giant maze, he suddenly halted. He was looking at something with definite interest on his face. When I turned to see what it was, at first I thought it was an electric massage chair that was on display in front of a yuppie gadget shop.

"You want a massage chair?" I asked cheerlessly.

Kyung-hee shook his head with surprising vigor, then pointed. To the right of the gadget shop was a costume shop, and in the window was a child-sized dummy dressed in an elaborate black costume with a long satin cape spread out behind him as if the wind were blowing through it.

"Batman," he said, with awe in his voice.

His mother immediately started scolding him in Korean, saying only the phrase "wasting teacher's time" in English. Though I nearly agreed with her for once, I realized that if I questioned the boy's choice at all—if I made him at all conscious of having to please me with the choice—the effect would be utterly ruined. I mustered an expression of innocence and said, "Mrs. Kim, there's nothing wrong with that suit. If he likes it, I think it would be fine."

She looked at me in total confusion. Kyung-hee slipped away from us and wandered into the store. "That for Halloween!" Mrs. Kim said despairingly. "This for playing game! Why you always want him playing game, 'Jump like cat,' 'Wear funny suit'?"

"Mrs. Kim, music isn't like other jobs. You don't get good at it by making a serious face and pretending like you work in a big company. The only way he's going to become great and make money is if he enjoys music so much he can't do anything else. I'm trying to help your son, Mrs. Kim, I really am, and I know what I'm doing. I was just like your son, so I know what to do."

Her hands were clenched into little fists and she looked as if she was fighting back tears. "We move here so Kyung-hee and Kyung-ja have good life, not like in Korea. Here we gotta make dry cleaner, no speak English, everybody think we stupid people! Mr. Kim, he no want Kyung-hee playing music, he say Kyung-hee no make money. He want Kyung-hee be engineer. I want Kyung-hee be happy too, so I fighting all the time, I say let him do music but he do it serious way. You, you American! You say, 'Play game, be happy, you make money.' OK for you, but what if Kyung-hee play game, be happy, but not work hard enough? Then he got nothing!"

It was the longest speech I had ever heard her make, and I didn't know what to say. I understood her better now, but it wouldn't have done anyone any good for me to tailor Kyung-hee's lessons to suit his parents' interests. You either teach honestly or you don't.

She spared me from having to say anything by sighing

heavily and looking down at her purse. "Everybody say you good teacher, famous teacher. You nice to Kyung-hee, he like you." She shrugged. "You want to buy suit, you buy. Maybe Mr. Kim no have to see."

We walked into the store together and found Kyung-hee standing next to the display model. I tried to forget everything I'd just heard and asked, "Is that the suit you want? Don't worry about what I think. If it makes you happy, then you must have it."

Kyung-hee seemed to be considering it. His mother had embarrassed him, but I hoped not too much. After a few seconds he glanced at me and nodded with his eyes. I think he was trying to answer without his mother seeing.

I bought the suit. It was shockingly expensive, especially after the salesman, an aggressive kid with the letters XTC shaved into the back of his scalp, insisted that the costume wouldn't be complete unless it included the "utility belt," an accessory that aspiring Bat-persons simply cannot do without, as one heard him tell it. When we returned to the house I didn't ask if Kyung-hee would like to put it on for our lesson; I didn't see any need to put myself or Mrs. Kim through the sight of him practicing with that shiny cowl, with its permanently molded frown, perched on top of his head. I gave him my own version of the pep talk von Kempen had given me, amending it only in that he was to wear the suit for practice only, not lessons. He seemed genuinely excited, which delighted me.

We picked up where we had left off with the drills and they went well. At the end I gave him a pat of encouragement on the shoulder, and smiled at Mrs. Kim. She only shrugged.

19

The killer's father appeared as the second witness for the defense. He had been sitting in the gallery since the beginning of the trial, but I hadn't guessed that he was the father; I had thought he was a member of the press.

Mr. Weber told the court that he was the senior vice president of a multinational paper-goods company. From the moment he got on the stand you could see he was no stranger to confrontation. In spite of a considerable paunch, the loss of most of his hair and deep worry lines etched around his eyes, he looked like a powerful man, with his huge shoulders and barrel chest. He maintained a stern, controlled expression for almost the whole time he was on the stand. His son, I noticed, only glanced at him furtively. His beatific expression had vanished for the time being, and was replaced by something more like embarrassment.

Ms. Doppelt asked Mr. Weber to tell the court when his son's troubles at home and in school had started. The big man, who was sweating profusely in the air-conditioned courtroom, dabbed his forehead with a handkerchief and began by describing his wife's first hospitalization for mental illness.

"When Philip was three, Nancy started getting obsessive about cleaning the house. She'd always been a damn good housekeeper, but this was obviously not about having a clean house. She'd spend hours folding the clothes in a single drawer, over and over. Then one day I came home from work and found her in the bathroom, curled up in the bathtub and crying. Philip was in the bedroom—he hadn't been fed all day, he was screaming. That's when I had to call the doctor. They took her to the hospital, and she stayed there for twelve weeks.

"I had to get someone to take care of Philip. That's the way it was until he left for college. Nancy was always in and out of hospitals. When she was home, she was pretty much helpless, so she wasn't much of a mother. Because of my work, we moved around a lot, so we had to change nannies several times. I thought they were all adequate, but now . . . I don't know . . ."

Mr. Weber testified that his son had always been moody, but seemed to be managing just fine until college, when he dropped out suddenly after only one semester.

"He came home—we were living in Sacramento at that time—and, oh, I don't know, I think he said he wanted to write a novel, or screenplay, or something of that nature. I was skeptical. Some of his teachers said he was talented, but you don't know how to interpret that. It sounded to me like he was just looking for a way to avoid having to work. I said he could live at home for six months and give it a try, but at the end of the six months he'd be on his own."

Mr. Weber wasn't at home for a lot of this period because his job took him back and forth to Europe frequently at the time. But despite the absences, his relationship with his son got especially tense during these months. "As I say, he was always kind of . . . moody, quiet. But now it was more of a kind of . . . He sulked around the house all the time. He was going through one of those college-age attitudes where the father could do no right in his mind. He was very negative about me and my work."

"In what ways was he negative?" Ms. Doppelt asked abruptly. As usual, she was not demonstrating a good bed-side manner. With this witness, however, it didn't bother me; Mr. Weber seemed like a fairly unpleasant fellow, so it was almost satisfying to see him grilled this way.

"Oh, well, it's a paper company I run, right? So I cut down rain forests, I pollute rivers, I take owls' nests away—the whole nine yards."

"So would you say that most of your talks with Philip were actually arguments?"

"When we talked at all, yes. We had nothing in common, so it always felt like there was nothing to talk about."

I knew that situation well enough. By the time I was ten I could no longer hold meaningful conversation with my parents; neither of them knew enough about music to follow what I was saying, and I didn't know enough about life outside of music to talk about anything else. This didn't seem to bother my mother, who made enormous sacrifices to protect me from the outside world. Believing as she did that my talent came directly from God, she felt it was her solemn duty to watch over my gift, and to make sure I was always comfortable and safe from unpleasant distractions. Her role as guardian and manager kept her busy and appeared to compensate for the fact that instead of a friendship developing between us we formed a bond that was made up almost entirely of a sense of mutual obligation. Instead of talking with me, she generally issued reports on what she was doing for my benefit, and I reciprocated by allowing her to have her way in matters of policy, such as what I would eat and wear, where I would play and when, and whom I could meet.

My father took a different approach. Once he felt he was no longer of use to me as an adviser or confidant, which was around my tenth or eleventh year, he abruptly retreated. Whenever people recognized him after concerts or were told that he was my father, he would hunch up his shoulders, lower his head and answer their questions in short, tense phrases, and would usually excuse himself by saying to my mother, "I'll wait in the car." It was as if he didn't want to spoil things with his presence.

When I was very young I was embarrassed by him, but as I grew older his social awkwardness particularly irritated me. He wasn't a stupid man, so I felt he had no reason to act ashamed of himself. If he hadn't had to flee Germany with my mother he would have been a lawyer there; because of his poor English he wasn't able to pass the entrance exams to any law schools here and finally had to take a job as a clerk in a large shipping firm. I could understand his disappointment, but it hardly made him a failure as a human being. It made me angry that at my concerts and at the parties our family was invited to he would make himself so conspicuously unobtrusive, because, I felt, this made people assume he must have had good reason to do so, and then I really did feel ashamed of him.

The whole time I was growing up I never knew my father to have any friends. He never invited any co-workers over for dinner, and he never went out at night or on weekends with anyone. He came straight home from work every night, and stayed there every weekend, finding useful but entirely unnecessary things to do around the house. He would ask me how my studies were going, what music I planned to learn next and so on, but the few times I tried to talk to him about anything else he always found something to do with his hands so that he wouldn't have to look directly at me. He would move his eyebrows up and down and nod occasionally so that I would know he was listening, but he kept his eyes on his hands, which would fold things, twist things, arrange things, prune things, polish things or whittle things, and this—intentionally or not—always seemed to drain the emotional content out of what I was saying and turn it into polite, indirect chatter.

My father rarely discussed his early life with me. I knew from my mother that his parents, who had chosen not to leave Germany, had died in the Holocaust, but I was in my twenties before I heard the rest of the story from a cousin. Our uncle, my father's oldest brother, had been held at the same camp as my grandparents but had managed to survive. In the years after the war ended, consumed with guilt over having lived without being able to save his own parents, he became addicted to morphine and died of an overdose in 1949. I never spoke about this with my father, even after I'd heard the story. The only truly weighty conversation I ever had with him occurred when I asked if he thought America could survive having a poorly educated, morally confused former actor as its president.

"It depends," he said.

"On what?"

"Whether you're an optimist or a pessimist."

When I asked him to explain how he defined these two groups, he said, "Reinhart, when somebody gets born, it's like he got pushed off the top of one of those ski-slope places. There's only one way to go, and that's down. Optimists are the people who face backwards; they're looking up, but trying real hard not to notice that up is getting farther away. Pessimists are facing the direction they're going."

"So what are you, Dad?"

"I'm not looking."

At the end of the six months Mr. Weber asked his son to show him the novel, and the boy admitted that he hadn't written a line.

"I felt bad for Philip then, I really did. It broke my heart, because as a kid he was always slouching around the house, he had no friends, and the nanny said that all he did was watch TV all day and sleep on the couch."

"Objection!" Mr. Graham interrupted. "That's hearsay, your Honor."

"Sustained. Mr. Weber, just tell us what you know to be fact."

The anguished father nodded and continued: "This was my own son. But I felt I had to be firm with him; otherwise he might never take responsibility for himself. So I gave him five hundred dollars and told him he was on his own."

"Was that the last time you saw him before he was arrested this year?" Ms. Doppelt asked.

"No. He showed up about a year after I'd kicked him out. I came home from work one night and there he was, sitting in the living room. He looked terrible. He was thin and pale, and obviously something was wrong with him. He talked kind of slurred and wasn't always making full sentences. He was rambling about living in Los Angeles and how he was writing for some big movie company. I could tell that he was on drugs and I confronted him. He didn't deny it, just went pale and stormed out of the house. That was the last time I saw him. I assume he drove back to Los Angeles."

"Mr. Weber, I realize this is a difficult question, but I think you understand why I have to ask it. Do you feel you did the right thing by sending him off on his own when you did?"

Mr. Weber mopped his forehead and cleared his throat. "With the information I had then, I think I did the best I could," he said tightly. "But knowing what I do now, I would do it differently."

"What makes you say that?"

The man exhaled loudly. He seemed very uncomfortable about having to admit that he had made a mistake. "When Philip dropped out of college I thought he was just being difficult, that it was just a childish way of getting attention. He didn't act the way Nancy did during her bad spells, so I didn't think he had her mental problems. I guess I couldn't let myself think that was possible; it was too awful to think about. I thought that setting rules and being strict with him would make him grow up. I didn't want him to become one of those spoiled rich kids who become parasites as adults. Now I realize that he did have a problem, something of a mental nature. It wasn't his fault. I wish I had known that then. I would have sent him to doctors, and—"

Mr. Graham objected, saying this was all speculation, and the judge agreed.

Ms. Doppelt asked the father to read several passages aloud from a series of letters that Philip had addressed to his mother when he was living at the Zen Foundation. Mr. Weber had never passed them on to his wife because he felt they would only upset her. For the most part the letters alternated between rambling, immature sentiments about life's impermanence and dramatic promises to exert himself to his fullest until he became enlightened and fulfilled his vow "to save all sentient beings from suffering." The overall impression you got was that Philip was a painfully insecure young man trying desperately to impress his absent mother, but in pathetically fantastical, overblown ways.

A part of one letter, however, impressed and interested me. It read: ". . . sometimes when I'm sitting zazen in the main hall an intense thing happens, which happens to people who are on the brink of satori. I'll be listening to something, like the temple bell, or the garbage truck backing up every morning at around six, and if I hit a certain kind of state of mind, I can suddenly *see* the sound or taste it! Like the sound of the bell is dark green and shiny or it tastes like those slippery mushrooms that come in cans. The truck backing up has one of those beeping sounds when it goes backwards and the beep is bright yellow and has a metallic taste, but when he revs up the engine that's black, and for some reason it doesn't have a flavor. This could be a makyo, which means a kind of illusion that advanced Zen students get and I'll have to push through it, or it may be an early taste of enlightenment."

This interested me because when I was very young one of the reasons I was able to hear a piece of music and then play it right back without having to look at a score was that for me each musical phrase had not so much a color or flavor as a texture, and if I could remember the sequence of textures, I could automatically reproduce the sounds. Philip's mention of "slippery mushrooms" suddenly brought a flood of memories for me. I could even recall a few of my textures, particularly the ones I associated with slow, haunting melodies.

There were phrases that felt like satin or feathers, and others that had the texture of coarse sand or polished marble. These memories were so pleasant that I fell into a grateful reverie for a while, where I remained until Judge Davis announced the morning break.

20

As the other jurors were standing up to file out, Maria-Teresa casually asked me if I would like to join her later for lunch. I was thrilled but nervous at the same time. Though there was nothing wrong with our eating together, there was the as yet unacknowledged fact that she was married. I knew, of course, that the only reason I'd gravitated toward her was the way she looked, but I certainly didn't intend to make a pass at her. I simply wanted to enjoy the fact that someone so physically attractive would pay attention to me.

I wasn't completely without experience around women; I had nearly fallen in love once, in my late twenties. Naomi was a violist who played in a semiprofessional quartet with Martin, the well-read violin instructor. He thought she and I might hit it off, so he invited Naomi and me and a few other musicians over for dinner one night. I was attracted to her, and Martin strongly encouraged me to call her up, assuring me that she was interested. As usual I felt hesitant about doing so; instead of calling her right away I experienced a surge of renewed determination and practiced until I thought my arms would drop off, hoping to make progress toward solving my problem so that I could at least tell her that I was preparing a concert. But when that effort brought no results, I yielded to Martin's exhortations and called her up.

We dated for several months, but it was an awkwardly platonic relationship. For most of our dates we went to concerts. When we didn't go to concerts, we talked about concerts or about music in general. She liked to talk about her quartet and solo work, but when she asked about my playing I could only discuss the past. Since we were both musicians, and had been nothing else since childhood, we had little else to share. We might have become great friends, but hanging over us was the expectation that we become something more than friends. Specifically, the expectation was that *I* should turn us into something more than just friends; she was a traditional-minded young lady and was clearly not going to initiate any of the activities I had in mind.

Whenever I got near Naomi I felt myself turn to ice. I couldn't help thinking how much easier it would have been for me to woo her, how much more confident I would have felt, if only I were a concert musician again instead of just a music teacher. To adapt my mother's analogy, if my stock had been as high as it had been when I was seventeen, I could easily believe that she would want to make love to me. As it was, however, I felt unable to make my intentions clear because I was convinced she would respond the way J. Alfred Prufrock's beloved did and say, "That is not what I meant at all, Reinhart. That is not it, at all."

The relationship ended predictably enough: suddenly she got busy. Whenever I called her she would sound happy to hear from me, but always had other plans. To be honest, I was relieved. After that I didn't let Martin set me up anymore. I figured that any woman with real character would eventually be turned off by my insecurity, and if she wasn't, I probably wouldn't want to date her for long. I decided to either wait until I was a successful performer again or just stay single.

It was hard to concentrate on the trial for the rest of the morning. When we sat down after the break, Maria-Teresa's hand brushed against my arm. It could easily have been unintentional, but it was very distracting. I was trying to listen to the prosecutor's cross-examination of the boy's father, but with only partial success. Mr. Graham's gentle voice and the witness's subdued responses faded in and out of my attention.

Just before lunch, however, the interview suddenly turned nasty. It started when Mr. Graham asked Mr. Weber when he began to believe that mental illness was the cause of Philip's problems, and ultimately of his violent behavior at the Zen church. Mr. Weber glared at the prosecutor with undisguised loathing. "When did I think Philip was mentally sick? When this happened, obviously! A sane man doesn't act that way, for Christ's sake. And look at him now," he said, jabbing a thick finger in his son's direction, "you can tell just by looking at him that he doesn't know what the hell's going on around him! He's on trial for murder and he's sitting there like he's on a school field trip, for God's sake."

Suddenly his exasperation with his son came tumbling out. "I mean," he said, gesturing with his chin at Ms. Doppelt, "no offense intended, but I wanted to hire a private lawyer to handle this, not a public defender, but Philip wouldn't—"

The prosecutor stopped Mr. Weber in mid-sentence and asked that the last comment be stricken from the record, saying that it was insulting to his colleague, Ms. Doppelt, and uncalled for. At first I thought this was a highly chivalrous gesture, but on further reflection it occurred to me that the fact that Philip Weber wouldn't let his father hire a more experienced lawyer did tend to support the defense's claim that Philip was not thinking clearly.

Mr. Graham turned back to the witness stand and had the court reporter read back the part of Mr. Weber's testimony where he discussed his son using drugs. Then he asked the father if he thought it was possible that the drugs had affected his son's mind.

"Objection, Your Honor," Ms. Doppelt protested. "Blood tests taken just after the incident showed that Philip was not using drugs at the time of the retreat. Furthermore, the witness is not an expert on drugs—there is no foundation for this line of questioning."

The prosecutor gently but firmly shot right back, "Just because the drugs weren't in his bloodstream that day doesn't mean that they couldn't have already affected his mind in some way."

Judge Davis agreed with him and overruled the objection. The senior Mr. Weber evaded the question by saying that since he wasn't a doctor, he couldn't possibly say where the drugs ended and the mental illness began. "I know one thing, though," he said, pointing his finger at the prosecutor now. "He was having these problems long before he got near any of those damn drugs. I know what you're getting at, though—you're going to make some fancy argument that Philip couldn't have been sick because any normal parent, especially one with a wife who was so sick, would have caught on to it a lot earlier. Well, the reason I didn't catch on to it earlier isn't because the problems weren't there; it's because I wasn't a normal parent, all right? I failed as a parent. I failed my son, and now he's paying for it."

You could see how hard it was for Mr. Weber to utter these words. He mopped his forehead again, and I could see his hands shaking. He was an unlikable man, but he had been loyal to his wife through eighteen years of mental illness, and was willing to accept responsibility for what had happened; he had been a poor father, but he didn't deserve anything like this. After this exchange I stopped listening; I couldn't bear to hear the rest of the interview.

"What's the verdict?" Maria-Teresa said as we sat down to eat.

"You mean do I think he's guilty?"

"I don't mean the trial, Reinhart. I'm talking about the tape I lent you—did you get a chance to listen to it?"

"Oh, the tape . . . Yes, I listened to it. It was incredible, all right."

She broke up laughing. "Come on, you didn't get into it at all?"

"Get into it? Of course I got into it—the problem is, I couldn't get out of it for forty-five minutes. I'd promised, after all."

I liked the way we could joke with each other. For most of my life I was so tired of being perceived as a talented youngster that I was constantly trying to act older than my age. How ironic it seemed that at the age of thirty-four and no longer talented, I was finding it enjoyable to act younger than my age.

• • •

For most of the lunch Maria-Teresa told me darkly amusing stories from her work: about people who called for ambulances when their miniature dachshunds threw up, oversized people who got wedged into their bathtubs and even a young gigolo calling for help when his aged and socially prominent client went into cardiac arrest during sex. The worst part of that episode, she said, was that the woman died wearing an outlandish leather outfit, leaving you to wonder what kind of scene occurred at the morgue when her grown children had to identify her.

When she lit her third cigarette of the lunch, I asked Maria-Teresa if she didn't worry about smoking too much. "I'm going to quit," she said, smiling, "but not quite yet. I made a New Year's resolution that if my daughter passes all her classes this year, then I'll quit smoking to celebrate. Until then, I need it."

"What grade is she in?"

"Ninth grade, do you believe it? Only, she's at one of those military schools. She was getting into trouble down here. Her dad's a career soldier, so she gets a break on tuition. They say you get a pretty good education there, but I don't know. . . . I feel sorry for her, having to salute all fucking day. Poor kid. She'll do OK, though. At least she's not in a gang."

"So your husband is in the military?" I asked, feeling a bit sorry that the subject had come up.

A relieved expression appeared on her face. "No way! That was my first husband. I married him when I was sixteen because I was pregnant. What do you know when you're sixteen? We got divorced in a year, but he kept the baby. He had a job and his family had some money, and I didn't. I guess I'm glad. I see Yolanda on weekends, except now that she's away at school, not so much anymore."

She picked up her napkin from her lap, folded it neatly and put it on the table, but then seemed to realize she was still eating and dropped it back on her lap. "So what about you? Have you ever been married?" she asked. I must have registered surprise, because she quickly laughed and apologized for seeming nosy. "It's none of my business, that's just me."

I didn't mind. I had been hoping she would ask me something personal. I told her that I hadn't ever been married, or even close to it.

She nodded without showing any reaction, inhaled deeply from her cigarette, looked momentarily satisfied and then ground it out in her ashtray. "You're lucky," she said. "It can sure pull you down if it doesn't work. Especially if you have a kid."

As soon as she'd said that she started to laugh at herself, and added, "I bet everybody says that to you, huh? 'You're lucky to be single.' And everybody I know that's single says they wish they were married. People are so screwed up. We can't do anything without making it seem hard." She laughed again. "Or maybe I should just speak for myself, huh?"

But I agreed with her. It was the oddest thing: I really had nothing in common with her, and I would never have imagined I could even hold a conversation with someone like her. It wasn't that she was dumb, and it certainly wasn't that she was unattractive, but she really seemed to be from another planet—and not one I'd particularly like to visit. And yet, though I couldn't imagine becoming seriously involved with her, I was certainly busy imagining what it would be like to be physically involved with her.

Walking back to the courthouse, she said nonchalantly, "I almost forgot what it was like—having a real conversation with a man. I mean, where the guy actually listened to what I had to say, too. That was fun—thanks."

I did pay the bill for that lunch.

In the afternoon a gaunt woman with severely short hair, one of the witnesses of the murder, testified for the defense. As she took her seat in the witness box, the small group of Japanese people in the gallery held a quick, whispered conference, then stood up together and quietly left the courtroom. They didn't make any unnecessary noise or commotion, but the gesture did not go unnoticed.

The witness, whose name was Fran DeLacy, said she was an artist and had first become interested in Zen for professional reasons. She had been studying with a Japanese ceramicist at the time, and her teacher had recommended Zen to help strengthen her concentration. Within a few years her interest in Zen grew to overshadow her interest in art, so she moved into the Zen Foundation in order to devote all her energy to practicing meditation full time. As she spoke I noticed that the defendant was shifting restlessly in his chair and avoiding looking at her. He seemed uncharacteristically tense during her testimony.

Ms. DeLacy recounted how Philip came to join their group. When Ms. Doppelt asked her to describe her early impressions of Philip, the witness said, "The first day he walked in I could tell he was 'off.' He needed a therapist, not Zen lessons." When she said this, Philip laughed out loud; it was the first time he had made any noise at all since the trial began.

"I remember," Ms. DeLacy continued, "that at the house

meeting where we were deciding whether to let him become a resident or not, I was against it."

"Did you express your concern?" Ms. Doppelt asked.

"Yeah. I said, 'Hey, we don't run a halfway house, we run a Zen center.' I thought it would be a problem to have him living there because he was obviously a mixed-up kid. But I got voted down."

Ms. DeLacy no longer lived at the Zen Foundation. She had left right after the murder, but she told us she had been planning to leave for some time. When asked why, she said it was because she disagreed with the late Zen master's teaching methods. She thought he put too much pressure on students to achieve enlightenment.

"Mr. Okakura was always saying, if you're really serious about Zen and really push yourself, you'll have a sudden enlightenment and it will be the greatest experience of your life. He said you had to practically kill yourself if you wanted to attain it." She sighed and ran her tongue over her lips as if to moisten them. A glass of water sat on the table next to her, but she didn't seem to notice it. "I got tired of that attitude, I guess. I think it's a macho thing. Zen teachers think that since they went through hell to get their knowledge, you have to go through hell too or you can't join their club. When you get someone like Philip, who's already kind of obsessive, and seems to be on the edge, and push someone like that . . . I mean, I'm right, aren't I? Look at what happened."

"So you feel that Mr. Okakura—or his methods, rather—pushed Mr. Weber over the edge, so to speak, during the retreat?"

The witness twisted her mouth to one side and looked around, thinking. "Well, not intentionally," she finally answered. "But I think the koan he assigned to Philip, the one about killing the Buddha in the road . . . I think it had something to do with it, yeah."

The reason the dead man's relatives left the courtroom became apparent during the cross-examination. In his usual polite but wry manner, Mr. Graham reported that a witness had mentioned in a prior statement that Philip had been quite upset, as many of the Zen Foundation members were, when a romantic relationship between the doomed Zen teacher and several students, including the witness, came to light in a very public way.

It turned out that the Zen teacher had been sleeping with several of the female members of his churches without letting them know about the others, and that one of them had even brought a sexual harassment suit against him that was settled out of court.

Ms. DeLacy did not seem surprised that this came out in the trial. The defense attorney must have prepared her for it. She said that yes, the scandal did upset a lot of people, including Philip. She said that one night, at an emergency house meeting, one woman said she thought that Okakura was a fraud, and that he should be banned from teaching. Philip didn't yell at her, but he did go up to his room and several of the members heard him crying. "There'd been a lot of crying around the foundation then, though," she added.

"Ms. DeLacy," Mr. Graham asked in his charming drawl, managing to seem polite even while asking the most intrusive questions, "before this incident came out in the open, did you have any reason to believe that Philip liked you? In the sense of having a crush, I mean?"

Again Philip laughed out loud when he heard the question.

When I looked at him he was shaking his head, with a forced-looking smile on his face.

"No, he didn't give me any reason to think so," the witness said. "In fact, he almost never looked me in the eye. He wouldn't talk to me unless I asked him something, and then he'd practically run away."

Mr. Graham nodded slowly, then glanced at Philip, who was frowning slightly and making notches in a pencil with his thumbnail. It got me thinking; if he'd had an immature crush on Ms. DeLacy that he couldn't express in an acceptable way, and he knew that the Zen master had slept with her and betrayed her, perhaps the murder wasn't entirely without motive after all.

21

"Have you been practicing with your suit on, Kyung-hee?" I asked as I tuned his cello for him.

He barely nodded, then said, "But I don't think the real Batman would play the cello."

"Why not?"

When he looked up at me, I noticed that his glasses had been repaired again with electrical tape, this time over the bridge holding them together. He moved his lips silently for a moment, as if rehearsing what he was going to say. He rarely spoke, and when he did he seemed to have a difficult time putting his thoughts into words.

"There's a bunch of superheroes," he began, frowning behind his damaged glasses. "Like Thing—he's made out of orange rocks, so he can't really get hurt if you punch him. Batman has all sorts of tools that he invents. Those guys have special powers for fighting bad guys. But playing the cello wouldn't be a good power because it wouldn't help them in a fight."

It was the most I'd ever heard him say. I was delighted, and wanted to encourage him to express himself more often, but at the same time I could hardly agree with what he was saying. "You have a point, Kyung-hee, but fighting and music are completely different. People fight in order to hurt other people, or to protect themselves, but people make music to feel good. It makes life worth living. Even those superheroes you mentioned have to do something besides fight, don't you think?"

He stared into space, concentrating, then in disagreement shook his head, which bobbed precariously on his narrow shoulders. "There's an awful lot of bad guys, Mr. Sundheimer."

"Well, OK, but let's talk about you. You don't fight bad guys, but you do have a special power. You have a special ability to understand music. You realize that, don't you?"

"Uh-huh."

"And in a way, your special power is greater than those comic-book characters', because all they can do is fight, but you can do so much more with music. With your playing, you can say a great deal to people, and give them beautiful moments so they can forget their hard work or remember things out of the past. I think that's the greatest power of all, don't you?"

Kyung-hee fell into deep thought again. When he resurfaced, he said gravely, "Well, if you don't have music you can still live and do other stuff, but if you get killed by a bad guy, you can't do anything. So maybe superpowers are still the best."

I couldn't fail to recognize the logic in what he was saying. Although I was disappointed to learn that he considered fighting more important than music, it relieved me to know that he was capable of reasoning appropriate for his age, and was not an idiot savant as I'd feared when I first met him.

"Well, perhaps it's foolish of me to make comparisons,

Kyung-hee. But let's talk about Batman—isn't he the one whose parents were killed by a bad guy, so then he decided to fight crime?" For once I was glad I had seen a popular movie.

"Uh-huh."

"So he's like you and me, isn't he? He's not superhuman—he's just very smart and determined."

"Uh-huh."

"So he might play the cello in his spare time, right?"

Kyung-hee's face suddenly froze; he looked as if something had dropped from the ceiling on his head.

"No!" he said with uncharacteristic vigor. "Batman wouldn't because the Batcave is where all the computers are and stuff, but he could have played cello when he was Bruce Wayne! In Wayne mansion! It would be perfect!"

"Why would it be perfect, Kyung-hee?"

"Because Wayne mansion *looks* like music! It has candles and old rugs and shining armor in it!"

Delighted that he was relating music to other aspects of human experience, even if it was only furniture, I asked him if the Wayne mansion looked like all music, or only a certain kind of music.

"Like Mozart!" he exclaimed. "Fancy, with a fireplace! And your house looks like Bach!" he added.

"Why?" I asked, feeling enormously complimented.

"Because everything in here, the chairs and desk . . . it's all . . ." He struggled for the words. "It's all skinny stuff!"

I realized that he meant the furniture was spare. "And that bookshelf," he continued, pointing to the set of shelves on the far wall, "it's the same on that side of the door as on the other side!"

In the matched pair of bookshelves on either side of the

door, he was apparently reminded of the harmonic symmetry that Bach had perfected.

I was so excited I could hardly stay seated. "Kyung-hee, let's try something. Keep thinking about music and houses for a moment." I got up and fetched several books of photographs from the shelves, hoping to find pictures of a wide variety of distinctive buildings and gardens. I showed Kyung-hee a photograph of the gardens at Versailles, and without an instant's hesitation he shouted, "Mozart!"

Next I found a picture of the Venice skyline, and once again, without any hesitation, he cried out, "Mozart!" When he looked at a picture of the Capitol in Washington, he immediately said, "Bach!"

As we went through more pictures, he identified anything remotely elaborate as being like Mozart and anything spare or classically symmetrical as being like Bach. I began to realize that these might be the only composers he was familiar with. When I showed him a picture of the ruins of an old castle, he stared at it for a long time, then said, "That doesn't look like music."

As an experiment, I pulled out a recording of Debussy's "Sunken Cathedral," an exquisite short piece for piano that features hauntingly liquid chords that were arranged to sound like the bells of an ancient church ringing under the waters of a deep, still lake. Kyung-hee listened without moving; when it was over, he looked down at the picture of the ruined castle, then back up at me, his pupils so dilated that his eyes looked like shiny black marbles. "It's incredible!" he said; the sound of his voice, coupled with the awed expression on his face, was both lovely and pitiful. The thought that had it not been for an elementary-school music teacher in Long Beach needing a cellist for the school orchestra, the Korean boy might have gone his whole life without ever discovering classical music made my whole body ache.

I knew then that my primary responsibility to Kyung-hee was not to improve his technique but to make sure that his talent was properly nourished by exposure to great music. I asked him what classical records or tapes he listened to at home; he answered that his family did not have a stereo. "We have two TVs, though," he said proudly.

I told him to have a seat on the couch, that for the first half of the lesson we were going to listen to music, and put on the Cleveland Orchestra's recording of Moussorgsky's *Pictures at an Exhibition.* Instead of giving him the traditional explanation for each of the movements right away, I spread out the books of photographs on the floor and invited him to find pictures in them that "looked like" what he was hearing.

Kyung-hee approached the problem in a way that at first didn't make sense to me. When the music began, he listened for only a few seconds, then jumped down onto the floor and started leafing through the books at such a fast pace that I was afraid he might tear some of the pages.

He didn't pause over any of the photographs, making me think that he hadn't understood me properly, and wasn't actually trying to relate them to the music. It didn't appear that he was paying any attention to the music at all. By the fifth movement, barely a third of the way through the piece, he had glanced at all of the pictures in every book, then climbed back up on the sofa.

I debated over whether to stop the music and repeat my instructions to him, but in the end felt it was more important that he hear the music straight through without interruption. After the last movement, the grand procession through the

Gate of Kiev, when the final notes had died away, I looked to see his reaction. He was looking at me with an expression of anxious concentration.

"What did you think, Kyung-hee?"

"Do you want me to show the pictures now?" he asked, fidgeting in his seat.

"Sure."

He pounced on the books, pushing all of them to one side except for one, a book of color photographs by Ernst Haas. "This one has the pictures that look the rightest," he said, flipping rapidly through the pages. Humming from memory the opening theme, the Promenade, which depicts the composer strolling from picture to picture at the exhibition where his late friend Victor Hartmann's paintings were hung, Kyung-hee settled without hesitation on a photograph of horse-drawn carriages in Central Park, their drivers wearing top hats and long coats.

"Old-fashioned," he explained, pointing at the top hats. "Then this part came." He flipped through the book humming the agitated theme of the second movement, Gnomus, which Moussorgsky composed based on Hartmann's painting of a misshapen dwarf. "This one," Kyung-hee announced, pointing to his choice of a photograph of storm clouds brewing in the sky above Nevada. Then he returned to the picture of Central Park. "This again," he said, correctly identifying the resumption of the Promenade theme.

The next movement, depicting troubadours performing in front of an old castle, has a mournful, Oriental-sounding theme carried mostly by the winds, particularly the oboes. Kyung-hee jumped to a photograph of a camel fair in India, saying, "They have to go on a long trip through the sand.

They can make snakes come out of baskets!" Without stopping to look up from the book to see my reaction, he went through all fifteen movements in perfect sequence, able to hum their melodies from memory. Later he explained that he could find the corresponding photographs quickly because he had memorized the page numbers.

His choices, though they did not correspond exactly to the images that Moussorgsky based his compositions upon, all fit the mood of each piece beautifully, proving that he was responding on an emotional level to the music. Perhaps most exciting was that he was able to relate those musical emotions to visual images; the difference between truly great musicians and skillful musical technicians, I believe, is that the musician is able to bring more than just the sense of hearing to his interpretations. When he plays or listens to music, he sees it, feels it, tastes it, and is able to season his performance with memories and fantasies of his own that may have nothing to do with strictly aural harmony.

"Kyung-hee," I asked at the end of our lesson, "have you ever gone to a concert? In a concert hall?"

He shook his head. A few minutes later, as he was maneuvering his rented cello into its threadbare cloth case, his mother returned from shopping in Koreatown. I asked her if she and her family would like to come into the city on Saturday night and be my guests at a performance by the Philharmonic. I reminded her of the international success of groups like the Philharmonic and the Boston Symphony, and said that it would be good for Kyung-hee to hear this type of music performed live. She seemed taken aback by my offer and delivered a long speech in Korean, at the end of which she nudged Kyung-hee and gestured in my direction with her chin. This was her usual signal for him to translate something into English. He didn't, however; instead he simply said, "My mom's embarrassed."

"Why?"

"You're the teacher!" he said, looking up at me and blinking. "We have to invite you to things. So she invited you over for dinner."

"Tell her that's very nice, and I'd love to do that soon, but what about the concert on Saturday? Can you come?"

"No, no!" Mrs. Kim answered directly, smiling nervously and waving her hand. "Mr. Sunhai too polite!"

When I assured her that my offer was genuine, that I wanted Kyung-hee to hear fine performances for his art's sake, and that I could get the tickets free (which wasn't true, but I thought it might help), she reminded me that the whole family worked at the cleaners on weekend nights. She hesitated, wringing her chapped hands and glancing at her son, then said, "But if you say important for Kyung-hee, maybe Kyung-hee go. I talk to Mr. Kim."

I was dumbfounded; it would have been absolutely unthinkable for my mother to let someone take me, at the age of nine, in a car to another city for dinner and a concert. Von Kempen seemed to have sensed this from the beginning, because he never made the mistake of inviting me anywhere without first inviting my mother. A less perceptive conductor in New York had once asked me to join him for lunch before our first rehearsal. I think he was nervous about working with such a young soloist and felt he should spend some time getting to know me before we worked together. I didn't need any special treatment; in fact, I preferred not having to socialize with conductors and orchestra musicians because I almost always sensed that they felt uncomfortable about having to treat a child as a colleague. Instead of speaking to us directly about it, this conductor had left a message for me at the hotel desk, which my mother received and read as we checked in. The note did not mention my mother at all. She called the conductor as soon as we got to our room and informed him coldly that *we* already had plans for lunch, and that in the future he might do *us* the favor of allowing more than an hour's notice for appointments.

"But how Kyung-hee get here?" Mrs. Kim asked. "Mr. Kim and me working Saturday."

Not wanting to let the opportunity pass, I offered to pick Kyung-hee up in the afternoon, take him to dinner and bring him back home right after the concert. Mrs. Kim went through the motions of being embarrassed again, protesting that I was being too polite and that the teacher shouldn't do favors for a student, but I persisted and eventually she said that if her husband approved, it would be all right.

22

Ms. Doppelt's next witness, Professor Grant Stribling, taught a course in comparative religions at Los Angeles Community College, looked close to retirement age and suffered badly from allergies. The gist of his testimony was that Zen is an iconoclastic sect of Buddhism that encourages impulsive, spontaneous behavior. Between bouts of sneezing ("It's the dust, not the smog," he kept saying, "same as in classrooms!") he told us that Zen was a nihilistic philosophy which teaches that everything is an illusion, and that all value judgments like good or bad, right or wrong, are meaningless. He said that Zen has no concept of sin, that the only reality is what is in your mind. If you do something bad and you recognize it as bad, you create bad "karma," which I understood to mean painful memories that burden you. If you do something without any idea of doing wrong, no bad karma is created; you don't have any regrets, in other words.

"So," Ms. Doppelt asked, letting just a bit too much excitement show through in her voice, "according to Zen, you could do anything and get away with it as long as you think it's OK? Even murder is not wrong if it's done with a clear mind?"

The professor rubbed at one of his eyes that was already raw from being irritated. "Right," he answered. "If you look at the samurais, your warrior class in old Japan, they had the ideal of being able to go into battle, or even to kill themselves, without any doubts or fear. Even in recent times, the kamikaze pilots during the Second World War used Zen philosophy to calm their minds before their suicide missions."

Ms. Doppelt nodded and, looking at us, said, "That leads to my last question, Professor. That puzzle about killing the Buddha in the road—are you familiar with it?"

"I've heard of it, yes."

"Can you tell us what it means?"

Mr. Stribling sneezed loudly again. "I'm sorry. . . . The koan about killing the Buddha, yes. Zen people like to insist that you can't explain koans in words, but I think that the general idea is that even if the Buddha himself appeared in front of you, in theory you ought to be able to cut him down without any second thoughts. It would be the extreme test of your calm state of mind. Like regular Buddhism, Zen puts a lot of emphasis on detachment."

It sounded to me like a kind of anesthesia. Why would anyone want to achieve such detachment? If you don't want to have any feelings or attachments to anything, it would seem that the easiest way to attain your goal would be to commit suicide. The impression I got from the professor was that Zen was an excruciatingly slow and difficult sort of psychological suicide. Why keep the body alive?

Yet I wondered, If Philip Weber wanted so badly to

achieve this state of detached bliss, who's to say that he hadn't? Maybe he really did attain his "enlightenment." If, as the professor said, Zen has no moral code, I couldn't see how killing the Zen master went against any of the principles of that religion. Presumably Ms. Doppelt called this witness to show us how vigorously amoral and bizarre the Zen cult was in order to support her claim that Philip Weber had been driven insane that day. It was a two-edged sword, however, because it also raised a question: What if Weber was just an exceptionally good Zen student? What if his psychological problems were, from the Zen church's point of view, actually valuable assets that helped push him toward a glorious enlightenment? Would he have been considered a great master if he had lived in Japan two hundred years ago?

During the cross-examination we learned that Professor Stribling's academic degree came from a seminary rather than a university, and that his degree was in theology rather than comparative religion. What he knew about Asian religions came from independent reading and research, and qualified him only to teach an introductory course called Religions of the World. Only one week of that course, it turned out, was devoted to all of Buddhism, including Zen. Mr. Graham stopped well short of calling the witness a fraud, but he did carry out an exercise that undermined the professor's testimony. Mr. Graham asked the professor a series of questions about Christianity, allowing the professor to give only yes or no answers.

Was it true that in some churches a service is performed where believers are invited to eat the flesh and drink the blood of their God? Yes. Doesn't the Bible tell us that God punished Lot's wife—for merely looking backward—by killing her and turning her into a pillar of salt? Yes. "Didn't Christ once say, Professor, that He had come into the world to set a man against his father, the daughter against her mother, and the daughter-in-law against her mother-in-law?"

The professor sneezed and shook his head angrily. "You're taking those quotations out of context, sir."

Mr. Graham freely admitted that he had, and apologized if he seemed to have insulted Christianity or the witness. "But, Professor, with all due respect, I must say that quite a bit of your testimony suffers from the same defect. For example, you made the point earlier that the kamikaze pilots used Zen to prepare themselves for battle. Your point, I assume, was intended to show us what can happen when people practice Zen. Need I remind you that Christianity was abused in precisely the same way during the Crusades and the Inquisition? What does that tell us about Christianity?"

Mr. Graham pointed out that Professor Stribling was a specialist not in the field of comparative religions but rather in Christian theology. I noticed that Mr. Graham's charisma only grew stronger as the trial wore on; his age, his slightly unkempt appearance, his paunch and gracious Southern manner all gave him a fine burnish, a warmth that made you trust him. Although she was obviously bright and well-spoken, Ms. Doppelt seemed too fresh and rough around the edges. Even when she made a good point, I found myself wondering if she wasn't manipulating us. She let her technique show; I could hear in her voice when she was setting a trap, which distracted me from the testimony itself.

During one of the breaks that day I followed Maria-Teresa out to the common room, where she was allowed to smoke. My strategy of reading during the breaks had gradually ceased to discourage Gary. He would sit down next to me, look over my shoulder at the pages and ask, "So how's the book going?" I complained to Maria-Teresa that I couldn't understand why he had latched onto me, considering that I'd never encouraged him, and had tried to seem lukewarm whenever he talked to me. Maria-Teresa said it was because I was the only person in there polite enough to pay any attention to him at all.

"Listen, I have to be around guys like that all day at work, so I learned not to bother being nice anymore. You always think they've gotta know, right? They've gotta know that they're boring, that they ought to work out a little, that they ought to brush their teeth more often. Let me tell you, and I know what I'm talking about, they don't have a clue, but that doesn't stop 'em from glomming all over you. Hell, no! Try being a woman sometime; it's a hundred times worse."

She puffed away, trying to get as much out of the cigarette as she could, then asked me where I had gone to high school. There it was, another question from her distant planet. I never saw the inside of a high school; I'd been tutored privately from the third grade on. Maria-Teresa was amazed by this and kept saying that it must have been an incredible way to grow up, that I must have felt like the Prince of the World when I was a kid.

Every child, it seems to me, thinks it would be more fun to be somebody else. I used to think it would be fun—the way most kids think it would be fun to live forever in a hotel—to go to a school and have lots of friends my own age whom I would know for years and years. My tutor in Germany, Andrew Halpern, was the closest thing I had to a playmate for several years, and he was a restless American in his twenties making some money while he pursued his main interests, which were dating European women, discussing the merits of existentialism with his expatriate friends in the café below his apartment in Kassel, and trying to spend as little time with me as possible.

The closest I felt to Andrew came the afternoon he introduced me to the philosophy of Ecclesiastes. "Listen to this, Reinhart," he said, quoting from memory. " 'In much wisdom is much grief, and he that increaseth knowledge increaseth sorrow.' Unfortunately, thanks to Plato, that advice was ignored for two thousand years."

"What did Plato do?" I asked, sensing that my tutor was about to entrust me with highly classified information.

"He was the one who said, 'Virtue is knowledge,' Renne. Ever since then most people have thought that knowledge was the answer to everything, even today. But all that was proven wrong. Now we know that there's no such thing as 'truth,' and that knowledge can't help us. Most people don't dare face that."

"You mean we know that all knowledge is wrong?" I asked, shaken.

"Well, just look at the world today, Renne. We can split atoms, but we can't stop people from making atom bombs. The human experiment simply hasn't worked out. Our big brains are kind of like the huge antlers on those prehistoric moose; they went extinct because they couldn't hold their heads up anymore from all that weight. We'd be a lot better off if we were a lot stupider—or a lot smarter."

"So what's the point of anything, then?" I asked.

A knowing grin came over Andrew's face and, looking around to make sure my mother could not overhear us, he whispered, "You'll find that out as soon as you get a girlfriend!"

I was not able to pursue this line of thinking with Andrew, however. Not long after that conversation he met an Italian girl, decided he had lived in Germany long enough, and announced his plans to move south and teach at an American school in Naples, where she lived. In view of my increasing success and my heavy concert schedule, my mother decided I did not need further tutoring, so Andrew was never replaced.

Maria-Teresa wanted to know about all the traveling. I told her about the time the small airplane carrying my mother and me from Rome to Paris for a concert couldn't get its landing gear down and had to land on its belly in a river.

"You must have been terrified!"

"Not really. For a kid, that's exciting. I was more worried about my cello than anything else. It got out fine; the captain himself grabbed it from the seat next to me and made sure it got off the plane."

"The captain bothered to save your cello?"

"Sure. He was Italian, and he'd talked to me on the flight. He knew that my cello was a Guarneri. No Italian would let a Guarneri get wet."

Maria-Teresa confessed that she'd never been out of the country. In fact, she admitted, looking a little abashed, the only time she'd been East was when she and her second husband went to visit Graceland on the tenth anniversary of Elvis Presley's death.

23

The last witness for the defense was a cute but nervous girl, nineteen years old, whom Philip had dated a few times just before moving into the Zen Foundation. She wore a pink dress that made her look even younger than she was, and she kept her hands folded on her lap the whole time she was on the stand. She and the defendant had met at a photocopy shop where he worked and had a brief romance, but when Philip moved into the Zen church he told her he couldn't see her anymore because he was becoming a monk.

"He was really into Zen, and I thought it sounded . . . weird sometimes but pretty interesting, I guess," she said in a minuscule voice. Judge Davis scowled and told her to speak up. Her eyes kept darting over to look at her former boyfriend; she seemed more fascinated than upset by the fact that he was on trial for murder. He smiled at her blandly; she didn't seem to interest him at all.

Ms. Doppelt asked the girl if Philip had ever said or done anything to suggest he was a violent person. "No," the witness said, her eyes opening wide, "he was the opposite. He didn't seem like he could hurt anybody."

"Can you think of any examples—incidents that might give us some idea of what Philip was like when you knew him?"

"Yeah . . . um . . . he bought me a goldfish for my birthday. Most people would give you jewelry or, you know, something like that, but he gave me something that was alive. . . . He was really into animals. He even saved spiders if they were on the sidewalk. He would pick them up in his hands and move them to a bush or something. Also, he would do funny things just to make me laugh."

"Such as?"

"Oh, he would tell me these Zen stories about guys who would do things like put their shoes on their heads, or say funny things because they were enlightened, and he would do stuff like that too. Once when he came to pick me up he was wearing his shirt on backwards, with the buttons on the back . . . it was just to make me laugh, you know? But it was also part of his philosophy, I think."

"When you heard about what happened at the Zen church, Miss Conway, what went through your mind? What did you think?"

The nervous girl sneaked another wide-eyed glance at Philip, who was sitting with his eyes closed as if he were meditating, then said, "I thought—Wow, he must really have gone crazy. He wouldn't do something like that, not the guy I knew."

When Mr. Graham asked Miss Conway if she ever saw Philip use drugs, she turned bright red and seemed to freeze. Mr. Graham gently assured her that the court wasn't interested in whether she had used drugs with him or not but only in whether *he* had ever used them. She glanced at Ms. Doppelt, who nodded as if to say it was all right for her to tell the truth.

"Yes, he sometimes did," she answered finally.

Mr. Graham pressed her to be more specific, and it gradually came out that Philip had used drugs fairly heavily. In fact, it sounded as if the two of them must have been intoxicated most of the time they were together, usually on marijuana, but occasionally with more serious drugs, such as LSD, mescaline and something called Ecstasy, which sounded like a kind of aphrodisiac. From looking and listening to her I would not have been able to identify her as a heavy user; she didn't seem to have been impaired by drugs. I wondered if they had affected Philip's mind, though, especially considering that he was unstable to begin with.

Mr. Graham looked confident when he called the state's first witness, Dr. Lawrence Carrillo, to the stand. We learned that Dr. Carrillo was a clinical psychiatrist who had worked in a state mental hospital for eighteen years. He looked to be in his late fifties, with a heavy mustache flecked with gray and hard, dark eyes. He looked muscular and strictly no-nonsense, the sort of man you would want to have around if a psychotic patient needed to be restrained.

"Dr. Carrillo, in your eighteen years at the state facility, did you treat patients there who were criminally insane? Whose mental illnesses led them to violent, criminal behavior?"

"Quite a few, yes."

"Were any of them schizophrenic?"

The doctor nodded almost sleepily. "Generally speaking,

schizophrenics tend to be too withdrawn to become violent, but occasionally, yes, we would see a schizophrenic who had turned violent during a bad spell."

Dr. Carrillo had been allowed to examine the defendant only once, but was given access to all the results of the tests administered by the defense's psychiatrist, along with all of the material evidence of the case. Mr. Graham created a slight pause in the testimony by going over to his desk and picking up a thick sheaf of papers. It was a short delay, but the break in rhythm got everyone's attention. It reminded me of how, just before playing a cadenza, I would freeze for a beat—the entire orchestra would have just gone silent and people in the audience would be on the edge of their seats, anticipating my climactic flight—and hold for maybe a half a second, creating an almost unbearable tension, then release the first note; I could almost hear them gasp, like someone taking a breath after staying underwater too long.

After his pause, Mr. Graham held up the sheaf of papers and said, "This is a copy of the report filed by the psychiatrist for the defense—Dr. Libertson, I think it was—who came to the conclusion that Philip Weber suffers from chronic undifferentiated schizophrenia. In your opinion, Doctor, is this diagnosis correct?"

The laconic witness nodded slowly and rubbed the corner of his eye with his ring finger. "Yep. He's schizophrenic, all right."

A commotion broke out in the courtroom gallery. The prosecutor's expert witness seemed to be corroborating the defense psychiatrist's testimony. By that time the courtroom was filled with spectators every day. In addition to the relatives of the deceased Zen master, at least a dozen journalists were present, and a growing number of curious onlookers, some of them shaven-headed, were starting to attend as well. There were even a few young women—they always sat in the first few rows—who seemed to have developed an almost romantic fascination for the defendant. The noise in the gallery forced Judge Davis to use his gavel in anger for the first time.

As the whispers died down I looked at the two lawyers to see if I could detect any reaction, but they both remained impassive. The judge threatened to eject the spectators if the talking didn't stop at once. It did, but a nearly audible tension remained in the courtroom. All eyes and ears were on the tired-looking psychiatrist, who had provided us with the most dramatic moment of the trial so far.

"He's schizophrenic, all right," the doctor repeated, looking right at the defendant, "but he isn't insane."

"Could you explain the distinction for us, Doctor?" Mr. Graham asked.

"Yes. Schizophrenia doesn't automatically make you insane, any more than having cancer makes you dead. Millions of people suffer from schizophrenia, but the disease affects people in different ways, and to different degrees."

Dr. Carrillo explained that mental illness hardly ever comes in "neat little packages." He said that it is far more common for patients to suffer from a combination of disorders, which is why treating them can be so complicated. He told us that in addition to schizophrenia, Philip showed symptoms of several personality disorders frequently seen in violent, antisocial criminals.

"But what you want to know, I assume, is whether or not Weber knew what he was doing that day, whether he was aware that he was killing a man, whether he could have done otherwise. And the answer is yes, he did know what he was doing. He suffers from borderline illness, which means that he approached psychosis, but he didn't cross that boundary. Weber's sick, all right, but he isn't crazy."

I noticed that this doctor always referred to the defendant by last name only, whereas the first psychiatrist had always used "Philip."

Mr. Graham asked the doctor how he could be certain that the defendant was not psychotic at the time. What in the evidence led him to that conclusion?

The witness grinned, as if to signal in advance that it would be a difficult question to answer. "You look at the whole picture," he said. "You don't just look at his answers on the tests. Let's talk about sanity for a minute. Most of us feel—our gut reaction, OK?—that anybody who commits a horrible crime must be out of his mind. If you commit a senseless murder, set a tenement on fire or try to kill the president, you must be crazy. But we still hold those people responsible for what they do, don't we?"

Dr. Carrillo shrugged in answer to his own question, then said, "Let's be honest here—it's an arbitrary judgment we make. No one really knows if the guy who chops his wife up and cooks her could have done otherwise. Given his genetic structure, his childhood experiences, his adult circumstances, we really don't know if he could have done better with his life. It's impossible to really *know,* but we have to draw the line somewhere, so we say: If someone is able to make rational choices most of the time, if they're able to exert self-control most of the time, then they should be held responsible for their actions. It may sound fancy, but it's really just common sense.

"It's the same for people with mental illnesses. As I said before, most of them do know the difference between right and wrong, and the exceptions are usually easy to spot. Classic examples would be the man who suddenly believes that everyone with a briefcase is a spy from another planet trying to kill him and who as a result murders his insurance agent thinking it's in self-defense. Or the man who strangles his wife thinking he's squeezing an orange. When you get borderline cases, though, you have to slow down a little. You want to be asking, Is the guy really psychotic, or is he only indulging his selfish fantasies? In those situations you have to look beyond just the fancy tests. You dig around and ask, What does he say about himself and about the crime, and how do those statements compare with the actual evidence from the crime? You look at the interviews, the case history—everything—and you get something like a collage. Then, when you step back and look at it all, you'd be surprised how often it forms a clear picture.

"In this case, the picture that emerges is of a lonely, insecure, selfish young man who wanted attention. He showed symptoms of mental illness before the crime—including schizophrenia—but on the whole, he had a good deal of self-control and self-awareness. It took a lot of self-control to wield that stick, let me tell you. It isn't easy to kill a man with a stick, even one that big. You have to hit the right places.

"Also, he's a fairly bright guy, and thinks pretty clearly. He stumbled on a gold mine when he discovered that Zen church because their philosophy, from what I've heard, seems to encourage 'doing your own thing.' He's not the only one to hop on that bandwagon, by the way; anybody remember the Beat poets? They were burping and scratching themselves at poetry readings and saying it was Zen for a while, but it went out of fashion pretty fast."

Several people in the courtroom chuckled at the poetry-reading image, particularly Gary, who snorted like a horse. Maria-Teresa nudged me with her elbow, motioning toward Gary with her eyes and rolling them scornfully.

"Weber's ideas, as unappealing as they are, are just too consistent and well organized to be coming out of a psychotic mind, I would say. Real psychotics may think they're geniuses, but they almost always make poor sense. The transcripts of Mr. Weber's interviews with the police, the other psychiatrist and me, on the other hand . . . Hell, if you published 'em, I'll bet you'd get a lot of people wanting to be this guy's disciple. He's got a dangerously clever mind."

24

It was disturbing testimony. I didn't have much time to consider how it affected my opinion of the case, however, because just before Judge Davis announced the lunch break, Maria-Teresa leaned over and asked, "I found a better place to eat—are you free today?"

Of course I was delighted that she wanted to have lunch with me for the third time, but I also worried that some of the others, particularly Mrs. Friedman, were starting to show interest in the fact that we were spending so much time together. As we filed out of the courtroom and dropped behind the others I asked if she'd noticed the whispers and sidelong glances.

"Oh, yeah. I don't care what they think—do you?"

It was the answer I wanted to hear, but shouldn't have wanted to hear. I knew by then that she was interested in me; better judgment was telling me that I should not be giving her such encouraging signals. Poorer judgment, however, insisted loudly that nothing bad could come of it, that it was exciting but safe. As soon as the trial ended I wouldn't ever see her again, and nothing serious could happen in such a short amount of time.

• • •

The restaurant was a little Indian place in an old hotel building. A tiny speaker nailed to the wall provided us with taped Indian music, which I found distracting. Hypnotic music makes my attention drift in and out, so that I feel as if I were hearing a mosquito making passes by my ear. I had the waiter move us to a table farther away from the speaker, but that only made it more annoying because then it really did sound like the buzz of insects.

Since I don't know Indian food, I let Maria-Teresa order. I'd tried it once in England when I was about fourteen and hated it, but I didn't like anything new then. I wanted my American hamburger for lunch every day, no matter what country I was in. Maria-Teresa ordered me a drink made of yogurt and mango juice; I tried to be open-minded about it, but yogurt makes me think of health food and all the desperately unhealthy-looking people who shop for it, so I let her have the drink and asked the waiter to bring me a martini.

Maria-Teresa laughed at the martini glass; apparently she found it amusing that someone my age would drink out of such a glass with a straight face. "Can I have your olive, though?"

"Not if you're going to make fun of my drink."

"I'm not making fun of your drink. I'm making fun of you."

I let her have it. She wiped the gin off it with her napkin and popped it into her mouth. "Yum. Ask me something now."

"What about?"

She unleashed that gorgeous smile—she had a slightly chipped tooth, and I was attracted even to that—and said, "Anything. Just ask me something—I want to talk."

I thought for a moment, then asked her what hobbies she had besides listening to proletarian music.

"Oh, all right. Are you gonna be disappointed if I say I don't have any good ones?" she asked.

"Why would I be disappointed?"

"Well, you lead this artistic life, and you're probably always around people who are interesting and creative. My life is just get up, go to work, stress out, come home, fix dinner, listen to the stereo, watch TV, then go to bed. On weekends I try to go out with my friends, but since they're all busy with their kids, it's hard to get together. My life is boring, in other words."

"What *would* you like to do, then?"

"If I could do anything? Oh, God . . . Let's see. I bet it's a pretty good life being rich and having a second house in South America, somewhere along the coast. Colombia has incredible beaches—my mother always talks about that—and I speak the language, so I could have a great time down there. Could you tell Spanish was my first language?"

I hadn't noticed any accent at all, but as soon as she mentioned it I started to hear one, and it made her even more attractive. I tried to visualize her in a hammock on the balcony of a South American villa, and, best of all, speaking Spanish on a cordless telephone. It was a delicious image.

"Or maybe a singer. I think it must be wild to be on a stage and have people watching, and getting into the song. I don't know—I'm sure there are downsides, but I think that must be a hell of a lot of fun. Plus, if you're in classical music you get all that respect, and you don't have to worry about getting too old for it like rock musicians do—you can be eighty and still play classical, right?"

Yes, I thought, but only if you can still play well. She asked me what it was like to play on a stage, and I told her that the whole day before a concert I couldn't eat or sit still. It wasn't from being nervous; it was impatience. I wanted to play, I didn't want to wait. I knew I was going to play well, so why wait? All day I'd be running through the music in my head. I'd wake up early that morning and jump out of bed—nothing could keep me lying there. I'd take long showers, I'd walk around inside the hotel, and then wander around the neighborhood with my mother. She and I would have lunch someplace nice, but I would have no appetite.

"So your mother went to all your concerts?" Maria-Teresa asked blandly. I could tell she was trying to hide something in her voice. I had to explain to her that the concerts I was describing all happened before my eighteenth birthday. Her face registered surprise, then relief.

She wanted to know if I was able to enjoy the concerts as I was playing, or if I had too much to think about to take it all in. I said that I wasn't able to think verbal thoughts like This sure is fun or Look at all those people in tuxedos listening to me, but I was able to enjoy a glorious sensation of power. I told her about seeing a documentary where a scuba diver was underwater filming whales when one swam right past him, and all of a sudden he reached out and grabbed one of its fins and hitched a ride. It was a spontaneous decision, the diver explained as he narrated over the footage, and it was the most incredible experience of his life. He said the feeling of being pulled along by such an immensely powerful creature was simply indescribable. I told Maria-Teresa that it couldn't have been that different from playing onstage.

Just talking about it to her gave me goose bumps; I rolled

up one of my sleeves to show her, and she was impressed. I can see now that the main reason I believed so strongly for so long that I would play onstage again was that I *had* to believe it. I was so unhappy as a nearly middle-aged virgin, a has-been concert musician giving cello lessons, that I simply had to believe great things would happen to me again someday. Otherwise how could I face myself? What else could I think?

Showing her my goose bumps seemed to embolden her. She leaned forward on her elbows, her chin resting on one hand, and asked, "You said you were never even close to being married. Is that true? You never had a serious girlfriend?"

Before that instant I would have thought that the closer one approached a morally corrupt situation, the more inner conflict one would feel. But it wasn't like that at all; the further things went with Maria-Teresa, the easier it felt to go the next step. When she asked me that question I felt intense pleasure, as if I'd been hoping that she would ask about my barren romantic life. Although I still couldn't imagine a relationship with her, other possibilities—fantasies I could briefly imagine—were starting to appear in my thoughts. I told her the truth, which was that until I was performing again, I couldn't see how anyone would want to date me, and I didn't want to put anyone through the embarrassment of turning me down. I wasn't trying to manipulate her feelings, but whether I intended it or not, she seemed to decide that I had just crossed an invisible boundary and had invited her to do the same.

"Life is short," she said, looking right at me with those sad, beautiful eyes. "Why waste it thinking about crap like whether you're famous enough or not when there's so much right in front of you? You're an extremely datable guy, if you ask me."

At that moment we were suspended. The situation could have gone either way. It hung there and swayed; it might have fallen over, but it tipped back toward the safe side. I don't even remember who talked first, but we fell into nervous chatter about how no one ever feels he or she deserves to be happy, how unfair life is and so on.

It didn't last long, however. The situation was still ripe; we were so close that the slightest push would have done it. On the way out of the hotel we saw a young couple sitting close together drive by in a convertible, and that was it. Suddenly Maria-Teresa stopped walking. I stopped also and looked at her achingly beautiful face, and my resistance utterly disappeared, like a puff of smoke. It was overwhelming; there was no room at all in me to think why I should not touch her.

I remember once seeing one of my colleagues in the faculty center having a Bloody Mary when suddenly, noiselessly, the bottom of his glass simply dropped out. One moment he was dry and happy; the next he looked as if he'd been gored by a bull. You couldn't have said precisely when it happened, and it took all of us, including him, several long seconds to figure out where all the red liquid had come from.

As on that occasion, it took me a few seconds to realize what exactly was going on. When I did, I found myself far along in the first passionate kiss of my life. It lasted for a long time. When it ended, I asked her if she would have dinner with me, and she agreed.

I wondered if the whole courtroom knew that something had happened. What with the excitement, the two drinks and that kiss, I'm sure I was blushing. Maria-Teresa looked sublimely content. Her face had the same color as usual, that of coffee and milk the way they serve it in Europe, but there was a patch at the base of her throat that was flushed deep red. We must have been quite a sight, floating there light as feathers among all those bored, morose jurors.

I don't remember much about Ms. Doppelt's cross-examination of the psychiatrist because I wasn't really paying attention. I know that she attacked the doctor's view that only a sane person could accomplish the complex psychological feat of using Zen to justify crazy behavior. "This is a religion that vigorously encourages people to act impulsively!" she said, exasperation showing in her voice. "Someone like my client, who you readily agree suffers from a grave mental disorder, who you said yourself stands poised on that fine line between sickness and craziness, could easily be pushed across that line under extreme conditions. And what do you call what they were doing at that religious retreat, where they were barely eating or sleeping and were obsessing on those puzzles?"

The doctor didn't seem shaken by this attack on his testimony. He continued to stroke his beard and insisted that regardless of what one thought about Buddhism, Philip Weber seemed to know what he was doing when he killed the Zen master. "The proof, for me," he said, "is Weber's claim that according to his enlightened view everything is an illusion. He says he felt no hesitation doing what he did, and now feels no remorse over killing the man because in his expanded view he wasn't killing a real man; it was all just part of this great illusion we call life. That's the giveaway for me. Psychotics don't play-act—it's all for real to them. Weber says he knew all along that none of what he was doing was real, that he did it as an inspired, religious gesture. I don't believe it."

During the afternoon break Maria-Teresa and I didn't say anything to each other; we had our date for dinner, and the rest was just waiting. She went out for her cigarette and I, for form's sake, sat with the other men and pretended to listen to Roy, the retired factory manager. He was complaining to the others about all the dirty tricks the Japanese were playing to upset the trade balance. Whenever his eyes met mine he gave me a slightly combative look, as if expecting me to challenge him. He'd been wary of me since the trial began—my age, my last name and the fact that I taught at a university no doubt put him on guard—and once, out in the shuttle lot, he'd pointed at my car and asked me if I planned to buy American next time. Yet I wasn't really following Roy's speech during the break; my mind was all over the place. I was trying to commit myself beforehand to a decision about that night so I wouldn't spend the whole evening wavering back and forth, only to freeze with indecision at the critical moment. I didn't have a specific moral problem with having an affair; if Maria-Teresa was unhappy in her marriage and was willing to stray from it, I wasn't going to try to convince her otherwise. I'd never been religious and I'd never been married, so neither of those institutions held much sway over me. The risks, if there were any, were hers to take.

My problem was that I knew I could never really see her as a companion. I felt like a prude for thinking in such grand terms, but I couldn't help it. If I had felt that there was even a remote chance of our having a long-term relationship, it would have satisfied my conscience—but there was no chance at all. I was not going to become seriously involved with a twice-married woman with a daughter in military school who liked music I couldn't stand. Although I enjoyed her company and enjoyed talking with her, most of that enjoyment came out of my intense physical attraction to her. I knew that once the novelty of her beauty wore off and we got to know each other better, we would have less and less to say to each other.

On the other hand, Maria-Teresa was bored with her life and had a right to enjoy herself; if sleeping with me would please her, and me, why should I prevent it from happening? I'd denied myself so many opportunities over the years by thinking fifty steps ahead, but had never bothered to really wonder if any of those women truly cared if I ever concertized again or would have insisted that I offer them marriage after a few dates.

My mother used to tell me what schmucks men were because they would take a girl out but then never call her again. She would tell me how girls would sit by the phones waiting for the phone call that never came while their hearts slowly broke. It was awful to contemplate. Unfortunately, this might have something to do with why I was so inexperienced with women; I rarely dared ask anyone out because I felt so strongly obliged to take them out a second, third and fourth time. But the few times I did so, out of politeness rather than sincere interest, it was much worse when I stopped calling because by then the woman had assumed I was serious about her. It almost seemed that it had to be marriage or nothing; otherwise you caused someone to suffer in the worst way by making her think she wasn't good enough to inspire love. You can't make it up to someone once you've done that.

The other, less abstract problem for me had always been

that I felt unable to make my carnal intentions clear. I could talk fairly easily with a woman, could even come to know her quite well, but at the point where I had to tell her I was attracted to her, or touch her in more than just a friendly way, I turned to ice. I always felt acutely self-conscious then; it seemed to me that I might as well just unzip my pants, point downward and say, "Would you mind if we included this in our plans?"

I felt I could only make that transition if it happened gradually, if I knew it was a mutual decision. I didn't want to shock or disgust anyone, and I certainly didn't want to be let down under such circumstances. I'd much rather be turned down in a restaurant or on a doorstep than while sitting on a sofa with my hand up someone's shirt. The right opportunity never came to cross that boundary. There was friendship, the exchange of ideas, art appreciation and the enjoyment of good food and wine . . . and then, it seemed, there were genitals. I never got to that part, even with Naomi. In other words, I was a coward.

Meeting Maria-Teresa threw me into turmoil. She didn't appear to have any indecision about crossing boundaries. She'd been married twice and had a kid; I knew I could count on her not to burst into tears after having sex, or to seem shocked if I tried to unbutton her shirt. But what if I made a fool of myself because of my inexperience? I was a virgin, after all, and not just in the purely sexual sense; if it showed, wouldn't it seem ludicrous to someone like her, who'd had so much life experience? The thought of being ridiculed or held in contempt by her terrified me. Even if I could make love to her successfully, what if she became attached to me? What would I say to her? Would she accuse me of continuing the relationship just so I could see what it felt like to have intercourse with her? Which of course was the truth.

But what if she only wanted to see what it felt like to have intercourse with me? Why did I have to assume she was burdened with the same cloying myths about sexuality that I carried around with me, the myths that weld sex to the notion of virtue? Maybe she simply liked sex, and didn't think it necessarily had to lead to anything else. If so, I'd be a jackass to call the whole thing off—I would be denying both of us the chance to enjoy ourselves, and it would be purely out of fear.

Needless to say, my attempts to carve out a decision only unearthed deeper layers of conflict. At last I resigned myself to having dinner with her without a plan and to see what happened.

25

The last witness, Mr. Tokku Hayashi, was a Japanese American man who looked to be in his early sixties. He had silver-gray hair combed neatly back, wore a modest gray suit and shoes polished to military standards. He was a commercial architect, but had also completed four terms as director of the Los Angeles Japanese Buddhist Association, and had published a book and several articles about Zen in English.

Mr. Graham began by asking if he had known Kazuo Okakura, the murdered founder of the Los Angeles Zen Foundation.

"Yes. I first met him ten years ago, just after he came to this country."

"In your opinion, was he qualified to teach Zen Buddhism?"

The witness nodded and answered in a clear, pleasant voice, "Yes. Mr. Okakura was qualified."

"Mr. Hayashi, the defense is arguing that Mr. Okakura, by assigning the puzzle about killing the Buddha, provoked Philip Weber to violence—that supposedly, Zen approves of and even encourages impulsive, irrational behavior, so Philip

Weber shouldn't be held responsible if Zen drove him to commit murder. Would you care to comment on that argument?"

The old gentleman cleared his throat politely and agreed to do his best, but said that it was never easy to determine where religious experience ends and delusion begins. His unaffected manner reminded me of von Kempen, who could, without any trace of contrivance, lend dignity to even the most ordinary situations. Just the way he entered a room put other people on their best behavior.

Mr. Hayashi began by explaining that Zen was not a religion, in the sense of worshiping a god or supreme being, but was more a kind of therapy for people who worried too much. He said that for the purposes of simplicity all those worries could be represented by one question, which he phrased as Why don't I feel free?

He paused to take a drink of water from the glass on the witness stand. He was the first witness to take advantage of this convenience; the others had looked at the glass or moved it around in front of them, but had all seemed too nervous to drink from it.

"Let's say," Mr. Hayashi continued, "that a fish is happily swimming along in the ocean and doesn't have any worries beyond finding things to eat. One day somebody tells the fish, 'You know what? The ocean is only so big, and you are trapped in it. You can't live outside the ocean, so you will never be free.' Suddenly the fish feels constrained, and resents his fate. He's trapped forever, after all.

"Now let's talk about human beings. Most people resent the fact that they cannot always do what they like. Some days even the most privileged of us feel we have no freedom at all. Zen is like medicine for that kind of thinking. Zen tells you,

Yes, you are limited by society and by your body and mind, but so what? Within those limitations you can find endless variety and opportunities."

Then the witness quoted Gandhi, who apparently once said, "Satisfaction lies in the effort, not in the attainment." Mr. Hayashi told us that Zen meditation was an exercise for people who wanted to learn how to make a greater effort in their ordinary moments, as opposed to only their extreme moments. He said that the entire purpose of Zen was to get you in the habit of paying attention and feeling more involved in your ordinary life, with all its limitations and shortcomings.

"But, Mr. Hayashi," the prosecutor asked, "what about the puzzle? To most of us, I'm afraid, it's difficult to imagine how that puzzle would make someone more involved in ordinary life."

The witness paused to adjust his sitting position, as if giving testimony were a physical activity that required good posture and sound placement on the chair. "First of all, are we all familiar with the story in the Bible where Jesus said that if your eye offends you, you should pluck it out? Do Christians take that literally and tear their eyes out if they see something ugly? Not that I know of. I think the phrase means that if you feel an impulse or desire that you know is wrong, you should make an effort to put that evil desire out of your mind.

"The koan about killing the Buddha is not too different from that. If you are always daydreaming about how nice it would be to be an enlightened Buddha, and how everyone would look up to you then, that is exactly the kind of silly thinking that prevents you from appreciating yourself fully just as you are. You'd be like that poor fish wondering what it would be like to swim in a bigger ocean, and in the process missing out on what is right in front of him. If you think, I'm just an ordinary man, I'm nothing like a Buddha, I'll never experience what a Buddha experiences, the koan tells you to banish those thoughts right away. Kill this imaginary Buddha, this fantasy of enlightenment! Turn your attention right back to reality, to the present moment, to constructive action. Who are you right now? What are you doing? Think about that. This is the meaning of 'If you meet the Buddha in the road, kill him.' "

When it was her turn to cross-examine, Ms. Doppelt approached the stand slowly. She seemed unmistakably wary of the gentle witness.

"Mr. Hayashi, don't you think it's possible that a person with a severe mental illness could take the advice of Zen—to accept yourself as you are—and interpret this to mean that he should pay more attention to, say, those strange voices in his head?"

"I suppose it could, yes. In fact, I can even think of an example of that happening."

"Can you?" The defense attorney looked hopeful for the first time since Mr. Hayashi had taken the stand. Meanwhile, the prosecutor looked unhappy. He leaned forward, rested his chin on his palm and tapped his pencil on his desk rapidly. He appeared to be trying to make eye contact with the witness, but Mr. Hayashi, true to his principles, was giving the defense attorney his full, undivided attention.

"Yes, it happened when I was still a young monk living in Japan. A student who had some kind of nervous breakdown decided to burn down a Zen temple with himself in it. He did burn the temple, but changed his mind about suicide at the last minute and survived. He said at his trial that he was inspired by a koan about a monk who burned a wooden statue of the Buddha to keep warm on a cold night."

Ms. Doppelt looked enthusiastic now. "Let me ask you, then, Mr. Hayashi, if you willingly admit that a young man in Japan, because of his mental illness, was inspired by a Zen story to commit a crime, why do you feel that Mr. Weber could not have done the same? Why do you believe he must have been sane?"

"Did I ever say that?" the old man asked, looking genuinely puzzled. Mr. Graham winced.

"Well," Ms. Doppelt said, "I can only assume that the prosecutor put you on the stand to support his position that Mr. Weber was sane when he committed the crime. Am I mistaken about that?"

If Mr. Hayashi felt at all uncomfortable, it didn't show. "I'm not sure, Ms. Doppelt," he said graciously. "It was my understanding that I was to answer questions about Zen Buddhism. I don't believe I'm qualified to judge Mr. Weber's state of mind."

"I see. So you acknowledge, then, that Mr. Weber could have been pushed into a psychotic episode by the activities of the Zen retreat?"

"Yes, of course. Personally I hope that is the case. Then there might be some hope that if his illness can be treated, Mr. Weber could live to benefit society one day rather than to burden it."

"I couldn't agree more, Mr. Hayashi. Thank you very much."

26

Maria-Teresa got to the restaurant before I did. It was in Pasadena, where she wouldn't have to worry about bumping into anyone she knew. She'd ordered a martini for me already, and the waiter brought it when I sat down.

"I don't think I've ever been in such a beautiful restaurant," she said happily. She'd nearly finished a beer, and her cheeks were starting to glow a faint pink. "I have to ask you something," she went on.

"What?"

"What did you think of the Japanese guy this afternoon?"

I told her that I had enjoyed his testimony, but once it was over it left me feeling slightly depressed.

"Depressed? How come?"

"Oh, because he reminded me of my cello teacher, and I always get a little sad when I think about him. It makes me wish I could have known him when I was a little older. It's stupid to think like that, I know, but . . ."

"I guess so," she said, shaking her head. "I don't know . . . It sure related to me, what he said about people who think their lives are boring, and think that there's nothing they can do about it? God, that describes me perfectly. That's what my life has been since high school—boring, more boring, and then on weekends a little less boring. Go to work, come home, cook food, clean house. I'm like that fish he was talking about, only I'm not stuck in the ocean, I'm stuck in somebody's toilet. . . . Sometimes I wonder, Is this all there is? Why can't I have a more interesting life? Maybe I oughta become a Buddhist, huh? Would I look good bald?"

She finished her beer and I ordered a bottle of wine for the two of us. I didn't want to get drunk, but I did want to become less sober.

"You know what?" she asked, practically cooking me with her gaze. My whole body felt warm when she had her eyes on me. "It almost seems like fate that all this happened today, you know? I was starting to worry the last few days, thinking that maybe I shouldn't be having this friendship with you. I was thinking, Is this wrong? Should I feel guilty? Even this afternoon, after we said we'd have this dinner, I was thinking OK, we'll have dinner, but we should leave it at that. But listening to that guy talk this afternoon made me think, Why shouldn't I? You're probably the most interesting person I ever met—certainly the nicest man. I was thinking that even if I can only know you for as long as the trial goes on, I should make the most of it, right? Why not?"

I was ecstatic. "Maria-Teresa, what you just said makes me feel so relieved. . . ."

"Why?"

"Because I'm terribly attracted to you, but I've been . . . I've been . . ."

Suddenly I started to laugh. What was I saying to her? I decided to stop before I ruined the whole evening. I'd already been through all this in my mind at least a hundred times, and I'd decided to play everything by ear and not try to work out any plans. "Forget what I just said!" I blurted out. "I'm having a wonderful time, and that's all I'm going to think about. Here's to Mr. Hayashi and his enlightened fish." We toasted the old man, then ordered dinner.

I had mussels in broth to start with, then soft-shell crabs. Maria-Teresa tried the carpaccio—it was the first time she'd had it—and then salmon baked in paper. Every mouthful of that dinner, every sip of wine seemed like the best I'd ever tasted. We hardly talked; our waiter must have thought we looked ridiculous. When he asked if we would like dessert or coffee, Maria-Teresa said, no, she had good coffee and some dessert at home. That settled it. I asked if it would really be all right for me to go there and she told me not to worry; besides, her place was much closer. I followed her in my car.

As soon as we got through the door to her messy house, she turned to face me. She stood completely still and closed her eyes. A thought bubbled up out of all the chaos. It was such a simple, fragile thought that I could almost see it as words flashed on a screen: "Don't ask." It summed up everything—this situation, this overwhelming sensation, this loss of control. I was aware of everything; I was making it happen, but as far as I could tell without ever having decided it was a good idea.

That thought dissolved; I kissed her, and we both melted. There was no thought of anything, no talking, no resistance.

I unbuttoned her blouse right there in the living room. Watching it slide over her shoulders gave me such a jolt that I actually shook. When I put my hands on her breasts and felt their weight and heard her sigh, I thought I might cry for sheer joy. So this is what it's like, I thought. This is what everybody's been talking about, this is why so much happens, so much that you hear about and read about. This is what having a body is really like; this is how every living thing feels when it finally gets to mate.

I felt as if I were making love to her just by looking at her. Every curve was a gift, every strand of hair, every fold, sent chills through me and made me wonder how I could ever have gone so long without knowing.

Once we reached the bedroom, though, it was less easy. I noticed a photograph in a plastic frame on the bureau near her bed. It must have been Maria-Teresa's mother. She had a puffy, bloated figure stuffed into a gaudy blouse and polyester shorts; she was wearing sandals and holding a can of beer. She had the same dark circles under her eyes that Maria-Teresa did, except that on the mother they made her look dull and exhausted. The picture had been taken at a picnic; in the background I could see a throng of people sitting around a fold-out table. My imagination provided the sounds of competing portable radios and crying children.

All of a sudden my nakedness embarrassed me, and when I looked at Maria-Teresa I realized she excited me less than when she'd had her clothes on. Instead of being overwhelmed by the sight of her beautiful nude body—and she was beautiful—I found myself noticing little flaws in her skin, bulges that marred her perfection. I began to look at her body too closely, the way I listened to my own playing. I rapidly became self-conscious, and then I wondered if I was going to be able to go through with it.

As soon as that thought appeared in my mind, I was finished. I tried with all my strength to concentrate, I pleaded with myself, I cursed myself, I tried everything I could to make myself excited again, but it was useless.

Maria-Teresa was kind about it; she said it was no big deal and I shouldn't worry about it, but I was devastated. She asked if it had ever happened to me before, and I said no. Something in my voice must have tipped her off, because suddenly she pulled back and asked, "Have you ever been with a woman before?"

I confessed that I hadn't.

She made the coffee she'd promised and we drank it in bed. She lay with her head resting on my chest and at times, as when I felt one of her eyelashes brush against my nipple, or when a knot of her chestnut-brown hair slid down across my neck and tumbled onto the pillow, I was able to forget for a moment how dismayed and ashamed I felt. Those moments faded quickly, however, and were immediately replaced by a growing sense of strangeness and deep anxiety. Everything started to look wrong; the jars of facial cream on the nightstand, her shoes strewn chaotically in one corner of the room, her ashtray in the shape of a frog, the slightly faded curtains, a trace of cobweb swaying from the far corner of the ceiling. The objects in the room started to loom in my mind, and even seemed to emit a kind of sound, an increasingly dissonant hum. Everything around me, including Maria-Teresa, became gratingly, fiercely wrong.

This sensation became more and more acute as time went on, until it was almost unbearable. I was smiling and chatting with her, but felt like screaming. At last I was able to put on my clothes, with my hands shaking from the tension. We kissed good-bye and I left, making a conscious effort not to appear to be hurrying. But I was so relieved to be out of her house that I wanted to break into a run. I could hear several of her neighbors arguing loudly in Spanish. Across the street a dog with a splint on its leg barked loudly at me when I opened my car door. I nearly caused an accident driving back to my apartment; I was in such a hurry to get home that I went through a red light without even seeing it and barely missed another car.

27

A contemporary of Bach's described attending a large party at which the host, a musical amateur, entertained his guests by playing the harpsichord. Arriving late, Bach entered the room during one of the player's improvisations. When the amateur became aware of the presence of the great master, he sprang up and left off with a dissonant chord. Bach found this so intolerable that he rushed by the man to the harpsichord to resolve the chord. Only then did he approach his host and make his bow of greeting.

Bach had the good sense to limit himself to resolving musical dissonances with his art, but I, foolishly thinking I could impose harmony on the emotional dissonance that had started in Maria-Teresa's bedroom, went straight to my practice room to play. I felt an unfamiliar twinge of dread as I tuned the instrument, then started with a few scales and arpeggios to warm up. I had to stop after only a few minutes. It wasn't just the intonation this time—there was something new. Playing the cello at this moment seemed an utterly trivial and wrongheaded thing to do. I went into the kitchen and made coffee; I read the paper; I turned on the radio. I would have tried anything to keep at bay the terrifying, painful thoughts that were running over and over in my head. All of them bore the same message; I would be alone all my life.

After a sleepless night I returned to the studio, and this time recoiled just at the sight of the cello. Suddenly I felt violently angry, and I knew I had to get out of the apartment. I didn't even want to listen to music.

I panicked. I'd never felt this way before, not even after the worst moments I'd had onstage. Even then I'd still wanted to play; in fact, the day after that last concert in Chicago I went right back to the practice room because I believed that practicing was my only hope. Whatever my problem was, neurological or psychological, I vowed to compensate for it with more practice. I would get to the point where I could play well regardless of whether I heard the music properly or not.

When asked how he became so proficient in the art of music, Bach would only say, "I have had to work hard; anyone who works as hard will get just as far." Von Kempen likewise believed that music was a craft as much as an art, and frequently warned me not to allow my talent to seduce me into thinking that I could eliminate rigorous, unglamorous technical studies from my daily practice. He especially loved to quote the passage from Bach's biography in which Forkel addresses those wishing to follow in the great composer's footsteps: "The greatest genius, with the most unconquerable propensity to an art, is in its original nature never more than a disposition, or a fruitful soil upon which an art can never properly thrive except it be cultivated with indefatigable pains. . . . Bach's ardent genius was attended by an equally ardent industry, which incessantly impelled him, when he could not yet succeed by his own strength, to seek aid from the models existing in his time." The model existing in my time was von Kempen, who still practiced every day beyond his ninetieth year, in spite of the certainty that he would never perform again.

That explains part of my discipline, but not all of it. It wasn't just a matter of training and willpower that kept me practicing for so many years after my career had exhausted itself; it was also a matter of there being no alternative. I had been labeled from childhood as an extraordinary artist, I had developed a musical technique that allowed me to communicate at a world-class level, and communicating at that level was both euphoric and self-defining. That state of musical emotion was the me that virtually everyone I had contact with thought of, spoke about or spoke to. I had little experience communicating in other ways, or in having any identity beyond my musical self. When I lost my ability to perform, regaining it became a matter of life and death. What was my life, after all, without music?

For most of my adult life I had wondered every single day: Who am I if I am not a musician? After my experience with Maria-Teresa, I began projecting that question backward in time: if my musical voice and identity, which had been so clear, so unwavering and pure, was really mine to begin with, then how could the voice that was reflected in my personal life possibly be so feeble and inarticulate in comparison? Since I had proven myself unable to participate in even that most fundamental of human dialogues, didn't this suggest that perhaps I had been deceived, along with everyone else, into thinking I was a genuine artist rather than just a precocious imitator? How much of my musical voice, my musical identity, actually reflected me, and how much of it was merely the composer's and my teacher's voices channeled through a remarkable childhood gift for mimicry?

While I debated these awful questions, Mrs. Kim left a conspiratorial message on my answering machine saying that Mr. Kim had decided to let Kyung-hee go to the symphony, and that she hoped it wasn't 'too-late notice.' Struggling through her fractured English, she said that "Kyung-hee, he so sad" when initially told he could not go that his father evidently had to change his mind. I gathered from her subdued voice that it had been an unpleasant family matter. Why? I wondered. If the man was so obsessed with having his son make money, why wouldn't he want the boy to have every possible chance to develop into a stellar performer? I was in no mood to be philosophical about it; I was disgusted. Cursing the Kims and their grotesque values, I decided not even to bother to return their call and stormed out of the apartment to take a walk. Three blocks from my building it sank in that, knowing what I did about his family, Kyung-hee must have been very upset to have changed his father's mind. He obviously wanted to go to the concert. Immediately I pictured him sitting at home in his little sport jacket waiting for me in vain. Stung with frustration and self-loathing, I rushed back to the house, called his mother and said I would pick him up at four-thirty.

The Kims' apartment was in a dull, flat area of Long Beach surrounded by strip malls and shabby one-story office buildings. Almost all the store signs were written in Oriental characters, and everyone I saw, including the people in cars, was Asian. The Kims lived in a small house with badly rotted eaves overhead, a rusted van with an underinflated tire parked out front and a battered chain-link fence encircling the property. Every square foot of the tiny front yard was used for cultivation, although there were no flowering plants visible—only beans growing up stick frames, eggplant, peas, carrots, rosemary, parsley, watercress and several other herbs I couldn't identify. The other houses on the street, I noticed, either had practical gardens like the Kims' or had been allowed to go completely to weeds and wheel rims.

When I knocked at the door Mrs. Kim answered, let me inside and called for Kyung-hee. While waiting I glanced around the living room, noticing that it was spotless. The furniture, though of the ghastly Sears-showroom variety, all looked either brand-new or meticulously cared for. The centerpiece of the room was the sofa, upholstered with crushed velvet and trimmed with elaborate antimacassars on the arms, all of which was covered with plastic and looked as if no one had ever sat on it. Two framed silk embroideries hung above it, each showing a pair of mandarin ducks swimming under the drooping branches of willow trees. A dark, heavy coffee table in front of the sofa supported a bowl piled high with oranges. I could see through to the kitchen, which looked more lived in than the living room. The house was fragrant with a mixture of incense, garlic, bitter herbs and a smoky, burned-cooking-oil smell.

Sitting at a little Formica table in the kitchen, behind a pile of magazines, Kyung-hee's sister was hunched over some books. "Homework," Mrs. Kim said proudly, noticing my glance. The daughter did not look up at me. The kitchen walls were practically wallpapered with long, scroll-type calendars that appeared to serve as advertisements for Asian business establishments; the few English words I could see on them proclaimed, "Great Ocean Auto Repair" or "Bul-Koki Barbeque Sauce," and each calendar featured an Oriental girl posing as if she were chasing butterflies. Worst of all was the noise. A television was turned on loud in the living room, even though no one appeared to be watching it, and a smaller one—the second set Kyung-hee had been so proud of—was on in the kitchen, tuned to a separate channel. Kyung-hee's sister seemed to be oblivious to both of them as she worked. The thought of Kyung-hee having to hear this racket nauseated me. Mrs. Kim yelled for Kyung-hee again, and at last he walked into the living room, wearing his sport coat just as I'd pictured. His mother sent him into the kitchen and he returned with a cup of tea in a large mug that had a ceramic lid, which he set down on the coffee table in front of me.

"You sit down, have tea first," Mrs. Kim said cheerfully, showing a rare smile and pointing at the sofa. I obeyed and had my cup of tea. Kyung-hee sat on a chair across the room with his feet dangling above the ground, and Mrs. Kim disappeared into the kitchen, only to reappear with a tray covered with pieces of several different kinds of cake. "Mr. Kim sorry he not here to see you," she said, speaking with her hand in front of her mouth in what appeared to be a gesture of remorse. "He so busy!"

After eating a piece of cake, I thanked her for the snacks but said that Kyung-hee and I should really get on the freeway as soon as possible if we wanted to beat traffic and have time for dinner. Mrs. Kim responded by refilling my cup from a large teapot resting snugly in a box lined with red velvet, then disappearing into the kitchen again. This time she came out with sliced fruit, elaborately arranged on a round serving plate.

She said something to Kyung-hee, who translated, "My mom says Americans don't like skin, so she peeled it for you." I thanked her for going to all the trouble, but she shook her head and said only, "No, no! Nothing!" Then she sat down next to Kyung-hee, folded her hands in front of her and watched me. I ate as much as I could and complimented her in particular on the pear slices, which were unusually crisp, but then regretted it when she leaped up from her seat, disappeared into the kitchen and returned with a plastic grocery bag filled with them. "You take home," she insisted. I tried to say that I could never finish them on my own, but she only shook her head again and waved her hand as if she were fanning a small fire.

When I had finished the second cup of tea I stood up as a signal that we should be going. Mrs. Kim looked almost alarmed, bolting upright and holding the teapot out toward me as if to assure me that there really was more in it, but when I assured her I'd had plenty she put the teapot back in its velvet case, gave Kyung-hee some final instructions in Korean, then allowed us to go. When we got in the car I saw that somehow she had managed to give Kyung-hee a second bag of pears for me.

On the drive to Los Angeles I asked Kyung-hee how he liked school.

"It's OK."

"What subjects do you like best?"

"They're all OK, I guess. I like math."

"Do you have some good friends at school?"

"I guess."

Every response was on that level, and he never initiated any conversation. It made me feel defeated; I wanted him to have a good time, to enjoy himself, to brighten up during our road trip so that I could be cheered up, but I couldn't seem to make it happen. By the time we reached Los Angeles I was beginning to wish I were at home in my own room drinking;

the cost of the tickets was seeming less and less important. But when I brought up the subject of dinner, Kyung-hee became more communicative. When I asked what kind of food he liked, he turned and glanced at me for an instant, then looked down at his lap.

"I like . . ." he said, his voice trailing off to an inaudible mumble.

"I'm sorry, I didn't hear you—what do you like?"

"I like Wendy's," he repeated, grinning sheepishly.

"You mean the fast-food place? We have plenty of time; we don't have to rush through dinner."

"OK."

"Do you like eating in restaurants, Kyung-hee?"

"Yeah. But we have to eat at home every day. My friends at school get to eat out all the time, though."

"I'll bet your mother's a good cook."

He nodded, and then said, "I like American food sometimes."

"Would you like to try another kind of Western food, then? How about French—have you ever had that?"

"No," he said, but he looked interested.

"France is where Debussy, Rameau and Ravel were from, and a lot of people think French food is the best in the world. Would you like to try it?"

"OK."

In fact I had already made a reservation for us at a quiet place I knew near the concert hall; I wanted all aspects of his first night at the symphony to be memorable. But when we sat down and he looked at the menu, instead of seeming impressed by all the strange dishes, he looked gravely worried. When I asked him if anything was wrong, he pulled a crumpled ten-dollar bill out of his jacket pocket and said, suddenly fighting back tears, "My mom didn't give me enough."

I told him to put away the money, that I was treating him and that he could have whatever he wanted. He still seemed afraid to order, however, so I took his menu away and asked what he liked best—chicken, beef or seafood. He said chicken, so I ordered him coq au vin and a shrimp cocktail appetizer.

While waiting for our food, I noticed that Kyung-hee kept sneaking glances at something going on behind me. I asked what was catching his attention, and he whispered to me, "That man walks funny." I turned around to see the maître d' seating a pair of women. I couldn't see anything unusual in his walk, but Kyung-hee couldn't take his eyes off him.

"What's funny about the way he walks?" I asked quietly.

"Look!" was all he would say. I turned around again, but from what I could tell, the man's gait looked perfectly normal.

"Not just his walking!" Kyung-hee said. "Everything's slow!" Now I realized that he was referring to the man's deliberately smooth movements, which one expects from maître d's and waiters in good restaurants. Apparently he had never seen someone who took pride in moving gracefully for the sake of creating a subdued atmosphere.

I explained to him that in a good restaurant the staff tries to make everything about the experience relaxing and beautiful—that was why, for example, our silverware and glasses were so carefully arranged in front of us. Just then our appetizers arrived. His shrimp were spread out on the plate in front of him in a circular pattern.

"You see?" I said, pointing to the shrimp. "The chef took time to put them all in the right place. Isn't that nice?"

His open mouth signaled that he was appropriately impressed. When he did not make any sort of move toward eating the shrimp, however, I worried that perhaps I had made too much of the presentation and frightened him into thinking it would be shameful to disturb the dish by actually eating any of it. When I urged him not to be polite and to eat, though, he turned red with embarrassment and asked, "How?"

I showed him how to use the tiny fork to dip the shrimp into the cocktail sauce.

"How come the fork is so small?" he asked me.

"Because it's an appetizer fork. The appetizer is a small meal before the main course, so the fork has to be small too!" I thought it was a clever answer, but he argued that the shrimp on his plate were the largest he had ever seen, so shouldn't the fork be even bigger than normal? I confessed that perhaps there was no good reason for the fork to be so small but that he shouldn't be bothered by it. He shrugged and took a tiny bite, which he held in his mouth without chewing; I was afraid he might spit it out, but that fear vanished when he stuffed the rest into his mouth and speared the next shrimp before even swallowing. Likewise his entree—he gobbled it up as if he might never have the chance to eat again. He had an impressive appetite for a nine-year-old.

However, the highlight of the meal came when the maître d' wheeled a fancy tray next to our table and introduced the desserts for the evening. When Kyung-hee saw all those slices of cake and pie, the custards, fruit tarts and cups filled with chocolate mousse, I thought he might have an insulin fit. He looked at each piece carefully, and, as I might have guessed, chose the one that looked biggest, a layered chocolate cake with chocolate truffles on top. He finished it so quickly that I worried he might give himself an upset stomach, but he felt well enough to ask if he could order another piece. I agreed, but on the condition that the waiter pack it up so that he could take it home and have it the next day. It would have been an awful setback, I thought, if he got sick during the concert and had to be taken home early to spend the night of his first concert throwing up in the bathroom.

On the short drive to the concert hall, I described the program to Kyung-hee and told him that he didn't have to think about any pictures this time; he was only to listen and enjoy. The first half would be Berio's *Sinfonia,* a modern piece that I'd never heard, and the second half would be Strauss's dramatic tone poem *Also Sprach Zarathustra.* When we took our seats in the hall, he looked around him in undisguised wonder. The clothing of the audience, particularly the women, seemed to impress him, as did the high ceiling, the chandeliers in the lobby and the bright, polished wooden floor of the stage.

Like most music in the classical tradition written since the First World War, the first piece was disappointing. The orchestra and singers did a heroic job trying to do justice to it, but no matter how well you play or sing, you can't make disappointing music sound inspiring. References to Mahler, Debussy, Strauss, Schoenberg, Stravinsky and Berg appear in the piece, along with musical depictions of Martin Luther King and the Paris student protests, in what was charitably described in the program notes as a "fascinating collage." Because of the debacle of the night before, I was especially impatient; I could hardly wait for it to end. Also, I was anxious to hear Kyung-hee's first impressions of a live symphony performance. Out of the corner of my eye I noticed he sat completely still during the piece, his face taut with concentration. During the applause he turned to me and said excitedly, "There are seventy-three people in the orchestra!"

"Yes, a big group, isn't it? And what did you think of the music?"

"Good!" A positive response, to be sure, but I had been hoping for something more specific.

As we strolled in the lobby during intermission, Kyung-hee tugged at my sleeve several times to point out sights that he found interesting. "Look at that lady's dress!" he said, staring at a woman in a gold lamé outfit. "It must be worth a million dollars!"

"No, not that much. Probably only a thousand."

"A thousand dollars! Wow!"

I bought him a Coke at the bar, and for myself a shot of whiskey. An older man standing next to us asked his companion, "How's your drink?" She replied that it was a little dry. I asked Kyung-hee, "And how's your drink?" He straightened up, seeming to appreciate the chance to talk like a grown-up. "Good," he said, which was what he had said about the Berio piece. Since the *Sinfonia* purports to depict the events of the 1960s, I decided that comparing it to a popular soft drink was probably appropriate.

The main treat of the evening was *Also Sprach Zarathustra.* It was conceived as a musical complement to Friedrich Nietzsche's book *Thus Spake Zarathustra: A Book for All or None,* although Strauss later said about the piece, "I did not intend to write philosophical music or to portray Nietzsche's great work musically. I meant to convey by means of music an idea of the development of the human race from its origin, through the various phases of its development, religious as well as scientific, up to Nietzsche's idea of the Superman."

The dramatic opening, with its low pedal point in the orchestra and its distinctive trumpet call—known to so many people now as the theme from the movie *2001*—made Kyung-hee's body go rigid. The first section depicts people who seek comfort in religion, as Zarathustra himself once did. In the second section, Strauss uses the cellos and bassoons to represent "great yearning" with a haunting, ascending theme. The third, called "Of Happiness and Passions," refers to a passage in Nietzsche's book in which Zarathustra reflects on how, thanks to strenuous self-discipline and wise direction, his dark passions have been turned into sources of virtue.

There follows a section called the "Grave Song," carried by the oboe, which is a meditation on death. "Of Science," the next movement, depicts the complexities of modern life, and "The Convalescent" evokes the restrained joy of spiritual awakening. "The Dance Song" reflects Zarathustra's happiness at seeing Cupid and wood nymphs dancing together. His joy gives way in the final movement of the piece, titled the "Song of the Night Wanderer," in which we hear twelve heavy strokes of an ancient bell, accompanied by octaves in the strings, that gradually die away.

As the last note faded into silence and the audience burst into applause, Kyung-hee looked at me with an expression of utter puzzlement. His face was drenched in sweat.

"It isn't done!" he cried over all the noise.

"What do you mean? That was the ending, Kyung-hee."

"No! It wasn't—it wasn't closed! He didn't finish it right!"

I realized with excitement that he was referring to the fact that Strauss ended the work in two keys, a device that also startled the first audiences to hear it nearly one hundred years ago. The upper woodwinds and strings play in the key of B while the basses hold steady in the key of C. Strauss himself never explained this ending, leading most people to conclude that this lack of harmonic resolution denotes Zarathustra's realization that in spite of all his knowledge, life remains a mystery. I tried to explain this to Kyung-hee, but to no avail.

"He should have finished it," he kept saying, his hands shaking with emotion. "It was so good until the end. . . . It was so good. . . ." He looked as if he had been swindled.

I had hoped that his first night at the symphony would be a more unreservedly joyous occasion, though certainly the experience had not been a failure. In fact, the more I thought about it, the more his reaction pleased me. It showed that he responded deeply to music as an emotional experience, and that he expected more from it than mere distraction. It also demonstrated a natural affinity for classical harmonic structure, best represented by Bach and Mozart, which requires that a piece be harmonically resolved according to the rules of counterpoint. Bach, for example, would have finished (or closed, as Kyung-hee put it) *Also Sprach Zarathustra* in only one key, and it would have had to be in the key of the tonic, in this case C, established at the very beginning of the piece. Since I shared Kyung-hee's attraction to strict harmonic design, I was delighted by his annoyance, and had to restrain myself from saying aloud that if Strauss had had Kyung-hee's natural talent he might have written better music.

In spite of the success of the evening, I ended up drinking heavily all day Sunday. Brooding over my barren social life, it infuriated me that I'd thrown away my entire childhood and youth, thinking that music was all-important. Look where it had landed me, I thought; I was a failure by the time I was eighteen, and had spent the sixteen years since then becoming steadily more ignorant of how to carry on the kind of relationships that human beings were designed for. I couldn't even manage sex with a beautiful woman who was starved for affection.

28

I was hung over Monday morning and was the last juror to get to the courthouse. Maria-Teresa noticed that I didn't look well and asked what was wrong. I told her I must have picked up a bug, and that I'd been wiped out all weekend with it.

She looked relieved and said, "God, I was afraid it was because of me."

"No, no, it had nothing to do with you. How could it?"

She smiled at me and said, "I hope not." I wished she hadn't been so nice about it; it would have been much easier if she had ridiculed me or been angry, because then at least I could have felt indignant or hurt or—anything but that sense of failure. I could hardly bear looking at her.

The day crept along unbearably. With all of the testimony and evidence out of the way, there were only closing arguments to hear before starting our deliberations.

Ms. Doppelt went first. She began by saying that by now we all knew that Philip Weber suffered from mental disease; this was an unrefuted fact. The only real question was whether we should send this mentally ill person to a hospital or to a prison. If she had asked for my opinion just then, I would have said, Who gives a damn? Why should we spend so much time and money on one spectacular lost cause, when those of us who become lost causes gradually are expected to shuffle out of sight without disturbing anyone?

Although I did try, I couldn't pay attention during most of Ms. Doppelt's speech. The only part of it that I really heard was the ending, where her voice suddenly dropped low and she said, "I have a particular reason for believing that Philip didn't know what he was doing that day. Do you remember that during the voir dire Mr. Graham dismissed anyone who had a relative with mental illness? Well, there's a reason for that. If someone in your family has this problem, then you know how awful it is, how innocent the people with the disease are, and how they suffer. I wouldn't qualify to sit in that jury box with you—Mr. Graham would have kicked me off it. I have a sister with a mental illness. It's destroyed her life, and it isn't her fault at all. I had to watch it happen, so I know what it does to a person."

She rubbed her forehead with her palm, then dropped her arms back to her sides stiffly. "Philip Weber's future—and possibly the future of other innocent people he will have contact with during the course of his life—is in your hands now. All I ask is that before you make your final decision and judge him, ask yourself this one question: If justice is meant to protect and enhance the lives of good people in society, what verdict in this case best protects and enhances our lives? Keeping a dangerously ill man out of society for a while—probably a short while—by locking him in a cell for an arbitrary period, or keeping a dangerously ill man out of society by putting him in a secure hospital for as long as it takes to heal him? I realize that this is a difficult question to answer, but I hope that this trial will force you to answer it.

"Remember that Philip never claimed to be insane. He was judged to be insane by a qualified specialist, and I have defended him on the basis of that evaluation and the other evidence. He hasn't assisted me in his defense at all. As you learned, he refused the services of a private lawyer because, as he said to me, 'I don't want my father to have to pay for this. I don't need to be defended, because there's nobody here to defend!' He is not someone who committed a crime, then thought, I know how to get out of this—I'll say I was insane! The day I met him I could tell immediately that something was terribly wrong, so I hired a psychiatrist to evaluate him. It was on the basis of that evaluation that I chose the insanity defense. If you feel any resentment about having to sit through an insanity-defense trial, blame me for it, not Philip. He honestly thinks that the outcome of this trial is utterly irrelevant. He is now, as he was on January fourth, clearly not sane and is unable to grasp the significance of what he's done, or to recognize the difference between right and wrong. To put him in jail would be like throwing a five-year-old in jail—it wouldn't bring Mr. Okakura back to life, it wouldn't help Mr. Okakura's family, it wouldn't help us, it wouldn't be punishment, and it would be a meaningless gesture. I honestly believe that."

Maria-Teresa slipped me a piece of paper that had "Indian restaurant again?" scrawled on it. I nodded and tried to look enthusiastic, but felt nauseated. I didn't even hear Mr. Graham's closing argument.

Lunch was a disaster. Maria-Teresa tried to cheer me up, but that made matters worse. Her attention only made me feel pathetic in addition to all the other negatives. At last she became exasperated and asked, "So just because we didn't have sex that night you don't want to talk to me? I didn't think it was such a big deal, but if you're going to act like it's the end of the world, it's *gonna* be a big deal, you know? Relax, will you?"

I didn't blame her at all for getting irritated with me, but I couldn't do anything about it. I felt as if I were bound, gagged and chained to a table, and now someone was asking me to socialize. I couldn't even form complete sentences. She finally grew too frustrated to try anymore, and we trudged back to the courtroom in deafening silence.

"First thing is we elect a new foreman," Mrs. Friedman said.

"Why? You did just fine before, Ruth."

"I don't want to have to do it twice. I nominate Mr. Anderson."

No one else volunteered, so Dwight Anderson, the black ex-Marine, took charge. He suggested that we start with a secret ballot, as we had before.

I wrote "Undecided." I did believe Weber had been out of his mind, but didn't necessarily want to have to make a stand. Hearing the other jurors' comments in the hallways and the men's room, and from looking at some of their faces as they rushed to write "Guilty" in bold letters on their slips of paper, I was afraid I might be the only dissenting vote; if so, I wanted the option of being able to change my vote quietly if I thought it wasn't worth fighting over.

"Eleven guilty, one undecided."

"Does it have to be all twelve to make a verdict?" Mathilda, the nervous woman, asked.

"Yes," Dwight said, "that's what the judge said; since it's a murder trial, it has to be unanimous."

"Oh, boy," she groaned. In the tense silence following her comment, I realized that everyone assumed that the one dissenting vote was hers, just as before. I nearly smiled at the misunderstanding, though it wasn't really funny.

"The next step, then," Dwight said, "is to go over the evidence. We'll go around the room and list all the main points of both sides. Then we'll take another secret ballot to see if the vote has changed."

"Why don't we just say who voted how," Roy asked. He was the retired plant manager, the redneck. "The one voting not guilty is going to have to explain her reasons anyway, right?" From the way he said it, I got the feeling that he simply didn't like taking instructions from Dwight.

"Well," answered Rose, the large black woman, "in those jury instructions they suggest we do it this way. There must be some reason."

Dwight nodded and said, "It's too early to put one person on the spot. We got to take our time here. It's murder we're talking about." Everyone was too polite at this point to grumble. "So let's get started, then. Rose? You want to start?"

"What is it we're starting now?" Mathilda interrupted, "I'm a little confused."

Several people exhaled loudly. Patiently Dwight explained that we were going to start reviewing the evidence that suggested he was sane; then we would talk about the evidence that suggested he was insane.

Mathilda was becoming flustered already. "I guess I'm the dumb one, because no one else ever has any questions. I guess I should just shut up."

"You're not dumb," Jesusita, the nurse's aide, said, smiling at her. "Relax."

During all of this, Maria-Teresa didn't look at me. She seemed to be going from being hurt to being angry, for which I was both sorry and thankful.

"Should somebody be taking notes as we go?" Grace, the soft-spoken widow, asked. "It might make things easier in the long run."

"Good idea. Who can write fast?"

No one wanted to volunteer. "Come on," Dwight prodded, "somebody has to be able to take good notes—Rose?"

"Hey, mister, I have to do that every day at work! It's bad enough being in this trial, but at least I get out of taking dictation for a while."

"Yeah, but you can do it better than any of us," Roy said. I was afraid he and Rose might start arguing, so I offered to do it. I also figured it might help me to think more clearly, in a more structured way, about the evidence, and it would keep my mind off the fact that Maria-Teresa was ignoring me so conspicuously. By this time everyone must have noticed our rift, which only added to my sense of discomfort.

Dwight passed me a big yellow pad and a pen. "We're talking about evidence of sanity," he resumed. "I'm starting, and we might as well go around the table like last time. First of all, there's what the second psychiatrist said—that the kid was sick, but not crazy. That psychiatrist thought the kid definitely did know what he was doing."

"Yeah," Gary, the meter reader, said, "and then there's the way he was so on target with that stick. Somebody nuts would be swinging wild, running around, panicking, saying he was Napoleon or . . ."

Roy nodded. "Yep. And he was able to lead a normal enough life—he kept a job for a while and paid rent. That kid knew enough to talk his old man into letting him goof off and smoke pot at home for six months. He didn't act very insane before that day."

Jesusita seemed convinced that the drug use was responsible. "Even if he wasn't doing it that day . . . I know people who do the drugs, then stop, but still there's something wrong with their mind, you know? A lot of 'em were pretty calm people before they got into dope, but after, they can't control their temper."

"You know what else is going through my mind?" Roy asked. "It's—if this guy really thinks he's God, and he says he doesn't care where he goes, then he might as well go to jail, right? Because—" he added, thumping on the table with a stubby forefinger, "if he's guilty and he's just faking that he's crazy, then he'll pay the price, but if he really is nuts, he won't know the damn difference! He'll be just as happy in jail. So guilty is the safest way to go, no matter what."

"That may be true," Dwight said, a touch of disdain beginning to show in his voice, "but we have to stick to answering the question of whether he was sane or insane."

"You can't ever prove what's in a guy's head," Roy shot back, looking around for support. "It seems to me we just gotta do what seems best, and what seems best to me is that this guy goes to jail."

Dwight didn't let anyone come to his rescue. "If we can't decide if he's sane or not," he said firmly, "we have to tell that to the judge, and they'll have to do the whole thing over. But even that'd be better than making a decision for the wrong reasons."

"I thought we weren't going to debate yet," Mrs. Friedman said. "Let's try to stay on track here, or we'll never get through this. We're only talking evidence now."

When it came her turn, Maria-Teresa said, "After he killed

the guy, he got tackled to the ground and he didn't complain. He got handcuffed and busted, but didn't resist. He got taken to jail and talked to his lawyer and to all these doctors, and now he sits in a courthouse for a couple of weeks while people talk about how crazy he is. . . . All those situations are pretty stressful, right? But he was calm through all of it. If you're insane, you're supposed to be out of control, right? He doesn't seem out of control to me."

A soft voice said, "And then there's the puzzle." It was Grace, whose late husband had worked at the jet lab. "The one about killing the Buddha. If the puzzle talked about killing, and the boy admits that killing the teacher was his answer to the puzzle, then . . . he knew he was killing, right? It seems to me that this weakens the argument that he didn't know what he was doing."

"Fritz? What about you?"

The old janitor scratched his head. "I can't think of anything right now. I'm trying, though."

I mentioned the fact that he had been able to sit still, in complete silence for hours at a time, every day for nearly a year before this had happened. That struck me as something a schizophrenic might have a hard time doing.

"Betty?" Dwight asked.

"I didn't like the fact that he didn't testify at all. If he's innocent, why didn't his lawyer put him on the stand? It seems like the lawyer is trying to hide something that way."

"Mathilda?"

All eyes turned on poor Mathilda. She fidgeted, then said in a pained voice, "All of the above, I guess. I don't know how we're supposed to know all this stuff by heart." I was thankful for her confusion this time because it kept me anonymous for a while longer. I needed time to think; after an agonizingly slow trial, the decision-making part seemed to be moving too quickly, and I didn't feel prepared to make a final decision yet. We'd been in the jury room only a few minutes, and already it seemed that everyone but me wanted to vote guilty and go home.

"I thought of something," Fritz said, drawing the heat away from Mathilda.

"He was a smart boy—everybody said so. It seems like he was too . . . regular to be crazy. Crazy people, you can tell so easy. They just . . . You can just see from the way they walk and talk. They don't seem smart."

No one else had any comments for the time being. I showed my notes to Dwight and he said, "OK, that's a good list. Now let's talk about the evidence that suggests he was insane. I might as well start again. Whether we think he acted like a real crazy person or not, it seems like it's a fact that he has schizophrenia. Both doctors agreed on that. So we're not talking about someone who just, out of the blue, says, 'I went crazy all of a sudden.' He was getting worse as the years went by, even though he was managing to keep out of trouble. We have to consider that he really does have this disease. . . . So a guy with this disease was living at this church where he had to go along with the strict discipline. And during that retreat they got very little sleep, no talking out loud, and hour after hour of sitting still. Remember what that first doctor said? Something about how that could drive even a normal person nuts?"

This time around the pauses between contributions were much longer. Jesusita was the next one to speak. "Well, I have to say . . . the Japanese man who was so nice—Mr. Hayashi, right? He made their religion sound peaceful, but I don't know. . . . The teacher that got killed sounded kind of weird. You hear on TV, you know, how every once in a while a kid who seems normal gets into some religion and suddenly he does crazy things. You ever heard of Santeria? They're crazy—they kill animals, and sometimes people . . . So if this Philip was really sick, maybe the religion threw him off."

After another long pause, I tried to mention casually that the fact that the defendant had been so violent with the teacher and then suddenly so calm afterward seemed curious. If he was really controlling himself, willing himself to kill for selfish reasons, he'd have had to work himself up to quite a frenzy, wouldn't he? Wouldn't it be hard to turn something like that off all of a sudden? And not be worried or defensive or contradict himself at all during any of the aftermath? That would seem to require either superhuman planning and self-control, which he had never before shown in his life, or a mind that had become unpredictable and out of control. As I said this, I realized I was directly contradicting what Maria-Teresa had said a few minutes earlier. She gave me a vacant look, then turned her eyes away.

After another pause Rose turned to Mathilda and, sounding as encouraging as possible, asked, "What about you, Mathilda? Can you think of any other evidence that says he's not guilty?"

Mathilda frowned and said, "If you're going to wait till the end to call on me every time, how is there supposed to be anything left for me to say? I—"

"You aren't the last person to be called on," Mrs. Friedman said abruptly. She was beginning to lose patience with the hapless Mathilda. "There are still plenty of people who haven't spoken."

"Fine! Well, I can't think of anything."

People squirmed noisily in their chairs; Mathilda was really getting them angry. They all assumed that she was the hold-out, and resented her not even contributing an explanation of her position. Mrs. Friedman frowned and made a little smacking sound with her lips, but said nothing. Tension hung in the air until Grace said in her quiet voice, "Up until he killed that man, this boy didn't seem like a mean person. Not like a killer. He wanted attention, but couldn't get it the regular ways. He had a bad family life, what with his mother being so sick and a father who didn't seem to be aware of what was going on in his family. When you think about all that put together, it makes you wonder."

"Wonder what?" Mathilda asked.

"If everything was really that boy's fault."

"It doesn't make me wonder," Roy said. "He's twenty-one years old, he lived away from home for years, he holds a job and he can put his own pants on. You can't blame his old man for what he does now."

When it became clear that no one else had anything to add, Dwight said, "Then let's do the blind ballot again."

"You mean the secret ballot?" Mathilda asked, sounding panicked.

"Blind ballot, secret ballot, whatever," Mrs. Friedman said through clenched teeth.

I wrote down "Not guilty" this time. I'm not sure why; I wasn't even thinking about convincing any of the others, but the more I thought about it, the more sure I felt that Philip had been insane. Dwight counted the slips again. Without registering any surprise or annoyance he said, "This time it's ten guilty, two not guilty." A few people sighed heavily, and Roy groaned out loud. I felt so grateful for the second vote that I had to control myself from asking whom to thank.

"Well, does anyone object if we have a show-of-hands vote at this point?" Mrs. Friedman asked. No one objected. There wouldn't have been much point in any case, because only two people in the room would have had any reason to object. "All right, then. Who voted guilty?"

Ten hands went up. I felt my heart pound as I kept my hand on my lap. Maria-Teresa glanced at me for a second when she saw that I was one of the bleeding hearts, but looked away without showing any reaction. I leaned forward and turned to my left, looking toward Mathilda, but saw that her hand was raised higher than anyone else's and was actually waving vigorously. I turned right and saw that the other dissenter was Dwight, the defense-plant investigator and our foreman.

I wasn't the only one who was surprised. Most of the others glanced curiously at the two of us out of the corner of their eyes, except for Roy, who shook his head and made a snickering noise, and Mrs. Friedman, who stared at me as if to say that she knew all along because it fit perfectly with everything else she knew about me.

"Do you want to start?" Dwight asked me.

"I was hoping you would—I'm not sure I can put an argument together just now," I said. He laughed easily and said that he had the same problem. I asked to see the copy of the judge's instructions. I wasn't sure what I was looking for; I was really only stalling for time. I read it over, but the excruciating pressure made it impossible to think. The words jumped around on the page, so that by the time I got to the end of a sentence, I couldn't remember how it had begun. I closed my eyes and took a deep breath, but it didn't help. "I'm sorry," I said, "I'm having difficulty concentrating."

"Nobody said we had to do it in ten minutes or under," Rose said helpfully. "Should we break for a few minutes? That way you guys could have some time to think, and I know at least two of us could use a cigarette." She smiled at Maria-Teresa.

As the others milled around or went to the rest rooms, I closed my eyes and tried to think—What is it? What was I seeing that the others weren't? Or what *wasn't* I seeing? Why wasn't I just voting guilty; I could not have cared less about Philip Weber at this point. I wanted to know what made Dwight change his mind, but he'd been one of the first out of the room at the break.

I looked at the judge's instructions again. If I wasn't truly certain that Weber was insane, I had to go along with the others. And I wanted to go along with the others. I wanted the trial to end as much as I'd ever wanted anything. What was it, I wondered, that made me feel so strongly that Weber was insane?

The harder I tried to concentrate, the more my mind darted around uselessly. I leaned back in the chair and rubbed my forehead, then my temples and eyes. I decided to put the whole issue aside for a few minutes; I wasn't getting anywhere, and I needed to get away from it, even if only for a short time.

Naturally, every few seconds my thoughts turned back to Maria-Teresa, and I wondered how I could have been so foolish and irresponsible as to become intimate with her in the first place. What was I thinking, trying to sleep with a married woman in her husband's bed? It suddenly seemed a mystery to me how I'd ever reached that point, how I could ever have done something so unlike me. Thinking along those lines led me to recall that strange moment in Chicago when I walked away from the cab—another example of a time I had not been myself. Scolding myself for indulging in a pathetic self-examination when I should have been thinking about the trial, I tried to shake myself out of it and get back to the far more important task of understanding why I felt convinced that Philip Weber was insane. However, my mind kept going back to that dreamlike episode, and slowly I began to see a connection.

When the others returned I said, "The reason I voted not guilty is that I know there have been times when I did things that I wouldn't normally do, things that surprised even me."

I had to make a supreme effort to keep from looking at Maria-Teresa as I said this. Even so, out of the corner of my eye, I could see her stiffen. I continued nervously, "So I look at this young man, whose mind is damaged by a disease to begin with, and I see him growing up the way he did; then I see him drifting for a couple of years and becoming more lonely and more socially inept; then I see him living in this church and trying to keep up with their discipline and their confusing philosophy . . . and I think it's very believable that he could have done something like this without understanding what he was doing. I think the testimony we've heard adds up to say that this was a person who lost his mind, who was no longer what we would call sane."

"Can you give us some examples? I mean of things you've done?" Gary teased, drawing a few chuckles out of the group. "Don't hold back!" he said, laughing through his nose.

I declined the invitation but asked them, "Haven't you ever said or done something that was wrong or unnecessary just because, say, you had a splitting headache that day or you were carsick? I know these are little things, but they're examples. Or have you ever been in a situation so awful, so stressful, that you did something that you later regretted, or could not explain to yourself? Well, I have, and so I think about a person like this Mr. Weber, who had been under stress and on drugs and mentally exhausted for years, and then put himself through that retreat . . . Doesn't anyone else think it makes sense that eventually he would have cracked and lost control of himself?"

"It's possible," Grace said softly, "but didn't the judge say we're not supposed to decide on the basis of possibilities? We have to be *certain* that he was insane in order to acquit him, and what you're saying doesn't make me feel certain."

I looked over at Dwight to see if he was going to back me up. He adjusted his watchband, rested his forearms on the table and turned to look at me. "Until a little while ago, I didn't think his mental problems were an excuse for what he did. I had the feeling his lawyer was . . . oh, playing that up for the sake of getting him off the hook. And she just wasn't as believable as the prosecutor to begin with. I voted guilty the first time—partly because I want the guy to be punished, you know? If a man kills another man for no good reason, you punish him. It makes sense. I was hoping that everybody else would vote that way, and my conscience would have been clear. But there was that one undecided vote, and it spoiled things for me. Now I know I have to think this through more carefully before I can convict a man of murder, and what you just said maybe makes sense to me. . . ."

Dwight leaned back in his chair and sighed. "I knew somebody once, when I was in the service, who lost it all of a sudden. It was in Vietnam, when a lot of people were losing it. One day he was OK, the next he went completely bullshit and shot some innocent people. So I know this can happen.

But the question is, did it happen here? As Grace just pointed out, we have to be certain. I can't say I'm certain yet, but I'm not ready to convict him either."

"I have another question," Grace said almost apologetically. "Mr. Sundheimer, you were saying before that you felt convinced the young man couldn't control himself that day. I know what you mean about losing control—I've certainly done some foolish things in my life, impulsive things. But I thought the main issue is whether or not the boy knew he was killing a man, isn't that it? He just had to be aware of what he was doing, I thought. He certainly seemed to be aware. He was able to talk about it to those doctors, and to the police."

"That's right," Rose agreed. "We can't say if he could have controlled himself, and we don't have to. We only have to know if the guy was aware that he was killing somebody."

"Exactly."

"Uh-huh."

"Yeah."

I pointed to the copy of the judge's instructions and said, "I thought that way too until I read this over. I noticed that Judge Davis put the definition of legal insanity in here for us. It says a person is legally insane if 'as a result of mental disease or defect, he lacks substantial capacity *either* to appreciate the criminality of his conduct *or* to conform his conduct to the requirements of law.' Those words 'either' and 'or' give us some leeway here."

Roy was shaking his head again. "Look, he was able to, uh, *confirm* his conduct to the requirements of the law for almost every other moment of his life, including after killing the guy. Why should we believe that just for that one instant he lost his mind? Just for long enough to do something that would guarantee he'd go down in history as the guru to beat all gurus, or whatever the hell they call themselves? It seems awfully convenient to me that he had his one instant of insanity at such a perfect time."

"Yeah."

"Good point."

"Yeah," Gary added, "you know, it's like the guy who has a crummy job all his life and who's jealous of his boss, so he shoots the boss and says, 'Hey, man, I'm sorry, I went insane—but I'm OK now, so do you mind if I take his job?' This Weber guy might get out of the hospital in a year or two, start his own cult of people like him who think that it's cool to walk on the wild side a bit, and—"

"We had guys like that at the plant, believe me," Roy said. "One day they're welding, the next they got some lawyer calling in shouting for worker's comp, sayin' their client has emotional suffering—you name it. So we had to have doctors take a look, and guess what, most of 'em were faking it. You can't just start letting anybody who says, 'Oops, I lost my mind,' get off, or everybody'll jump on the bandwagon."

"Uh-huh."

"I still think it's the drugs," Jesusita said.

"But what if the drugs aggravated the mental illness and made it worse?" I asked. "Do we hold that against him?"

"I'll tell you one thing," Rose said, shaking her head. "If this guy was black and from South Central, we wouldn't be sitting here even asking the question. He'd be convicted in a minute. But you get a white kid smoking dope and beating somebody to death, you've got an army of people talking about his father didn't love him enough, doctors arguing for hours, and even religious experts coming in here arguing about the meaning of life. I tell you, I don't know whether to laugh or cry."

"That may be true," I said, "but that doesn't make it right. Should we rush through this and call this man guilty just because another man wouldn't get a fair trial?"

"Yes!" she answered, flashing an angry glance at me. "The law should be the same for everybody, and if it's one way for blacks, then it oughta be the same for whites too, because that's the only way things will change if they're lousy. You know what I'm saying?"

"So you believe that convicting him would be lousy justice, then? You agree with me?"

"I'm not saying that at all. I'm saying a black man would be convicted, and that helps me make a decision. I'm voting guilty, and I don't have any second thoughts about it."

We continued arguing for another two hours over Philip Weber's sanity, but without any real progress; by five o'clock we were only repeating ourselves, and the room had become unbearably close. I was exhausted from the tension. Ten people in that room badly wanted to be done with this trial after almost three weeks of sitting in court. One of them in particular probably wanted to be done with me, and they all honestly believed that Philip Weber was guilty. But Dwight and I had a different view, and we were holding the others prisoner. Their lives were being put on hold while we clung to our minority opinion. It was an almost unbearable situation, but I took solace in the fact that at least one other juror shared the burden with me.

At last we decided to call it a day and resume the next morning, since we obviously weren't going to bring in a verdict that night. Several of the jurors groaned at the thought of having to go through another day of jury duty just to convince two overcautious men that their concern was misplaced. I have a feeling that some of them believed that Dwight and I were holding out just to be stubborn, or simply to enjoy an opportunity to wield power over ten other people.

29

By eight o'clock the next morning it was already 90 degrees out and a first-stage smog alert had been declared. Immediately after getting up I had called the Kims to cancel Kyung-hee's lessons for the week. After the weekend I'd just had and the way the deliberations had gone the day before, I knew that even if the trial ended later that morning I would be too exhausted to think about teaching for at least several days. Mrs. Kim sounded concerned; she said that Kyung-hee had been very excited since Saturday night's concert and was eager get back to his lessons. I apologized, but assured her that we could resume at the latest by Monday of the next week.

The traffic was even worse than usual. I saw one man who had been in a minor accident literally hopping up and down in frustration; at first I thought he was joking because it looked so comical, but as I got closer I saw that he was purple in the face with rage.

Even though the courthouse was air-conditioned, the jury room was already stuffy, and Mrs. Friedman was fanning herself with a piece of cardboard. The custodian announced that we would have to wait for Betty, whose car had overheated on the way and who was still waiting for a tow truck.

I couldn't stand the tension in the room, the feeling that so many people were angry with me. I tried to tell a funny story, hoping to give them the impression that I was not an unreasonable man. I told about the time I gave a concert with an orchestra in Rome on an especially humid summer night, when I thought that nothing could surpass the discomfort of the heat. Suddenly the unthinkable happened: my chair was placed on the fixed part of the stage along with the rest of the orchestra, but the spike of my cello rested on an extended platform that could be raised or lowered by throwing a switch backstage. The stagehand, an ancient fellow, was overcome by the heat and fell asleep, slumping forward onto the switch and setting the platform in motion. I could see the audience react in horror as the platform started to descend. The conductor couldn't see it, so he and the orchestra kept going. I didn't want to be the one to stop, so I didn't stop as the cello sank. The cadenza—my solo—arrived, and I kept playing. The cello sank so low that at one point I was doubled over with my chest touching my knees. Fortunately the kettledrum player realized what had happened and rushed backstage to throw the switch in reverse, so the platform slowly came back up again. I got through the cadenza without missing a note, we finished the concerto, and I got a thunderous standing ovation. The Italians love a spectacle, so I became an instant celebrity when the story and photos hit the local papers.

I hoped that telling the story would make it possible for me to debate the verdict without drawing hostility from anyone. A few of them laughed at the story, but I think my plan backfired; apparently some of them thought I was telling it as a conciliatory gesture before admitting that I had been wrong yesterday and was now ready to vote with the majority. When Betty finally arrived, in a terrible mood over being put through all this, Roy smiled at me hopefully and asked, "So, any change of heart since yesterday?"

Everyone turned to look at me, and they were all smiling, except for Maria-Teresa, who was looking at me without any expression at all.

"Not really."

A collective sigh of exasperation let me know that my hope for debate without frustration was an unrealistic one.

"What about you, Mr. Anderson?"

Dwight glanced at me, then leaned back in his chair and crossed his arms in front of him. "I thought about it a lot last night. Especially about what Reinhart said about how, if even normal people can lose control under pressure situations, then a guy with mental problems could be pushed out of control a lot easier. And I thought about my example of the guy in Vietnam who lost it from battle fatigue, and all the guys who've lost it even after the war ended because the stress finally got to 'em and twisted their minds into knots. But then I had a problem."

"What problem?"

"Well, soldiers get put into hellish situations because it's in the line of duty. They have to wade through that swamp, or crawl through that field where they could get shot or blown up, because they're under orders, they have to complete their mission. When a person not in a war situation does something strange, when he loses control, you have to ask what the situation was. Was it something he could have avoided before he lost control? Do you see what I'm getting at?"

"No, I don't." Mathilda complained. "Are we . . . are you talking about war now?"

"I'll give you an example, ma'am. When someone's drunk, really stone-dead drunk, they lose all control of their reflexes and their judgment. They stumble around, they act rude, they do stupid things and regret it in the morning—if they remember at all, that is. They're out of control, right? A drunk man can't suddenly straighten up and control himself, right? But we convict drunk drivers. Not because they knew what they were doing when they were driving, but because they knew what they were doing when they did all the drinking. If they knew they had to drive, they could have thought about that when they were sober and not had so much to drink.

"My problem with our Mr. Weber is that while I'm willing to believe that at the time he killed the Zen guy he was out of control, I think the fact that he chose to participate in that retreat when he knew how tough it would be, and knew how strange all the puzzles would be, that's where he loses my sympathy. A guy like this, who's dropped out of college, who's been jerkin' around with dope, who has brains and can use 'em when he wants to, had plenty of opportunities to improve himself rather than make himself worse. So he lost my sympathy when he joined this group instead of, say, going to a counselor or a drug clinic."

"That's what I was gonna say," Jesusita said.

"Yes," Grace added quietly, "I didn't think of it that way, but now that you mention it . . . He could have done so many constructive things, or at least tried to, but instead he chose to join a group where he could sit around all day and think about himself. I don't think we have to feel sorry for people who make this kind of choice, especially when it leads to murder."

"Right."

"So you'd vote guilty now?"

"Yes," Dwight said, to my great disappointment, "I'm convinced that it would be the right thing to do."

I was all alone. No one was looking at me, but it was obvious that I was the center of everyone's attention.

"What do you think of what Dwight said?" Roy asked me, grinning as if our foreman's change of opinion were a personal victory.

I said it made sense, and that I would certainly give it my full attention.

"It doesn't change your mind, though?" Gary asked.

"Not yet."

"Can you say why not? Or try to?"

"I . . . I think that . . . It may not be a fair analogy, but this boy has . . . a physical disease, something he was born with—"

"But he chose to join that church!" Roy practically yelled, "and this is a religion where their saints hit people with sticks! He decided to join that bunch, just like he decided to drop out of school and loaf around the house smoking pot! You can't blame it all on a disease, for Chris'sake."

"No, I'm not saying that everything can be explained by his disease. He joined the group of his own free will, it's true, but that shouldn't be counted against him. You talk as if joining that church only proves that he's a bad person!"

"But it does! It's not a normal religion you're talking about. Maybe it's normal for people over in Japan, but not here."

Dwight's analogy of the drunk driver came up again; it was a good point. But something about it didn't seem right. I struggled to figure out why it didn't convince me, then offered another analogy to counter it. "What if a man is at home . . . he's drinking at home and he has no intention of going out. Then he gets a phone call from a hospital. His wife has been in an accident and she's badly hurt. The man jumps in his car to go to the hospital; if he were sober, or if it weren't an emergency, he might think clearly enough to call a cab. But he panics; he runs out to his car, drives it and causes a bad accident. OK? Now he's on trial for manslaughter. . . . Granted, he caused an accident; he was driving drunk and it was his fault. But is he as guilty as the guy who goes to a bar and gets drunk for fun, then drives?"

"No, but—"

"What are you saying, Reinhart?" It was Maria-Teresa asking me. Her voice sounded tired.

"I'm saying," I said, feeling hopelessly bullied, "that this isn't . . . It's not a matter of black or white, absolutely guilty or absolutely innocent. It's more like a gray area, and I think the insanity defense fits here. It seems to fit this boy and what he did. It wouldn't be just setting him free, it would be more like . . . I mean, he obviously needs to be locked up, but this way he'd get treated, and since he never got to see a doctor when he was growing up, I think he deserves the benefit . . . I think he deserves the chance to get treated. Doesn't that seem fair to you?"

"No it doesn't," Roy grumbled. "Look at what you're saying! You're saying that all the rest of us—all eleven of us—are totally wrong about this guy, but you're the only one who sees it clearly. Doesn't this strike you as being . . . Doesn't it make you think that maybe you're being unreasonable, that maybe *you're* the wrong one?"

"Of course it makes me think that!" I said, slapping my hand on the long table in frustration. "Do you think I enjoy this? I'd love to vote guilty and go home! You're staring and yelling at me as if I'm doing this on purpose just to inconvenience you. I'm not. I'm examining as hard as I can everything I'm saying, and if I see I'm wrong I'll be happy to admit it! I'm doing what I think I have to do. Am I wrong about this? Aren't we supposed to take this seriously, and vote honestly? This is a murder trial we're talking about, and I can't vote guilty just yet. I can't live with the idea that I'd be convicting a man of murder just because eleven people were annoyed at me. Can you possibly try to understand that?"

One thing that none of the jury-room dramas I'd seen or read prepared me for was the silence, the tense periods between exchanges that could last for minutes at a time. I kept thinking of the movie *Twelve Angry Men*, where Henry Fonda found himself arguing against eleven men, but at least there they kept talking the whole time. Having someone to argue with was far better than those interminable pauses, where no one said anything and I felt it was my obligation, as the sole holdout, to keep the debate moving. My mind would grasp wildly for new ideas, while at the same time I was asking myself, Is this really necessary? Would it really be wrong for me to change my vote?

The other thing that surprised me was discovering what sort of points contributed to the jury's impression of the case, and to their decisions to vote for conviction. The lawyers' clothing, mannerisms and accents counted heavily. Ms. Doppelt struck most of them as being "cold" and "pushy," whereas Mr. Graham seemed "nice," "a regular guy, not trying to put anything over on anybody," "reasonable." The fact that the defendant looked oblivious and smiled vacantly worked against him. The first psychiatrist was too young; he was a smarty-pants, an intellectual, too smart for his own good. The state's psychiatrist was no-nonsense, another regular guy. The Japanese man's eloquent, almost poetic testimony had grated on many people's nerves, it turned out. They thought he was snobbish, and acted superior. I got the impression it was because they didn't like seeing a foreigner, particularly an Asian man, using bigger words than they did.

I really did think about changing my vote just to get it over with; I considered it all the time, over and over. If eleven people thought he was guilty and I couldn't change all their minds, why bother voting against them? None of the others seemed to be hearing anything of what I'd been saying. It was as if I were speaking another language; when I spoke they all looked down at the table with barely concealed irritation. If I stuck to my vote it would mean that the trial would have to be done all over again. The lawyers would have to start all over, the witnesses would all have to come back, a new judge would have to be assigned, another courtroom would be needed, another jury would be selected, a whole new trial would occur, all because my conscience wouldn't let me send a man who killed another man to jail. It would probably be a futile and expensive gesture.

I wondered if the hospital would really be so different from prison. I also wondered if treatment now could help this boy much after all. Both doctors had said that schizophrenia can't be cured, and he looked perfectly satisfied with the way he was. Maybe he wouldn't pay any attention to the treatment. Maybe it would make him even more self-satisfied. The worst part of it was that I really didn't care what happened to him. I didn't have much sympathy for him or feel that one day he would contribute to society. I assumed he would always be a burden to us all. He had killed someone, after all. He took someone's life away forever, and he was irritating even to look at.

Just before my first solo appearance with a full symphony von Kempen told me that an orchestral composition is like a piece of elaborately woven fabric. If you damage even one of the threads, the others around it start to unravel and the whole fabric can disintegrate. This is why individual members of the orchestra must be vigilant and maintain their concentration, even during passages when they don't play at all. Von Kempen believed that if a single musician became distracted and thought of something other than the piece, he could feel it pulling the music down. I think that maybe society, not just music, is like that. When a man like Philip Weber punches a hole in the fabric, threads start to unravel. The damage spreads, far beyond the Zen church or the Japanese man's family. Considering the damage he had caused, I wondered, was it really humanitarian to focus so much concern on him? Would it be better, perhaps, to focus attention on repairing the damage? One way to do so would be to send him to jail. Society likes to see people who have hurt other people be punished. It heals the fabric.

But just because society likes to see such people punished doesn't mean that in the long run it's the right thing to do. You wouldn't repair a silk embroidery with fishing line. Just because the sort of people sitting on this jury with me, eleven people of average ignorance, more or less, wanted an eye for an eye wouldn't necessarily make it a good outcome.

In the end, this was why I couldn't change my vote. Since I couldn't possibly know what was right, and since I couldn't know what the consequences of either verdict would be, I had no choice but to vote as I believed. It was really the only viable basis for a decision.

Which is what I told them over and over, grueling hour after grueling hour. I said it before lunch, I said it after lunch, I said it all day. And as I became more and more exhausted they became more and more exasperated. By the end of the second day it wasn't just Maria-Teresa who could hardly bring herself to look at me. At nearly six o'clock that afternoon we agreed to go home and come back for one more day, and if I still felt I couldn't change my mind, we would announce a hung jury.

30

After less than an hour the next day the others voted to declare themselves a hung jury. We filed back into the courtroom, where Dwight stood up and told the judge we were deadlocked, eleven to one, and that we hadn't gotten anywhere at all in two days of painful deliberations. The courtroom burst into confusion and noise; the dead man's mother began crying and had to be led by her family out of the room.

Once she left the room I thought the worst was over, but to everyone's surprise and dismay, Judge Davis refused to accept our decision. After bringing the court to order he frowned at the jury so hard that his eyes nearly disappeared, and he rebuked us in booming tones for not trying hard enough. He reminded us that this was a murder trial, and that it had cost the courts, not to mention the witnesses and lawyers, a great deal of time and money to put on, and he wasn't going to let us give up and go home after only two days. He sent us back to the jury room and told us not to return until we had fulfilled our obligation to serve justice and had reached a verdict.

I thought the deliberations had gone badly before, but I

didn't know what bad was until I lived through what came next. We stayed in that room for four more days, forcing me to cancel Kyung-hee's lessons for the second Monday in a row. One by one the jurors abandoned all pretense of having any respect for me or my opinions, making each day more uncomfortable than the last. I felt violently torn between the desire to change my vote and the fear that if I did it would haunt me for the rest of my life. I believed that Philip Weber was out of his mind and that the right thing to do was to send him to a medical institution, regardless of how viscerally unsatisfying that might have been. I felt that sending him to jail would be demoralizing in the long run. Our social conscience is nourished whenever we live up to the agreement we have made with one another not to punish people who don't deserve to be punished, including people who are incapable of being responsible for their actions. Was I sure that Weber couldn't have stopped himself? No, not absolutely sure, but reasonably so, and if it is true that in the United States someone is innocent until proven guilty, and that as a society we have agreed that it is better to let a hundred guilty men go free than to send one innocent man to jail, on what basis could I have voted guilty? If I was an innocent man wrongly accused of a crime, I would certainly hope that at least one member of my jury adhered to those ideals. How could I have changed my vote, as the others were asking me to do, in order to save taxpayers the expense of another trial? That shouldn't be a consideration at all.

During the worst moments, when I thought I might go insane myself from the tension, I remembered that von Kempen had lived through this and far worse. Every day of the last twenty-five years of his life he had to live with the knowledge that his name had come to be associated with one of the most shameful periods in recorded history. Believing that it would do more harm than good to struggle against those accusations, and probably also out of guilt that he had not taken a more vigorous stand against fascism as Casals had, he responded with dignified sacrifice. For a man like him to silence his instrument was surely as painful as for an ordinary person to cut out his or her own tongue, but instead of redeeming him, his sacrifice led to his being merely forgotten. In spite of all this, he never gave in to despair or breathed a word of complaint to anyone.

In the jury room we asked for transcripts of the testimony and went over the evidence of the trial so many times that I learned most of it by heart. One quote in particular, originally from an American Bar Association report, summed up the whole trial, as well as our dilemma as jurors: "There is no objective basis for distinguishing between offenders who were undeterrable and those who were undeterred, between the impulse that was irresistible and the impulse not resisted, or between substantial impairment of capacity and some lesser impairment . . . the question is unanswerable or, at best, can be answered only by moral guesses."

Eleven people, one of them the only woman I'd ever tried to make love to, guessed that Philip Weber was deterrable, I guessed that he was not. For an entire week we argued over whose guess was better. Maria-Teresa rarely spoke to me during the arguments, but occasionally when I would say something, she would click her tongue and close her eyes, hold her breath for half a second and then sigh, as if she couldn't believe what I was turning out to be like. Her nonverbal commentary hurt me far more than the others' blunter criticism. Once, when I said that I couldn't see punishing a man for losing his mind, since no one loses his mind on purpose, I caught her sharing a look of disgust with Rose. It was the final blow; I couldn't actually hate her, but from then on I felt numb toward her.

To make matters worse, Betty, whose husband was supposed to work "in sales," confided to me bitterly that he was actually a drunk and had no steady income, and that they were living off her undeclared income as a domestic. She couldn't admit this during the voir dire because she was terrified of being caught and having to pay taxes on it. Every day of the trial was money she wasn't bringing home to her family, and she told me that her customers were starting to hint that they might have to look elsewhere for help.

While all this was going on I was trying every night to practice, believing music was my only hope. Bach, I reminded myself, hadn't even published any music until after his fortieth year; I was still young, there was still hope, the deliberations would end soon, and this dreadful experience, along with my devastating encounter with Maria-Teresa, would soon fade into the past. But the sound of the cello, even the smell of rosin, was torture for me. I often wished I could scream or throw something or cry, but nothing came out. I've never known how to express my strongest feelings except through music, and now even that channel was blocked.

On the last morning of the trial, however, I stepped into the shower before going to court and had my head under the hot water when the strange thought occurred to me that no one could possibly see me under all that water. A ridiculous thought, since no one could have seen me in the shower stall of my apartment anyway, but the water seemed to form a tangible, comforting screen, and I was able to cry for a few minutes with my hands gripped around the shower head. It felt so good that I actually laughed at the same time.

I went to court that day knowing that my conscience could not possibly allow me to change my vote. As soon as I entered the jury room I suggested going before Judge Davis again, and said that if necessary I would be willing to identify myself as the lone dissenter and answer any questions the judge might want to put to me. We sent word to Judge Davis, the clerk summoned us into the courtroom, and Dwight explained for the second time that we were a hung jury. Once again the judge ordered us back to the jury room, only this time without any comments or instructions. We waited for several long minutes, unsure of what to do next, but then the clerk came into the room and explained that the judge wanted to see us in the courtroom one at a time.

Dwight went first. He came back after a few minutes, then Rose was called. Gary went after her, and then Mathilda. I was the tenth to be called. The clerk led me into the courtroom and I sat down by myself in the jury box. The entire courtroom was looking at me while Judge Davis asked firmly, "Mr. Sundheimer, what's going on in there?"

I nearly panicked, wondering if he knew that I was the holdout and wanted me to explain myself. Struggling to keep calm, I answered, "We seem to be deadlocked."

"Yes, I know that. What I want to know is, have the deliberations stopped in there? Are the twelve of you still trying?"

"We've been deliberating the whole time, Your Honor."

"Is there any chance of your reaching a verdict if you were to keep trying?"

"I believe not."

"What do you mean, you believe not? Mr. Sundheimer, I am not going to declare a mistrial if there is any chance that further deliberations will result in a verdict. Is there any chance that a verdict can be reached?"

When I said that I felt there was no chance of this happening, Judge Davis dismissed me, and the clerk led me back into the room.

After all twelve of us had been through this process, the judge summoned us back as a group and, starting with Dwight, asked us the same questions.

"Mr. Anderson, are you still willing to deliberate?"

"Yes, sir."

"Is there any chance that further deliberations will result in a verdict?"

"I believe not."

When it came his turn, Roy answered the questions in the same way, but then requested permission to ask a question himself. Judge Davis allowed him one question.

"Your Honor, what I want to know is, if one juror isn't willing to deliberate, could he be replaced with an alternate?"

The judge suddenly turned purple with rage. "It is against the law to refuse to deliberate on a jury!" he boomed. "If one of your members refuses to deliberate, he or she must be dismissed at once. In that case, one of the alternates would be chosen, and the deliberations would have to begin from scratch. I just asked each one of you individually if you were still willing to deliberate, and you each answered in the affirmative. I want to know right now—what's going on in there? Is anyone not willing to deliberate?"

Roy leaned forward in his seat, turned toward me and

glared. One by one, the other jurors either glanced or turned to stare at me. My anonymity was stripped away in an instant; the whole courtroom now knew that I was the one.

"Mr. Sundheimer, are you no longer willing to deliberate?" Judge Davis asked.

Everyone was looking at me: the judge, the jury, the sheriff's deputies, the good-natured prosecutor, the clerks, reporters and courtroom visitors, including a group of high school students with their social studies teacher. Although intellectually prepared for the consequences of my decision, I was emotionally devastated. Being the focus of such strong disapproval, particularly in the somber atmosphere of the courtroom, was astonishingly painful—more painful, I believe, than if I had been physically beaten. I felt myself start to tremble, and thought that I might collapse under the strain. Then I looked at the defendant's table. The defendant himself wasn't looking at me; his eyes were closed and he appeared to be whispering to himself. His attorney was looking at me, however, and a gesture of hers caught my eye. Ms. Doppelt was wearing a pair of simple pearl earrings, and she was fingering one of them nervously. That slight movement drew my attention to her face. I could see in her expression a combination of respect and gratitude so sincere that the worst of my panic subsided, and I was able to gather myself enough to answer the judge.

"I'm not unwilling to deliberate, Your Honor. I think the other jurors are just extremely frustrated that I don't share their opinion."

"Are you honestly listening to their opinions, Mr. Sundheimer?"

"Yes, I am."

"And you honestly feel that there is no chance of your changing your mind?"

"Your Honor, the deliberations have become repetitive—we're not getting anywhere. We've covered all the points many times. The disagreement between me and the other eleven jurors is fundamental, not a disagreement over details."

The judge paused for a long time, then exchanged a weary glance with the prosecutor. He sighed heavily, leaned forward in his seat and, addressing the whole courtroom, said, "The jurors having been polled, the court finds that further deliberations would be meaningless and that the jury is hopelessly deadlocked. The court declares a mistrial, and the jury is excused."

All of a sudden it was over. This time the dead Zen master's mother was not in the gallery. Ms. Doppelt nodded gratefully at me, but I couldn't imagine that she had much to celebrate. Now she was going to have to do the whole thing over again.

Philip Weber smiled in the same bland way he had throughout the trial. His father reached forward and touched him on the shoulder, but it was an awkward gesture, and Philip didn't seem to react to it at all. He looked over at the jury box, and I'm sure he could tell that I was the one—maybe because I was the only one looking at him. Our eyes met, and after a pause of a few seconds, he shrugged, as if to say, Who knows? It was a very unsatisfying ending.

They say that after reaching a verdict, most juries are able to reconcile their differences, heal the wounds created during the most heated arguments and leave with a generally positive feeling. Not so our jury; we had failed, and everyone went home angry. Toward the end of the deliberations only two people remained polite to me: Grace, who seemed incapable of raising her voice at anyone, and Dwight, who remained controlled during the whole procedure. I suspect it had something to do with his military background; he'd had to keep his head under worse conditions, I'm sure. Maria-Teresa had never yelled at me, but she had made no effort to conceal her exasperation.

When Judge Davis declared the trial over, only Dwight said good-bye to me before leaving the courthouse; he said something about knowing what I must have felt like through the ordeal. He even shook my hand. I didn't see Maria-Teresa leave; I could understand why she would want to get out of there without having to talk to me again. I waited in the empty room for about twenty minutes so I wouldn't have to ride on the shuttle with any of the others, then left the courthouse. I was halfway down the front steps when I heard someone call my name.

It was Ms. Doppelt. She walked up to me and said, "I just wanted to say thank you. I've never had to go through what you had to go through, and I don't know that I could. That was a hard trial to sit through, and a very hard one to understand clearly. You did, though, and you did a very important thing, and under unbelievably bad circumstances. I won't ever forget it."

I was unable to tell her how much her appreciation meant to me. We shook hands, and my experience as a juror at last came to an end.

31

After a few days I called Kyung-hee's mother to resume his lessons, but right away I sensed that she felt uncomfortable talking to me. "Sorry for trouble you," she said, "but Kyung-hee no more coming your house for lessons. Kyung-hee very sorry."

I asked why and she seemed hesitant to discuss it, but finally I was able to learn that her husband had had mixed feelings about lessons with me from the beginning. He felt that it was too expensive for them, for one thing, and involved too much driving time for Mrs. Kim. But, most important, he wanted Kyung-hee to spend more time on his math. For the first time, I learned that the boy showed as much promise in that subject as in music. Which explained, at last, how the Kims could be so perversely unenthusiastic about Kyung-hee's musical ability. Faced with their child's two extraordinary gifts, they worried that trying to pursue both might be a mistake. Now Mr. Kim had, perhaps understandably, decided that music was the more expendable of the two. In view of this, he had decided that Kyung-hee should study the cello once a week rather than twice, and with a local cello teacher who was less demanding and who charged a more reasonable fee of eight dollars for forty-five minutes.

In spite of my deep disappointment, I did not try to persuade Mrs. Kim to change her husband's mind. After the ordeal of the trial I didn't have the energy to argue with anyone, and even if I did—offering to teach their son for free, for example—I would still have had to cope with Mr. Kim's resentful suspicions that I was leading his son into poverty, and I did not want to find myself in that situation.

I stopped practicing entirely after the trial ended. The few times I forced myself to try, it was like playing with mittens on my hands.

Toward the end of that summer I moved out of my apartment and found a place in the hills up north, away from campus and the city. Fall came and went, then winter, and I still didn't play. I taught without using my cello at all. I don't remember much about that time. It was as if for seven or eight months my mind was full of static, a cloud of soft noise, and I had only a slight awareness of what lay on the periphery. It was like a dream where you want to look at something but your eyes can see everywhere but right in front of you. For that whole period my cello stayed in its case in my bedroom closet.

Then, in February, Mrs. Kim called and asked if I was still teaching. She said that Kyung-hee didn't like his new cello teacher at all, and indicated that his grades in math had suffered rather than benefited from the shift in emphasis away from music. Also, she said several times that he had never stopped begging to be allowed to study with me again, and Mr. Kim had finally given his wife permission to call me. In view of my having stopped playing altogether, along with my general state of mind at the time, I was not sure I could be a good teacher for Kyung-hee anymore, but it gave me some pleasure to know that he had missed me, as I had missed him, so I agreed to try again. He and his mother came over to the new apartment on Saturday morning and I felt genuinely happy to see him. He seemed almost afraid to look at me that first day, however, probably from embarrassment over my having been fired by his parents the year before.

I asked Kyung-hee what he'd been working on with his other teacher, and his shoulders drooped a little. He reported that they had been playing a lot of Popper and Grützmacher—dull student exercises, for the most part. But, he said, on his own he'd been practicing the Bach suites I'd given him, and he wanted to play the fifth for me.

From the moment his bow touched the strings I could see that he had matured; he was more relaxed, and had obviously benefited from his technical studies. By the time he finished the suite twenty minutes later, something in me had changed. Perhaps it sounds mystical, but I really did feel something move in me; it was both a physical and an emotional sensation. Never in my life have I cried in front of a student while he was playing, but that morning I did. Imagine! In front of a small boy like that. Fortunately, he was so intensely absorbed in the music that he didn't seem to notice my reaction, and I managed to control my emotions before he finished.

While Kyung-hee played, the music seemed to have hands that reached into my chest, took a firm grip and shook me savagely—so hard that I felt as though I were really waking up from a dream. It was like waking up from a dream only to realize that you are in another dream, but then finally you wake up for real, and there is something unmistakable about that reality—you are really waking up. That was what I felt like; it was so strong that it was like a hallucination. When I opened my eyes and looked around me, what I saw was a tiny boy playing the cello, and I felt engulfed, swept away by something immediately familiar. It was the experience of music I had felt almost every day for the first half of my life. As he played I remembered what it felt like to be playing the music myself. Then I had a strange thought. I said to myself, It's so simple and so obvious: when he plays, the music goes into my ears, resonates in my mind and becomes a part of me! It becomes my music too. When I thought about it that way, the boy's awkward personality, his appearance, his unfortunate situation at home—everything about him—became irrelevant except for the music. I had a delicious sense that teaching Kyung-hee might just possibly be enough. It could fill in the blanks; it could satisfy me.

After Kyung-hee left that afternoon I took a drive up into the mountains to the east, to Mt. Wilson, where there is a huge observatory housing a telescope with a mirror a hundred inches in diameter. I'd read in one of my books that it was while looking through this telescope that Edwin Hubble discovered that the universe is expanding, and had all started from one unimaginably large explosion at a single, infinitesimal point. I parked at a turnout in the road near the observatory, got out of the car and looked down at the ocean to the west and the city directly to the south.

From the mountains or from a plane the smog has distinct boundaries and real substance to it. It's toxic and depressing, but all the same there's something cozy about the way it looks. It's like a soft brown comforter draped over the city.

I wanted to sit on the ground at the edge of the turnout,

but at first I couldn't bring myself to do it in my good pants. I'd still not forgotten to dress up for lessons. But then I thought, What do I care, no one's going to see me up here. So I sat down. It felt so funny that I laughed aloud. It must have been twenty years since I'd sat on the ground.

The city spread out in all directions, a huge basin of stucco buildings, parking lots and swimming pools, with a tight cluster of high rises stranded in the middle. Suddenly those downtown buildings reminded me of the Rodin sculpture "The Burghers of Calais": five or six figures standing close together, with horrible expressions on their faces because they're about to be executed. The high rises aren't ugly in themselves, but hemmed in by all of that crap surrounding them it was easy to imagine that they were leaning toward one another in despair.

The white dome of the observatory behind me made me think of one winter afternoon in Ederstausee, just after my eleventh birthday, when von Kempen asked my mother and me to stay on for a while after the lesson to see what he called "a celestial performance." When the grandfather clock upstairs in his music room struck five o'clock, the three of us looked out the bay windows over his garden and saw the full moon, newly risen over the reservoir, glowing a dull, copperish red.

"Mondfinsternis," he said reverently—a lunar eclipse.

I asked what this meant and he explained that the sun, the earth and the moon were now perfectly aligned so that the moon was now entirely in the earth's shadow; it could receive no direct light from the sun.

"So why can we still see it?" I asked.

The old master looked genuinely puzzled and limped over to his desk, where he picked up a newspaper, held it under a light and, using a huge magnifying glass, read what was apparently a brief article about the eclipse.

"Ah, yes. Dear boy—such a fine, inquiring mind!—the paper tells us that the moon receives a bit of indirect sunlight thanks to our own earth's atmosphere, which deflects the light and sends some of it toward the moon."

In spite of the moon's diminished brightness, I could see details on its surface more clearly than I ever had before, perhaps for the same reason that distant trees and mountains look sharper when seen through darkened glasses. Von Kempen returned to the window to admire the scene further, then chuckled to himself. "I just thought of something," he said, opening a fresh can of blended tobacco. "The moon and I, we have something in common. Can you guess what it is?"

"No, Herr Professor."

"Oh, come! Take a guess, at least."

I could never think quickly when put on the spot. My mind went blank, but to satisfy my expectant teacher I blurted out, "You both have reddish faces?"

The old cellist laughed out loud, but my mother was horrified. "What a thing to say!" she said loudly in English.

Thankfully, von Kempen leaped to my defense before she could scold me any further. "Not at all, *meine liebe Frau Sundheimer*. The young maestro is quite right. But I was thinking of something else." He lit his pipe, puffed at it dreamily, and then laughed quietly once again. "I am still visible because of you—that is why I am like the moon. How fortunate I am that you play the cello."

Nearly a quarter century later I understood all too well what he meant. I heard myself think, My old life is done now—it's over. I didn't know whether to be afraid, delighted or worried. It was such an unexpected thought that I didn't know how to feel at all. At that moment, I finally ceased to be a concert cellist. I felt detached from myself, if that makes any sense, but at the same time I was all there. Who else, after all, was this man sitting on the ground in his good pants?

I suppose I'd always thought of myself as a good man, a talented man, a professional musician with the right ideas about important matters, one who would never do anything really wrong. I've always simply assumed this; I could make small mistakes of judgment, I could have little accidents, but I would always make great music and never willfully do anything really foolish or bad. Sitting on the edge of the turnout, though, I began to suspect that maybe I wasn't that man after all. I felt that now I could see my life from several different perspectives, giving me views of myself that were not all flattering. My failed career, the way I'd avoided my parents since leaving home, the way I'd resented my students' successes, my clumsiness with women. I did not become upset, however; it didn't hurt to think about these things. I just sat there and observed, completely enthralled. It was like that television program where the fat critic and the skinny one argue about movies. Except that here it was many critics, and the movie was me.

On that day I began to have a different idea about why I couldn't play onstage anymore. I'd always assumed it had to do with my sense of pitch, because that was certainly what I'd noticed had changed. I couldn't hold on to the dead center of notes anymore because my pitch had become too sensitive; my fingers couldn't keep the notes pure enough. It felt like trying to split hairs with a butter knife. But now I started to think that maybe the problem had nothing to do with my ears.

When I was a child performer I could do no wrong. Anything I did pleased an audience; I had no fear at all of making mistakes. There was also no question that I was going to get even better; everyone told me so, it was promised to me. When I was sent to von Kempen, I was going to become the next von Kempen. I was even going to surpass him; he himself predicted that, joyfully. But what had once been limitless expression for me suddenly acquired boundaries. I was the unfinished version of some greater perfection. I had no choice but to try to search deeper and deeper until I found that perfection and brought it to the surface. So I tried; I searched, I went deeper, but I felt like a diver jumping into the deepest part of the ocean without equipment and trying to find a sunken galleon. No matter how deep I went, there was not only no treasure, but no bottom. And that was when von Kempen died, just at the crucial time. When I needed him most he was taken away from me, and that made it much worse. With him gone, the expectation that I would bring his music to life in all its glory, to restore his honor and incomparable voice and at the same time establish my own, grew much stronger. It came from all sides—my parents, critics, music patrons and, most of all, me.

If a thirty-year-old man were to play exactly the way I did at fifteen, no one would have insisted that he become better. No one would have said, "I can't wait to hear you when you're forty!" Now I think I know what happened to me. Since musically I couldn't see how to improve, any more than one can willfully improve one's capacity for hunger or joy, I turned my attention to the only aspect I could control, which was intonation. I knew that, for example, musicians can become used to minor thirds that are too large. I became obsessed with locating any such habits in my own playing, and for all practical purposes forgot that absolute intonation does not exist. As my mind focused on the impossible goal of achieving pure intonation, I became unable to feel the music. It was the same problem as what happened when I was staring at Maria-Teresa's family pictures and trying to make love to her at the same time.

When you play music well, you are transported. However, my experience has been that you cannot make great music happen; you can only *prepare* yourself for it to happen. To a degree, your preparation determines what will happen, but once it starts happening you have to surrender yourself to it. Once you do so you are free, except that you are free only within the boundaries you created through your preparation. When, at eighteen, I started trying to force great music to happen I ended up making awful music; in fact, it wasn't even music anymore.

It seemed as if that boy who killed his Zen teacher also wanted to achieve an impossible sort of purity. Before the incident during the retreat, he apparently hoped that Zen would help him transcend his imperfect life all at once, in a flash; he wanted to become somebody else, somebody whose wisdom allowed him to experience perfect freedom. Maybe he did experience a kind of freedom when he lost his mind, but from any point of view other than his own it was a lousy kind of freedom.

I thought of the trial the year before, and wondered if my brief sense of detachment sitting under the observatory was anything like what that young man had felt, a perspective that allowed him to know he had committed murder, yet have no sense of guilt or anger about it. Maybe that was why he refused to let his father hire an expensive lawyer; maybe he really didn't care what happened to him.

After half an hour or so my epiphany dimmed until it was only a subtle glow, a light, refreshing feeling; it was as if I had just shed a suit of chain mail. On the drive home every breath seemed luxurious, I swayed with every turn in the road. With utterly unwarranted conviction, I felt that even the commuters around me, expressionless in their cars in the heavy traffic, were all on the verge of laughter.

I had not become the heir to von Kempen's musical tradition, but I hadn't betrayed his legacy completely. I had done something that I believed was right even though it might have been a futile gesture. Perhaps if von Kempen were alive he would say that by doing what I did, I validated his work with me. He was always saying that there should be no separation between one's musical life and one's spiritual, social or political life. Those little speeches about unifying one's life with one's art, about animating one's life with one's art and making one's very life art—those were the speeches that used to make me think he was getting senile. I'd forgotten all of that for many years, but now I remember. I don't feel that my apprenticeship is incomplete anymore; I tell myself now that my experience during the trial was my graduate recital.

32

One improvement in my life since that day has been the acquisition of a pet. Knowing how badly Kyung-hee wanted a cat, I thought I might as well get one for him to play with when he came for lessons. Also I'd always heard that cats were the easiest pets to keep. At first I planned to go to a pet store and buy one, but when I mentioned this to Martin he advised me to choose one from the pound instead. He gave me an informative lecture about the animal overpopulation in our city and why adoption from the pound was more socially responsible than buying one in a store. He also said that many of the cats in commercial pet stores were raised in miserable kitty farms under harsh conditions, and that they encourage the propagation of exotic, specialized breeds, which tend to suffer from cruel birth defects as a result of all the inbreeding. He had even memorized statistics, although I don't recall what they referred to. Most convincingly from my point of view, he told me that by bringing a cat home from the pound I would almost certainly be saving it from being put to sleep. Furthermore, at the pound I could select an older cat, so that if it turned out I didn't enjoy having it, I wouldn't have to take care of it for very long.

The pound in my neighborhood had separate areas for cats and dogs. To get to the cat house, I had to walk down a long aisle past cage after cage with dogs in them barking and whining piteously. I tried not to look directly at any of them because I felt terrible passing them by.

There were twenty or thirty cats. Some of them were obviously feral, crouching as far back in their cages as possible and hissing at whoever entered the room. Little cards under their cages identified them as strays and offered such comments as "Not very tame," "Needs lots of patience" or, simply, "Aggressive." But most of them seemed tame and affectionate. Several of them mewed to get my attention and rubbed their sides against the bars of their cages when I looked at them. Still, the enthusiastic ones were almost all very young. I looked at a few older cats and had nearly settled on a fat tabby named Mango when a volunteer attendant, a teenaged boy with a baseball cap worn backward, pointed out that there were a few more cages just around the corner. In one of these I saw a small, ink-black cat with long fur and green eyes. Her name was Smoky and the card under her cage said, "Ten years old. Owner passed away. Spayed, declawed. Very gentle pet." I felt particularly sorry for her. Knowing that she had once been owned and loved by someone, that she had experienced a comfortable life as someone's companion but was now suddenly alone, made her seem more pitiful than the cats that had known life only on the street. Also I couldn't help finding an unfortunate parallel between Smoky's change of status and mine as a failed prodigy. The attendant, who was changing the water bowls in the cages, paused to stand next to me for a minute and glanced at the date written at the bottom of Smoky's card. "Today's her last day," he said matter-of-factly. I asked what he meant, and he explained that spring was kitten season, and that because of the overwhelming number of cats coming into the pound, each one had only three days to be adopted before being put down. I checked Mango's card and saw that he still had a day to go, so I adopted Smoky.

She took charge of the house almost immediately. When Kyung-hee and his mother walked in the door five days later, Smoky (I didn't like the name but couldn't get her attention with any of the new ones I came up with) meandered into the studio and gazed, unimpressed, at the intruders. She gave me a harsh look, as if to ask why I wasn't chasing them out.

"Is that yours?" Kyung-hee asked me, pushing his glasses closer to his eyes as if to make sure he wasn't just looking at a cat-shaped smudge on the lenses.

"Yes. Her name is Smoky."

"Could I touch her?"

"Sure. Just take it slow, so she can get used to you."

He inched toward the old cat, stuck out his hand uncertainly, as if afraid she might bite, then touched her head with his fingertips.

"Wow," he said, his voice suffused with awe, and then started sneezing.

Sadly, it turns out that Kyung-hee is mildly allergic to cats. This doesn't seem to discourage him at all, however; he has already fallen in love with Smoky and isn't about to forsake her just to keep his nose from running. It only means that now he has to wait until the end of his lessons to play with her. One unexpected benefit of giving him this playmate has been that it gives me a chance to talk with his mother. We've been discussing having Kyung-hee give a small recital at the university, which I think would be a good warm-up before making a professional appearance. Also we would be assured of a supportive audience there; a good response will be crucial for the shy boy, and might also have a positive effect on his father.

The real surprise with Smoky, however, has been my reaction to her. I adopted her primarily as a way to improve my relationship with Kyung-hee, and assumed that beyond feeding her and cleaning the litter box, I wouldn't have to think about her much. It appears, however, that this cat was accustomed to sitting in someone's lap for several hours a day, and within a few days of moving into my apartment she began demanding the same arrangement with me. Wherever I would move in the apartment she would follow, waiting for me to sit down. The moment I sank down into a chair she would look at me and wait for five or ten seconds, as if making sure it wasn't a false alarm and that I wasn't going to pop right back up again. But if I stayed put she would bob her head, contemplate the exhausting leap from the floor and then jump. The poor animal was so old and needed to make such an effort to reach my lap that I would force myself to sit still for at least twenty minutes before getting up. When I'd finally try to lift her, her ears would flick back and she would look up at me with an expression of such confusion and disappointment that more often than not I would set her back down on my lap and sit for another half hour, scratching her behind the ears and under the chin.

I discovered that I enjoyed touching Smoky at least as much as she enjoyed being touched by me. Just to stroke her fur made me breathe a little deeper and feel oddly content. Still, I began to feel manipulated by her, so I had to set ground rules. We have established a pattern now: every morning she sits on my lap for an hour while I have my coffee and read, and every night she sits there for another hour or two while I listen to recordings. Other opportunities during the day are strictly optional, and I don't let myself feel guilty for shooing her away if I feel like it. I realize that my negotiations with Smoky are almost comically simplistic when compared with what married couples or families undergo every day, but I still take pride in my relationship with her.

When it came time to choose a veterinarian for Smoky, I asked around the department and got a few recommendations from people who already have pets. I didn't want to just choose a name out of the phone book. Gwen, the pianist who shares an office with Martin, gave the strongest and most unusual recommendation; she told me that if she could only find an obstetrician as good as her veterinarian, she might think about having children. I made an appointment right away and brought Smoky in, carrying her in a box that I'd lined with thick towels and furnished with toy mice and dried snacks. An assistant led me into an office and told me that the doctor was finishing up a surgical emergency and would be ready in just a moment. As I waited I noticed with pleasure that taped classical music was playing in the background.

Dr. Polk slid open the door and apologized for the delay. She was younger than I had expected; the way Gwen had talked about her I had expected a Jane Goodall figure: tall and thin, with graying hair and plenty of creases etched in her forehead from years of compassionate worry on behalf of animals. Instead she was short and appeared to be closer to my age, with dark hair and smooth, pale skin. She wasn't pretty in the ordinary sense, but as soon as she began examining Smoky I understood why Gwen was so enthusiastic about her. My poor cat, who probably thought she was back at the pound, was trembling with fear when I first took her out of the box, but in a remarkably short time Dr. Polk had her purring and sitting comfortably on her lap. Her voice seemed to have an especially soothing effect. Toward the end of the examination, when I complimented her on her choice of office music, her eyes lit up; "Do you like classical music?" she asked.

I ended up making an appointment to bring Smoky in the following week for a tooth cleaning, and during that visit I invited the doctor to be my guest at a recital of baroque chamber music next month, the main event of an early music festival I helped to organize. She seemed genuinely excited about it.

I don't really practice anymore, but I have established a little cellistic ritual I go through every day, and it makes me happy. It started when I finally took the cello out of its case a few months ago to make sure the strings still had some tension in them. If they get too slack the sound post can fall out of place, and in an older instrument this can cause serious problems. When I pulled it out I saw that it was covered with dust, so I lay it on its back across my knees to clean it off.

Smoky was fascinated by the cello. She hopped onto the sofa and sniffed the length of the instrument; realizing that no one could see me in the apartment, I tried sniffing it too. I couldn't detect much of an odor, but in bringing my face that close to the instrument I saw it in a way I never had before. It's odd that I've owned this cello for twenty years and had never really looked at it closely before; I had only used it. It was a gift to me from a wealthy patroness of the arts who heard one of my recitals and decided it was time I had an adequate instrument. My parents could never have afforded a good cello on their own.

The patroness invited my parents and me to her home for tea, along with a dealer in fine instruments. He brought six cellos, all of them magnificent. I played them all, then chose this one. I felt obliged to explain my choice, so I spoke at great length, extolling the virtues of the different instruments, coming around at last to why the virtues of this one in particular suited me. However, the truth was that I'd fallen in love with the color of the varnish. I was only thirteen.

The dealer, who was forever cleaning his teeth with an ivory pick, complimented me effusively on my fine ear. Thinking about it now, I suspect I chose the most expensive instrument, to his great delight. I never found out how much the old woman paid for it. My mother sat me down that night and made me write her a thank-you letter. I'm ashamed to admit that I found writing that letter to be just as tedious a responsibility as writing the annual thank-you letter to my grandmother for her traditional birthday gift of a new dollar bill. It's just one more of the many things I wish I could do over again.

Now, twenty years later, I was looking closely at the cello for the first time, discovering minute knots in the patterns of wood grain on the front, and seeing for the first time that the ebony fingerboard was not pitch-black as I'd always thought but had nearly invisible streaks of rich chestnut brown running down its length. You had to look very closely in strong light to see them. I ran my hands all over the instrument, and noted a difference in texture between the glassy varnish on the body and the duller but smoother surface of the neck, brought to a different sort of polish from three hundred years of thumbs sliding up and down it. How many left hands besides my own, I wondered, had gone about the consuming task of searching for the right notes?

An idea came to me, and I turned off the lights in the studio. In the darkness I put the cello's spike into a loose spot in the carpet, tightened the bow and drew it across the open strings. I took off my shirt and tried it again; it was the first time in my life I'd felt the instrument against my bare chest. I could feel the vibration of the strings travel through the body of the instrument to my own body. I'd never thought about that; music scholars always talk about the resonating properties of various instruments, but surely the performer's own body must have some effect on the sound. As I dug into the notes I imagined that my own chest and lungs were extensions of the sound box; I seemed to be able to alter the sound by changing the way I sat, and by varying the muscular tension in my upper body.

After improvising for a while, I started playing the D minor Bach suite, still in the darkness. Strangely freed of the task of finding the right phrasing, the right intonation, the right bowing, I heard the music through my skin. For the first time I didn't think about how it would sound to anyone else, and slowly, joyfully, gratefully, I started to hear again. The notes sang out, first like a trickle, then like a fountain of cool water bubbling up from a hole in the middle of a desert. After an hour or so I looked up, and in the darkness saw the outline of the cat sitting on the floor in front of me, cleaning her paws and purring loudly. I had an audience again, humble as it was.

So that's what I do now with my cello. At least once a day I find time to tune it, close my eyes and listen. It's probably not going to lead to the kind of comeback I'd fantasized about for so long—years of playing badly has left scars on my technique, and, practically speaking, classical musicians returning from obscurity are almost impossible to promote—but I might eventually try giving a recital if I feel up to it. Or better yet, I may play for Dr. Polk if our date at the concert goes well. Occasionally I feel a stab of longing, and wish I could give just one more concert on a great stage before my light blinks off, but that longing passes more quickly now. I take solace in the fact that, unlike the way I felt before, I can enjoy playing for myself now. I feel relaxed and expansive when I play, as if I could stretch out my arms and reach from one end of the apartment to the other. A feeling of completeness and dignity surrounds me and lifts me up. I've been thinking about this quite a bit lately, and I've decided that we all crave a sense of dignity in our lives, but most of us find it an elusive goal. For so long I'd tried to generate it by thinking of who I once was, what I used to be able to do or what I could be doing if certain things changed. Now I think there's something ugly about someone who thinks well of who he was, or of who he might be. (At the same time, there's something equally unpleasant about someone who thinks poorly of who he once was, or of who he will probably become.)

Maybe I've become like my father; maybe I just can't stand contemplating the larger picture, so I've taught myself to keep my eyes focused on the tips of my shoes. For my father it was caulking the tiles at home, cleaning the gutters, changing the oil in the car. For me it's drawing sound out of a wooden box, and teaching other people how to do it. I don't think about the past as much as I used to, and I hardly ever think further than a semester ahead. I'm not sure that's a bad thing, though. I'm starting to think that the larger picture is overrated.

ABOUT THE AUTHOR

MARK SALZMAN was born in Connecticut in 1959. He divides his time between writing, practicing martial arts and playing the cello. He and his wife—and their cats, birds and fish—have adapted to life in Los Angeles, especially since mastering the freeway system.

ABOUT THE TYPE

This book was set in Galliard, a typeface designed by Matthew Carter for the Mergenthaler Linotype Company in 1978. Galliard is based on the sixteenth-century typefaces of Robert Granjon, which give it classic lines yet interject a contemporary look.